OLD
FAMILIAR
PLACES

THE INNOCENT YEARS
★ ★ ★

Love and Glory
These Golden Days
Heart and Soul
Old Familiar Places

OLD FAMILIAR PLACES

ROBERT FUNDERBURK

BETHANY HOUSE PUBLISHERS
MINNEAPOLIS, MINNESOTA 55438

Old Familiar Places
Copyright © 1996
Robert W. Funderburk

Cover illustration by Joe Nordstrom

Published by Bethany House Publishers
A Ministry of Bethany Fellowship, Inc.
11300 Hampshire Avenue South
Minneapolis, Minnesota 55438

Printed in the United States of America.

Library of Congress Cataloging-in-Publication Data

Funderburk, Robert, 1942–
    Old familiar places / Robert W. Funderburk.
       p. cm. — (The innocent years ; book 4)

    I. Title. II. Series: Funderburk, Robert, 1942–
Innocent years; bk. 4.
PS3556.U59O43 1996   813'.54—dc20   96–4505
ISBN 1–55661–463–2   CIP

To
Terry Workman, our pastor.
A faithful shepherd—
even when the path grows
steep and stoney.

And to
Jasmine, his wife,
whose warm smile is always
a beacon of light in
a sometimes dark world.

ROBERT FUNDERBURK is the coauthor of six books with his friend Gilbert Morris. Much of the research for this series was gained through growing up in Baton Rouge and then working as a Louisana state probation and parole officer for twenty years. He and his wife have one daughter and live in Louisiana.

CONTENTS

★ ★ ★

PART THREE
A CHRISTMAS STORY

PART FOUR
THE WHIRLWIND

PROLOGUE

★ ★ ★

While he waited just offstage, he thought of his mother and of his lifelong—or so it seemed to him at the time—dream of buying a home for her. Since his birth in the tiny three-room house in Tupelo, Mississippi, on that cold afternoon in January of 1935, the milestones of his life had seemed little more than a long succession of shacks and project apartments and shabby rent houses—and of living with relatives while his father was in Parchman Prison.

Today he had combed his hair into glistening Captain Marvel, Jr. swirls, in the likeness of his favorite comic-book character, and had worn a red shirt borrowed from a friend. Almost six feet tall with soulful good looks, he had practiced his songs for anyone who would listen, determined that he would win the annual Humes High School Variety Show.

Eight years before, as a ten-year-old, he had sung at the Mississippi-Alabama Fair to an audience this big. Back then his dream had been little more than a

small, flickering possibility. But *this* was different—
this was Memphis! Somehow he felt that today was
the *real* beginning!

Backstage, he breathed in the smell of old floor
wax and slightly moldy curtains, watched the excitement of the other kids—jostling, bumping into each
other, hyping themselves up or calming themselves
down—and knew that he was the best, that he was going to win. He could almost see, like the long succession of shacks, a long succession of other stages, other
audiences, other—

Then it was his turn to perform.

In the front row, a sixteen-year-old with a blond
ponytail watched him slouch out onto the stage. Turning to her best friend, she whispered, "He's kind of
strange—don't you think? A *real* oddball."

"Maybe. He *does* wear those funny clothes, and
then there's all that long hair," the friend said as she
blinked behind her glasses, "but just wait till you hear
him *sing*!"

"Aw, he can't be *that* good," the blonde shot back,
but had to suppress a gasp when the boy in the red
shirt stepped before the microphone, propped his foot
on a chair, and suddenly slid his guitar around to the
front. She stared into his dark eyes, noticed the
slightly crooked smile, and sighed as he began to sing.
Halfway though the first number, she fainted.

When the thirty acts had finished their perform-
ances, Miss Scrivener, his homeroom and history
teacher, who produced the show, had decided that
only one act would be allowed the honor of an en-
core—the one declared the winner by getting the most
applause.

"It's you, Elvis," Miss Scrivener announced, turning to him with a smile.

But the torrential applause had already told him and, hidden by the curtain, he had set himself at the edge of the stage. Taking the stool once more, he strummed his guitar softly and sang "Old Shep," the song of his boyhood. No one fainted, but the lyrics and the feeling in his voice touched something inside his classmates. Some were wiping away tears by the time he had finished. The applause was deafening.

In moments like these, we speak whatever is deepest inside us. Responding to years of ridicule and teasing from many of his classmates, he could have said, "That'll teach 'em to make fun of me!" or, "I guess I showed 'em!" But he didn't.

"They liked me, Miss Scrivener," Elvis beamed as he left the stage. "They *really* liked me!"

PART ONE
★ ★ ★

THE APPOINTED
HOUR

ONE

SHARON

★ ★ ★

"I helped him with this speech, Mama." Sharon, at fifteen, looked very much like her father who was about to speak on the floor of the Louisiana House of Representatives. She had worn her new summer dress with tiny pink roses and lace-trimmed bodice for this very special occasion. "He told me I know more 'pretty' words than *he* does."

Catherine, wearing a lavender blouse and gray skirt, gazed into Sharon's eyes, as blue as her own. The cornflower blue eyes were the only physical trait that Catherine had passed on to her daughter. She liked to think, however, that she had something to do with Sharon's gentle spirit. "I know you did, sweetheart. Sometimes it takes a woman's touch with words to make other men swallow political speeches."

"I sure hope so," Sharon nodded, gazing from the visitors' section back toward her father. "Daddy said this is an important issue."

Lane Temple, his brown hair streaked with gray,

his ex-Ol' Miss quarterback's body still lean and hard from weekly exercise, unbuttoned the coat of his tan suit and loosened his tie. Stepping to the podium, he took stock of his audience. Messengers and pages made their appointed rounds among the representatives who were busy talking among themselves, reading bills, making telephone calls, and smoking cigarettes and cigars with dedicated fervor.

Gazing about at the elaborate chamber constructed of stone, bronze, and wood, with desks of walnut and Australian laurel and the intricate detail of Louisiana symbols such as pinecones and cattails, Lane wondered if there was a time past when the decorum of the House matched the elegant decor of the building. In his two years as a member of this somewhat less-than-august body, he had learned to deal with bedlam.

"What's Daddy waiting for down there, Mama?" A tiny vertical line creased Sharon's clear brow.

"He's just deciding how to start his speech," Catherine replied with a half smile, wondering what her husband would come up with this time.

Lane slipped the starter's pistol from his coat pocket, pointed it upward, and fired. The shot boomed throughout the chamber, reverberating off the lofty ceiling and the marble floors. Women screamed, men ducked beneath desks. Four uniformed Capitol policemen, their eyes wide with fear and disbelief, rushed toward the podium.

Holding the tiny pistol by the end of the barrel with his fingertips, Lane shouted, "Starter's pistol. Only uses blanks," and laid it on the edge of the podium.

A grizzled sergeant, his knotty fist raised in anger, growled, "I oughta run you in, Temple!"

Lane held out both hands in front of his waist, wrists close together.

"It's not worth all the paper work I'd have to do." The sergeant waved him off, turned, and stalked back up the aisle, grumbling. "Never know what's gonna happen around this place. I shoulda kept my job up at the insane asylum in Jackson where the people ain't so nutty nutty."

"Now!" Lane began, shuffling a few papers in front of him. "If it's all right with the rest of you, I'd like to take a quick shot at this gambling issue."

Out on the floor of the House, men were grumbling and cursing as they clambered from underneath desks, picked up their scattered copies of House and Senate bills, and generally gathered their wits about them. The shot had called to mind for many of them the death of Huey Long twenty years before in the hallway just outside their chamber.

"Somebody oughta take a shot at *you*, Temple," a sallow-faced man in the back shouted.

Lane smiled, knowing that he now had the attention of most of his fellow representatives. "Governor Kennon and Francis Grevemberg, the state police superintendent, have cracked down hard on gambling in this state over the past three years."

Suddenly, the chamber's heavy oak doors opened noisily and a dour-faced man appeared, holding onto an expensive unlit Cuban cigar. His brows were knit together in what appeared to be perpetual disapproval.

As she spotted him, Sharon nudged her mother and asked, "Who's that, Mama?" She pointed to the short, stocky man in a perfectly tailored blue suit. He stood rigidly just inside the main entrance, his dark eyes glinting with a cold light.

17

" . . . Especially in New Orleans," Lane said flatly, noticing André Catelon, his old nemesis, glaring at him from the rear of the chamber.

Catherine leaned forward, whispering in her daughter's ear. "That's André Catelon, the Senator from New Orleans."

Sharon caught her breath at the sound of the name, remembering that Catelon was the man who had framed her father and had him sent to prison. She recalled the night they took Lane away—the worst of her life. That night she came to realize the presence of genuine evil in the world.

"Some people," Catherine went on with a glance in Catelon's direction, "think he's got some gambling interests down in Jefferson Parish. Now, let's listen to what your daddy has to say."

"The governor and his men have busted up thousands of slot machines," Lane told the gathering. "They've closed down gambling houses like the Beverly Club and Southport down in Jefferson Parish, and just about put the lotteries and pinball operations out of business.

"But," Lane continued, glancing at his notes, "there's an ugly rumor going around that some of our colleagues over in the Senate want to pass a bill to make some types of gambling legal in this state."

Several of the House members turned around in their seats, their eyes riveted on the senator from New Orleans.

Red-faced now, Catelon whirled about and stormed out of the House Chambers.

Lane finished the body of his speech, shoved his single five-by-seven card aside, and walked out onto the House floor. "The very *thought* of someone considering legalizing gambling is incomprehensible to

18

me. It would be like turning a beast of prey loose to devour the poorest, weakest, and most vulnerable of our citizens."

"I helped him with this part," Sharon whispered.

Catherine smiled and patted her daughter's hand, then turned back to her husband. She knew that some of the legislators had already considered legalizing gambling in Louisiana, and that Lane would have to hit the issue hard to counteract the lure of the big-moneyed Las Vegas crowd.

Feeling very proud of her husband as she listened to his impassioned speech, Catherine noticed that the normal hustle-bustle on the House floor had slackened considerably. *Maybe it's not his speaking skills— maybe they're just watching to see what he'll pull off next.*

"Not only does gambling breed crime and corrupt government"—Lane paused to take stock of his audience—"but it's a false economy. Most of the so-called *profits* are taken out of Louisiana. What little money reaches the state coffers is more than offset by the decimation of families. Mortgage notes, rent payments, groceries, utilities, clothes for children, medical care—all sacrificed on the altars of roulette, dice, and blackjack."

Some of the legislators were now glancing about furtively at their colleagues.

"We live in a country and a state founded on Christian values," Lane concluded, walking back behind the podium. He gazed at a few of his fellow legislators, shifting about uneasily in their leather chairs. "And those who count themselves friends of the cardsharps will answer for it at the polls."

A smattering of applause ran though the crowd as Lane returned to his desk.

"He made a fine speech, didn't he, Mama?" Sharon's face glowed with pride in her father.

"He sure did, honey," Catherine agreed, "and it wouldn't have been nearly as good without your help."

★ ★ ★

"This is so much fun!" Sharon took a swallow of her Coke, then set the bottle down on the grass beside her. "I wish we could do this all the time."

Catherine had spread a flowered quilt in the shade of a young cypress that stood on the edge of Capitol Lake. As Sharon helped her unpack the basket, Catherine marveled that their daughter still wanted to spend time with her and Lane.

Recalling Jessie, their eldest daughter, as a fifteen-year-old, Catherine could still see her lying on the floor of her bedroom, curlers in her hair, bobby-soxed feet propped on the wall, talking endlessly to girlfriends or her latest beau. She and Lane had become little more than the wardens who cramped the style of her social life with their silly rules.

Lane took off his jacket and sprawled on the quilt, staring up at a puffy white cloud resembling a clown face that floated against the blue dome of the sky. "Ah, *this* is the life," he sighed. "I could lie here till nighttime if we didn't have that session facing us this afternoon."

"Just skip it," Sharon said offhandedly, although she was the most responsible of the four Temple children and would never consider shirking a duty herself.

"Listen to you." Lane propped up on one elbow, eyeing his daughter with mock gravity. "You wouldn't skip a class if somebody planted a bomb in it."

20

"Shows how much *you* know! Last week I was five minutes late for English!"

"Five minutes!" Lane turned to Catherine. "Cath, did you hear that? Our Sharon actually made a *mistake.*"

Catherine continued spooning potato salad from a glass bowl onto paper plates without looking up. "I'd better alert the media! Just let me finish here first."

Sharon smiled at her mother's dry sense of humor, then took the plate of potato salad along with a po' boy made with soft, warm French bread with a crispy crust. Thin slices of fried catfish were accompanied by sliced tomatoes, lettuce, and mayonnaise. "I could eat these every day," she mumbled, taking a big bite of the long, narrow sandwich.

Lane added Tabasco sauce to his po' boy and joined Sharon in the miniature feast.

After the meal, Lane and Catherine sipped coffee from a red Thermos bottle while Sharon finished the last of her Coke. A breeze off the river wrinkled the dark surface of the lake and touched the cattails in the shallows, causing them to wobble and sway against each other.

"How's the latest column for the *North Baton Rouge Journal* coming along, Monkey?"

"Daddy," Sharon corrected her father quickly. "You've got to stop calling me that!"

"You used to climb all over me like a monkey when you were little."

"That was a long time ago."

"Maybe for you." Lane, a soft light coming to his eyes, glanced at Catherine. "Not for me."

Sharon sat up straight and adjusted her gold-rimmed glasses on the bridge of her nose. "I'm doing a piece about the industrial development along the river from here all the way down to New Orleans."

"That's heady stuff for a tenth-grader," Lane observed, resting his arms across his knees.

"I think it's interesting. They're already calling it the 'Miracle Strip.' It's the fastest-growing industrial area in the country."

"Sometimes I wonder if it's all happening *too* fast," Catherine said as she repacked the wicker picnic hamper. "I kind of like Baton Rouge the way it is."

Lane lay back again on the shade-cooled quilt, hands clasped behind his head, staring at the sky. "We might end up like Los Angeles . . . with smog."

"With *what*?" Catherine asked, pausing with a jar of pickles halfway to the hamper.

"Smog, Mama," Sharon explained, gazing at a brightly colored mallard paddling in the lake next to a stand of grayish brown cypress knees. "It's a word somebody just made up a few months ago—a combination of smoke and fog—and it makes your eyes burn. Anybody with respiratory problems has a hard time when it gets bad."

Catherine turned her attention back to the hamper. "See, I knew bad things would happen when towns got too big. I don't like all this change."

"Well, I don't make value judgments in the article," Sharon explained. "I just report the facts."

" 'Just the facts, Ma'am,' " Lane teased. "You sound like Joe Friday on 'Dragnet.' "

Sharon smiled, then began slipping out of her stockings and shoes. "Do we have any bread left?"

Catherine reached into the hamper and handed her a hunk of the French bread.

"Thanks," Sharon said, eyes fixed on the mallard gliding close to the water's edge. "I hope he hasn't had his lunch yet." Sharon got up and walked slowly to the edge of the lake, sat down on the grassy bank, and dangled her feet in the water. Then she began tearing off small chunks of bread and tossing them out near the cypress knees.

The mallard turned away from this intruder, then, seeing the bread floating on the water, stopped and paddled slowly back for his free meal. Following the sodden white trail over to the bank, he soon was taking pieces out of Sharon's hand.

Catherine sat next to her husband, staring at their youngest daughter, the noonday drone of the city almost unnoticed in this small enclave of trees and grass and water. "She has such a placid nature."

"Uh-huh," Lane mumbled drowsily. "Think we could transplant some of it into Cass?"

"There's nothing wrong with Cass," Catherine defended, thinking of her youngest son, who had the same white-blond hair and small frame as Sharon, but was as volatile and unpredictable as the sudden summer storms of south Louisiana.

"I didn't say there was. But I'd sleep better at night if he was a little more like his sister or, even better, like Dalton. With that boy it's football practice, homework, and bed at ten—just like clockwork every day."

"Cass is going to do something . . . *unusual* with his life," Catherine offered. "Wait and see."

"I don't think there's any doubt about *that*," Lane agreed quickly.

Catherine patted him on the leg. "Well, I think all *four* of our children are special. Look what Jessie did. How many girls get to go on a USO tour with Bob Hope?"

"You're right," Lane yawned. "And I sure wish she'd get the bright lights and glitter out of her blood."

"Oh, she doesn't even *think* about that anymore."

23

"I wish that were true. But I don't think she'll be satisfied with teaching music just yet."

Catherine's voice carried a note of concern. "That's why she's getting her degree at LSU."

"She's twenty-two and still not finished either." Lane stretched and yawned.

"She missed a year while she was in Hollywood and Korea. Otherwise, she'd be finished."

Sitting up on the quilt, Lane rubbed his eyes. "I think she's just not interested."

Catherine let the disturbing conversation die, turning her attention back to Sharon. "I think Sharon's working too hard for a girl her age. She should be enjoying her vacation—having some fun instead of working for that newspaper."

"That's how she *has* fun, Cath."

"But she's starting to look a little pale to me." A shadow flickered across Catherine's brow.

"She's always been pale, but maybe she does need to take some time off," Lane sided with his wife. "She went right from school to that newspaper job."

"Why don't you talk to her about it," Catherine suggested. "She thinks the sun rises and sets in you."

★ ★ ★

"The ad calls ya'll 'Telephone Girls.' It says that you 'enjoy interesting and important jobs in a growing industry.'" Sharon held her yellow pencil close to the steno pad as she sat at the Formica-topped table in the break room. She wore brown penny loafers, jeans with rolled cuffs, and a white blouse. "It makes the job seem exciting, the way you use all this modern equipment for worldwide communication."

Across from Sharon, Joyce Whitley sipped her strong, Pet Milk-whitened coffee from a chipped mug.

Her reddish brown hair was pinned up and dark circles beneath her faded gray eyes gave them a raccoon-like appearance. "Important? Exciting?"

"That's what the advertisement said."

"Some Wall Street ad jockey must have written that," Joyce grunted, gazing through the plate glass that separated the break room from the dozens of operators plugging and unplugging wires at banks of switchboards.

Sharon glanced at Joyce, then out at the work area, then jotted down a few notes. "You don't sound too happy to be out in the workplace, Joyce."

"Workplace? You musta been reading one of them women's magazines—*Ladies' Home Journal* or something."

Taken aback by Joyce's tone of bitterness, Sharon plunged ahead anyway, determined to do her story. "No. It's just a term I picked up from reading about women working out of the home back during the war."

Joyce stared into her coffee cup. "Well, I can tell you I'd rather be home washing and ironing than coming to *this* place every day."

"You think you'd like staying home?"

"Don't really know," Joyce mumbled. "I was only married six months—then I had to get out and make a living."

Sharon felt herself being drawn into the misfortunes of Joyce Whitley. She knew as a reporter that she had to maintain her distance, but was already beginning to see how difficult and elusive an objective that could be.

"Soon as ol' Harold found out I was gonna have a baby, he up and took off. Haven't laid eyes on him since." Joyce sighed wistfully at the schoolhouse

25

clock on the wall. "I'd love to have one of them fancy homes in the suburbs with all them newfangled gadgets like a dishwasher, vacuum cleaner, electric toaster."

Sharon pictured her mother's polished-chrome-and-gleaming-tile kitchen.

"Instead," Joyce went on in her singsong voice, "I work a split shift at this place and walk around in a daze all the time 'cause I never can sleep right."

Sharon felt herself being dragged almost physically into Joyce's drab, tasteless world.

"Well," Joyce moaned, standing up and placing her cup in the sink behind the table, "it's time to get back to my public."

Rising from her chair, Sharon extended her hand. "I appreciate your time."

"*Why* did you say you wanted to talk to me, sugar?"

"I'm doing an article for the newspaper called 'Modern Women in the Workplace.'"

"Well, you can tell 'em for ol' Joyce that it ain't what it's cracked up to be." With a glance at Sharon's neatly pressed jeans and blouse, Joyce produced an especially pitiful expression on her sharp face. "I don't even know how I'm gonna afford milk for the baby tonight."

★ ★ ★

Catherine gazed out the screened back window of her kitchen. The dappled light spilling down through the live oak gave the whole yard a green-gold cast. Water flowed down the three-tiered fountain, playing a tinkling musical background for the thrush singing on one of the low spreading limbs. The warm June air carried the fragrance of the honeysuckle climbing a

trellis at the end of the gallery. "How did your first in-
terview go today?"

"I talked to a lady named Joyce." Sharon pried the
top off a Peter Pan jar and spread a thick coating of
peanut butter on a slice of fresh white bread. Then she
dipped the knife into a jar of Catherine's homemade
fig preserves.

"Sharon! Haven't I told you to use a clean knife for
that? Now, just look at the mess you've made of the
figs."

"Sorry."

Catherine watched her daughter rake the figs onto
the peanut butter, add another slice of bread, and bite
hungrily into the sandwich.

"Hmm, that's *so* good!" Sharon mumbled as she
pulled the cardboard top off a quart bottle and filled
a glass with frothy, cold milk.

Sharon had always been the most finicky eater of
her children and Catherine found herself staring with
surprise at the way she was devouring her sandwich.
She walked over to the table and sat down across from
her daughter. "You act like you haven't eaten all day."

"Missed breakfast," Sharon replied before taking
another big bite.

"What did you have for lunch?"

Sharon colored slightly, then pointed at her full
mouth and waved the question away.

"Well?" Catherine waited until she had finished
chewing and had taken a swallow of milk.

With a sheepish smile, Sharon stared out the window at a fox squirrel splayed against the rough bark
of the live oak. Its tail flicked a quick warning to its
cousins in nearby trees. *Something's amiss out there in
Squirrelsville,* Sharon thought.

Sharon stood up and walked over to the window.

27

"I thought that's what it was." She watched the neighbor's big orange cat slink gracefully across the lawn beneath the trees. "The whole squirrel tribe is on alert, now that Claude's on the prowl."

Catherine already suspected what had happened to Sharon's lunch money. Since childhood she had given her toys away to other children, her allowance to tramps who happened to wander into their neighborhood, and, on occasion, she had raided her own closet for clothes when one of her playmates looked particularly threadbare. She had quit scolding her overly generous daughter long ago, but her curiosity had been piqued.

"I gave my lunch money to Joyce," Sharon blurted out, then took another bite of her sandwich.

"This Joyce woman is working, I assume. Otherwise, you wouldn't have interviewed her."

Sharon's blue eyes darkened slightly. "Sure she is, but she's got this little boy who's sick a lot and her rent's awfully high and . . . well, she's just got a lot of problems." Wiping a smear of peanut butter from her upper lip with the tip of her forefinger, she gazed out the window as a cloud floated by overhead, casting the yard into shade and then back into sunlight.

"I don't mind your generous nature, sweetheart," Catherine reassured her daughter, "but I don't want to see you going hungry, either."

"Okay, Mama." Sharon swallowed and drank some milk. "Unless I see some ribs poking out through their skin, they don't get a dime out of me."

Catherine smiled and shook her head. "How'd the other interviews go?"

"I think most of the women who have jobs would rather stay home and raise children like you do."

"I worked at the school for a while—remember?"

Catherine thought back to the days when Lane had been called back into the marines to go to Korea and of how short money had been. "But I have to admit, I'd rather stay home."

Sharon finished her sandwich, swallowed the last of the milk and, with a sigh of contentment, sat back in her chair. "I talked to a lady who sells women's clothes at Goudchaux's, a secretary at Blake and Bowles Office Supply, and a clerk at Ourso's."

"That must have been interesting, meeting all those people," Catherine said, smiling.

"I guess," Sharon agreed, with a shrug. "Nobody cared about their jobs very much though, except the lady at Goudchaux's, and I think she just likes clothes a lot. The way she carried on, I think she'd work there for free."

"You think you'll like your work at the newspaper?"

"Oh yes. . . ." Sharon beamed.

Catherine noticed the white mustache of milk on her daughter's upper lip, suddenly remembering her as a toddler.

"I'll only be doing two or three short columns a week, but it'll be *such* good experience."

"When are you going to write this one?"

"Oh, I've already written it. Finished it down at the office before I left."

Catherine nodded her head, thinking of how Sharon had always stayed ahead of the rest of her class. She had pushed well beyond her years intellectually, but in some ways still seemed like a twelve-year-old. "I should have known. What's next?"

"They haven't given me anything yet, but I got this idea for a story last week."

Leaning her elbows on the table, Catherine rested

her chin in her cupped hands. "Is it about a little girl who gives all of her money away to strangers?"

"No, Mama," Sharon grinned. "It's about a little dog. I bet you've seen him." She pointed to the north. "He lives in that yellow house on Longfellow—you know, the one back behind Delmont Village."

"You mean that little brown-and-white fyce?"

"That's the one." Sharon walked across the kitchen and placed her knife and glass in the sink, then put the peanut butter and preserves away as she continued to talk. "Well, I've noticed for a long time now that he always lies down at the foot of the front steps around three-thirty every day. He's never missed, as many times as I've been by there."

"That's a story?"

"It is since I talked to Mrs. Dulany, the lady who lives in the house."

"I'm all ears."

Sharon sat back down across from her mother. "She said that Edgar—that's the dog's name—waited there on the front walk for her son to come home from school at three-thirty every day."

Catherine noticed the wonder and excitement in Sharon's eyes as she spoke.

"Well, after two years, Linton—that's her son—graduated from Istrouma High and joined the army"—Sharon's face clouded over—"then he got killed at the Battle of the Bulge."

"There were two boys from Sweetwater who died there," Catherine offered, then wondered why people always added their stories of death to others.

"She showed me pictures of when he was in school and some that he sent home from the army."

Catherine pushed aside memories of two wars that had separated her and Lane. "That sounds like it could be an interesting story."

Sharon stood up. "I'm going to work on it right now. It'll be the best thing I've ever written."

"Why don't you rest a bit first? You'll have plenty of time after supper."

"The Muse is upon me, Mother." After a quick pirouette on her toes, Sharon tilted her chin upward and cupped her hand behind her ear. "I must obey her siren call. Besides," she called back from the hall, "I want to watch 'Ozzie and Harriet' tonight on TV."

Catherine watched her youngest daughter skip up the stairs to her room. She tried to remember a time when Sharon had been disobedient or sullen or disrespectful. If there had been one, it was hidden in a mother's heart.

In her room, Sharon slipped her penny loafers off, sat down at her writing desk next to the window, and rolled a fresh sheet of paper into the twenty-year-old Royal typewriter that Lane had bought for her at one of the shops in the French Quarter down in New Orleans.

Through her window, Sharon could see the upper limbs of the live oak, their tendrils of Spanish moss lifting in the afternoon breeze.

Downstairs, Catherine had begun to prepare supper for her family. The familiar sounds drifting up the stairs gave Sharon a sense of comfort as her fingers flicked across the keys of the typewriter, transforming her thoughts into form and substance.

Edgar's Story

Drawn back to that same spot at the foot of the front steps every day, he waited for a master who would never return. For eleven years passersby would see him in the blistering afternoon sunlight, shivering in a cold winter rain, or watching autumn leaves scrape down the sidewalk in the wind—always faithful to the appointed hour, listening for that special voice calling his name.

Edgar wasn't much to look at when the fifteen-year-old boy found him, shivering and alone, behind . . .

TWO

REBEL

★ ★ ★

"Well, *that* was a complete waste of time." Austin Youngblood, his tan chinos stylishly rumpled, his white, button-down collar shirt in marked contrast to his deep tan, strolled out of the Paramount Theater next to Jessie.

"What do you mean, 'a waste of time'?" Jessie protested. Wearing a sleeveless summer dress, she shivered slightly in the night wind that blew in from the river. "I think James Dean's the best actor *ever*."

"You think he's *cute*," Austin corrected. "You can't really call what he did acting, can you? That hunkered-down, humped-over, mumbling and whining all the way through the show. An arrested-development adolescent."

"Hmmph." Jessie dismissed Austin's opinion with a toss of her head, the marquee lights flashing in her pale blond hair. "You think you're *so* smart with all your big-shot Harvard psychology!"

"I'm in law, remember? Not psychology. And this

character Dean played—you don't have to be a psy-
chologist to see what this guy's problem is."

"And what's that, Mr. Know-it-all?"

"He needs to get a job."

"What?"

"Sure. He's got a nice home, parents who love him,
and even his own car. By the way, I thought that 'Merc'
was the best part of the whole movie"—Austin
stopped at the curb, giving Jessie a sidelong glance—
"except maybe for Natalie Wood."

Jessie punched him playfully on the shoulder.
"What's so great about *her*?"

Austin paused, staring reflectively toward the
levee two blocks away. Then he tapped the side of his
head lightly with one forefinger. "She has such a fine
. . . mind."

Jessie turned away, her skirt whirling about her
slim legs, and started toward the parking garage.

With a muffled laugh, Austin started after her.
"C'mon, Jess. She's not *half* as pretty as you."

Jessie slowed until Austin caught up to her.

"I just thought the whole movie was shallow," Austin continued. "I mean, this guy's got *everything* and
all he does is complain."

Jessie's thoughts raced back to the years that she
and Austin were in high school together. She remembered what a rebel *he* had been, in spite of having rich
parents and his own car. She had to admit, though,
that he never did whine and mumble and complain.

Austin continued his critique of the movie. "His
stupidity even got his best friend ki—" His words
broke off abruptly.

Jessie had seen too late where Austin's words were
taking him—both of them. She could almost see the
heavy fog swirling above the river, could almost hear

the thundering roar of the locomotive barreling down on them.

Austin's face had gone slack with the memory of the terrible night years before on that towering dark trestle. He lapsed into silence as they walked across the street and waited for the attendant to bring his car down.

With a cry of tires on pavement, the young attendant, his skin the color of café au lait, swung the white convertible around the corner and down the last ramp. Stepping out, he straightened the black bow tie that matched his sharply creased trousers. "Fifty-five T-bird. Yas-suh. That's a *fine* automobile!" He produced a white handkerchief and wiped an imaginary speck off the fender. "Maybe someday. . . ."

Austin handed him a dollar bill, helped Jessie slide beneath the wheel onto the passenger's side, and got in. Pulling out onto Convention Street, he ran the red light at Lafayette and coasted down the hill toward the levee, turning left onto River Road.

"I thought you'd given up doing things like that."

"Oh, you mean running that red light? I guess old habits die hard."

Jessie listened to the lonesome sound of a tugboat whistle far out on the river. She hoped the evening wouldn't be ruined by the memories that had surprised both of them. After all the years and all the miles, it seemed as though that solitary night would haunt them for the rest of their lives.

Driving in silence, Austin reached over and flicked the radio on. The dial's amber glow was followed by the sound of a disc jockey extolling the musical prowess of the country's latest rock-and-roll sensation. "Now here he is, folks, soon to be the new King of Rock and Roll—Elvis Presley—singing the song that started it all, 'That's All Right Mama.' "

"Just listen to this *voice!*" Jessie swooned.

Austin had reached for the dial to change stations. "You actually *like* this guy?"

"Well, I have to admit the *song* could be better," Jessie admitted.

"Oh, I don't know; listen to those *meaningful* lyrics." Austin turned the volume up. "He's telling his mama that something's 'all right.' I don't quite understand why he has to tell her a hundred times—but then, it's *his* song."

Sighing, Jessie leaned back against the white leather seat. "I can't really explain what's so special about the way he does a song. I think you have to be a woman to understand."

"I guess so."

Jessie found herself coming to the young singer's defense. "I'm sure he'll have better songs to record after he develops his style a little more."

"Maybe." When the song was over, Austin punched a button to another station that had just begun to play "Secret Love" by Doris Day. "Now, *that's* more like it."

"It's nice," Jessie agreed halfheartedly, "but it's certainly not Elvis."

"Aw, come on. That guy won't last six months!"

"Yes, he will!" Jessie said the words with conviction, as though no alternative existed. "Rock-and-roll music has some real possibilities."

Austin turned up an embankment toward the entrance of the old Municipal Dock, now obsolete and abandoned. "You can't be serious?"

Jessie merely nodded.

"With all your musical training and experience, you think *that* stuff has merit?"

"All the songs aren't like 'Rock Around the Clock'

or 'Tutti Frutti' or 'Shake, Rattle, and Roll.'" Jessie
wondered why she found herself defending the na-
tion's latest musical fad when she seldom listened to
it herself. "There are a few good ones—'Earth Angel'
by the Penguins and 'Only You' by the Platters."

Austin grunted in reply. The white Thunderbird's
tires thrummed along the plank-floored runway. With
tin roof and wooden walls, it resembled a long, covered bridge and led from the levee out to the dock.

"I didn't say I thought rock and roll was great music or anything." Jessie stared at the windowpanes
flashing by in the dim interior of the runway. Some
had been shattered with only jagged shards remain-
ing around the edges of the frames. Others carried the
neat, round holes of .22-caliber rifle slugs. Glancing
ahead, she saw a brightening where the tunnel led out
onto the wide expanse of the main dock.

Pulling out onto the heavy timber flooring, Austin
braked the T-bird, letting its tires rest against a weathered eight-by-twelve that had been bolted to the edge
of the dock forty feet above the swirling muddy water.
"Sure is pretty at night."

Jessie glanced upriver at the glow of the downtown business district and beyond, toward the million
glittering lights of the vast Esso Standard Oil com-
plex. "It is, isn't it? We haven't been out here in such
a long time, I'd almost forgotten."

Austin killed the engine but left the radio on. "I'll
have my law degree next year, Jess."

A string section played the theme song from *Mou-
lin Rouge*.

"I know."

"And you'll be graduating from LSU."

"I guess."

"What do you mean, you *guess*?"

37

"Oh, I don't know." Jessie said, staring straight ahead at the grain elevator rising on the far shore. Across the surface of the river, the full moon had laid down a silvery path of light leading directly toward its brooding dark bulk. "Maybe I'll try something else."

Austin flicked the radio off. He reached for Jessie and touched the side of her face with the tips of two fingers, turning it toward him. "I hope that's supposed to be a joke."

Jessie placed her hand over Austin's, pressing it against her cheek. "Would it be so awful if it weren't?"

"Jessie, we've already been through this—the USO tour with Bob Hope, nightclubs, screen tests."

"But this wouldn't be anything like that," Jessie protested. "You know why I left Hollywood. They expected a girl to have a lot more than talent to break into the movies."

Austin took his hand away, shaking his head slowly back and forth. "What is it *this* time, Jess?"

"Don't act like that, sweetheart." Jessie took Austin's hand in both of hers and leaned her head against his shoulder. "We've got the rest of our lives to be together."

"Not if you end up chasing one rainbow after another, we don't."

"I just need to know if I can make it as a singer. Hollywood's out—so is New York. It may be even worse."

"What's left, then?"

"Memphis."

"Rock and roll."

"They're starting to sing a few ballad-type songs," Jessie argued, now that her secret was out in the open. "A good female vocalist just might stand a chance."

"How long have you been thinking about this?"

"Six months or so."

Austin watched a deep-water vessel pushing up-river, heading toward the Standard Oil docks located just south of the bridge. "Have you told your parents?"

"No," Jessie admitted. "I guess I just now decided it's what I want to do."

"I may not be around when you finish this one, Jess." Austin caught sight of a shadowy figure walking the deck of the huge ship. He could barely make out the profile of the sailor as he moved about and bent to his work.

Jessie felt a coldness in the pit of her stomach. *"Don't say that!"* She tried to bridge the gulf that had suddenly opened up between them. "You know we're going to spend our lives together. After all we've been through!"

"Maybe that's it. After all we've been through, maybe it's time we made some commitments."

"But I love you, Austin!" Jessie found her voice freighted with a tone of desperation. "I have, since that first day we met. Remember how—"

The roar of the Ford's engine drowned out the sound of Jessie's voice as Austin spun the car around backward, skidded on the slick wooden surface of the dock, and sped off down the darkened corridor toward the levee.

★ ★ ★

The cabin nestled in the shadows of virgin cypress trees, towering more than a hundred feet against a blue summer sky. Located deep in the vastness of the Atchafalaya Swamp, it rested on pilings seven feet above the tea-colored water and forty feet out from the shoreline. Cypress knees stood like jagged brown teeth in the shallows.

"I think this is the prettiest place in the world." Cassidy, his hair bleached almost white by the sun and rumpled from three days without the touch of a comb, sat in an ancient ladder-back chair on the little tin-roofed gallery.

Like his younger brother, Dalton wore only cut-off jeans, but his broad chest and heavily muscled arms and shoulders contrasted sharply with Cassidy's slim, wiry frame. "You'd think *anyplace* away from a schoolhouse was beautiful."

"Not so, dear brother." Cassidy waved his hand in a sweeping gesture toward the lake, its surface glittering in the morning sunlight. "I find this place invigorating!"

Dalton sat on the steps that led down to the little dock where a homemade pirogue drifted at the end of a cotton rope. "Where'd you learn words like that?"

"I don't spend all my time on football fields and in smelly locker rooms."

"Judging from your report card, you don't spend much time with your books, either."

Cassidy, unable to think of a snappy comeback, watched a snowy egret's solitary flight across the lake. Landing in the shadows of the forest near the opposite shore, it began stalking minnows on its stilt-like legs.

Dalton felt a twinge of guilt about his reply to his brother. "You know, Cass, if you'd put on a little weight, you could make the football team yourself."

"I don't like *team* sports."

"Aw, give it a try. Nobody else on the JV team is as fast as you are."

"Nobody on the varsity either," Cassidy replied matter-of-factly, glancing over his shoulder.

Dalton stood up quickly. "Oh, yeah. Well there's

two I know of—me and Billy."

"Cannon ain't human, so he don't count. I think he's half horse," Cassidy shot back.

"What about me?"

"I'm faster."

"You're a thirteen-year-old runt! I'm *seventeen*!" His physical prowess on the line now, Dalton forgot all about brotherly benevolence. "Nobody was faster than me in the hundred at the state finals last spring—"

"Except Billy." Dalton's reaction was better than Cassidy had hoped for.

"Yeah," Dalton grunted reluctantly, "but I just might take him this year."

Cassidy turned his head and grinned at the egret on the far shoreline. "Forget it."

Dalton stomped down the steps to the dock, glancing about at the water and the vast forest. "I wish there was someplace we could run. I'd wipe that smile off your face in ten seconds."

"No time, anyway."

"Why?"

"We used up all the crickets this morning. Gotta go dig some worms if we want to fish this afternoon."

Still fuming to himself, Dalton untied the pirogue. "Well, come on, then!"

Cassidy got up and stepped inside the cabin, pushing the screen door outward against its spring. Turning quickly, he watched Dalton scowl and shake his head when the door banged noisily against the jamb.

"Do you have to do that *every* time you go through that stupid door?"

Grinning, Cassidy buckled Lane's K-bar knife in its leather sheath around his waist. Hefting the marine-issue weapon by its handle, he thought as always, *I*

wonder if Daddy ever stuck any Japs with this thing.
His father had spoken little to him about his years of
combat in the South Pacific.

"C'mon, slowpoke!"

Cassidy dropped a rusty garden trowel into a
Campbell's Pork and Beans can and ran out the door,
making sure he shoved it wide for maximum noise
when it banged shut behind him.

Dalton sat in the bottom of the pirogue, his twelve-
gauge single-barrel shotgun resting across the gunwales.

"You bringing that cannon just to dig worms?"

"I don't go nowhere in cottonmouth country without Ol' Betsy here."

"Don't you ever watch 'Disneyland'?" Cassidy took
another tact, keeping the pressure on his brother.
"Fess Parker's already used that name for his rifle on
'Davy Crockett.' Can't you come up with something
more original?"

"Just get in the boat, will you?"

Cassidy stepped lightly into the fragile craft,
leaned back with his arms along the gunwales, and
stared up at the sky. "I just might go out for track."

Dalton used long, smooth strokes with the paddle
to propel them toward the shore, a V-shaped trail following across the dark surface of the lake. A half-
dozen fleecy white clouds were reflected in the water.
"Won't work."

"Why not?"

"You can't stay out of the principal's office long
enough to run track."

"I just might change my ways."

"And the sun just might turn around and set in the
east tonight." Dalton let the pirogue slip through the

reeds in the shallows and glide onto the low, muddy bank.

Ten minutes later, having convinced Dalton that he should scout around for a better place to dig for worms, Cassidy sat at the base of a huge tupelo gum. He stared upward, watching pale light filter down through the high, green canopy. It gave the forest floor a look of twilight rather than early afternoon.

Closing his eyes and leaning back against the massive tree trunk, Cassidy let the life of the forest flow through him: the dry scent of the Spanish moss and the green lichen on the bark of the trees; the damp, fecund smell of decaying leaves and limbs all about him. Off in the distance the cry of a solitary crow rang out across the trackless swamp.

Cassidy imagined himself as one with the creatures of this wild and savage land: a twelve-foot bull alligator slipping beneath the lake's dark surface; a bobcat making that final headlong rush after a fleeing rabbit; a fawn, timid and fragile and fearful, leaving the safety of the woods for a drink in the lake.

"Get out of here!"

Startled out of his reverie, Cassidy heard the sound of Dalton's voice from fifty feet away, followed by a snarling growl. He grabbed for the handle of the knife, as if by instinct. Instantly, he found himself plunging through a thicket, limbs and vines slapping and pulling at him as he ran. Breaking into the open, he froze.

On the opposite side of the little clearing, Dalton stood with his back against a sycamore, the twelve-gauge jammed against his shoulder. Fear glazed his eyes, but he held the shotgun rock-steady. Forty feet in front of him, a half-grown black bear shook its head, growled once, and charged.

Cassidy saw the smoke and fire burst forth at the end of the shotgun barrel, saw his brother's shoulder jerk backward from the recoil. The bear tumbled head over heels—then, covered with leaves, its chest spouting blood, it rose on its hind legs and stalked doggedly toward its new enemy.

Without thinking, Cassidy sprinted across the clearing after the bear, jerking the K-bar from its sheath as he ran. He could see Dalton, frantically breaking open the shotgun, pulling out the spent shell, digging into his pocket for a fresh one.

When he was directly behind the bear, Cassidy planted his feet, clutched the heavy ribbed handle of the knife with both hands, and drove it with all his strength into the bear's back at the base of its thick neck.

The bear let out a terrible roar of pain and rage, whirling around to face this latest tormentor. The back of one paw caught Cassidy across the chest, sending him sprawling and tumbling against the base of a tree.

Shaking his head to clear his vision, Cassidy struggled to get to his feet. He saw clearly the bear's white canines, long and sharp and gleaming with saliva and blood, smelled its fetid breath as it bore down on him from above—then the thunder of the twelve-gauge roared in his ears. The beast collapsed in a heap onto the soft ground next to his bare feet.

Breathing heavily, Dalton ran to his brother's side. "You okay, Cass?"

Cassidy opened his mouth, but could not seem to form any words or summon the breath to speak them. He stared at the slain bear, its back torn open by the second blast from Dalton's shotgun.

Dalton had already slipped a third shell into the

chamber. "Let's get out of here."

Forcing himself to take hold of the knife, Cassidy tugged it free of the bear's body, wiped it clean on his shirttail, and followed Dalton across the clearing and back toward the lake.

When they reached the water's edge, Cassidy stared down into the pirogue where the two rods and reels lay in the bottom. "We forgot the worms."

"Are you kidding?" Dalton glanced back into the shadowy woods. "I'm not going back *there*."

"You gonna let a dumb bear ruin our fishin'?" A sensation entirely different from anything he had ever experienced suddenly coursed through Cassidy's body. He could almost feel his hands gripping the handle of the big knife as he drove its blade deep into the bear's back, cutting through muscle and sinew and finally hitting against solid bone.

Dalton shook his head slowly. "You never know when you've had enough, do you?"

"*You* did him in, big brother," Cassidy grinned, the heady sensation still very much with him. "I'm not worried a *bit* with you and Ol' Betsy along."

★ ★ ★

"You're the most understanding man in Louisiana." Jessie felt the cool night wind blowing her hair about her face as she held on to Austin's arm.

Austin stared at the white lines flicking past him on the blacktop as he drove south on Highway 1 toward Plaquemine. "Maybe just the most gullible," he suggested, his eyes fixed on the road before him.

Jessie smiled out into the darkness, glad that the feud between them had cooled.

Located south of Baton Rouge on the west bank of the Mississippi, the little town of Plaquemine boasted of having once been the home of Louis Armstrong. On any Friday night, Red Mancuso's club—a mile north of the locks that joined Bayou Plaquemine with the river—was *the* place to be.

"Don't forget you owe me one of those big seafood platters at Bob and Jake's."

"That's our deal." Jessie glanced at Austin, noticing his dark hair in stark contrast to the white shirt, his gray eyes clear and intense in the amber glow of the dashboard. Something about him had always reminded her of Montgomery Clift—or more specifically, the character he had played in *From Here to Eternity*.

Thinking back on their years together as high-school sweethearts, Jessie realized that she had never truly considered marrying anyone else but Austin since they had met. *The time's just not right, though,* Jessie thought, aware she wasn't ready to take that step.

"I wish you'd given me a little more notice about this, Jess." Austin held his wristwatch sideways to the dashboard to catch the light. "I've got to get up at four in the morning to go fishing with my dad."

"I just found out today." Jessie gazed ahead at the glow of the nightclub that also served as a rollerrink. "A girl in my drama class said she heard on the radio that he was singing here tonight. I think he played up at the Louisiana Hayride last weekend."

"You know how I hate places like this."

"It's not like we were going to drink or anything," Jessie insisted. "I promise we'll get out of here just as soon as his first set is over."

Austin pulled off the road, into the Shell parking lot, finding a place between a battered Chevrolet pickup and a pink Cadillac convertible. "I wonder who'd drive a car like that?" He got out and walked around the Ford, opening the passenger-side door. "Nobody from around here—*that's* for sure!"

"I think it belongs to the man we're here to see." Jessie took Austin's arm, walking with him across the parking lot toward the main entrance, ringed with hundred-watt bulbs.

Staring up at the picture of Elvis Presley in his trademark posture—hair flying, arms reaching toward both heaven and earth, his guitar slung like a carbine at his back—Austin made a clicking sound with his tongue. "Um-uh. The things we do for love."

"Oh, come on, now!" Jessie laughed and squeezed his arm. "It can't be *that* bad. You might even *like* some of it."

"Yeah," Austin mumbled, guiding Jessie through the door, "like I enjoy root canals and Yankee food."

The din of two hundred voices and the scraping of tables and chairs as people found seats inside made normal conversation impossible. Jessie pointed out a small table in the back corner, and Austin led interference over to it. The three-piece band was warming up as Jessie and Austin ordered Cokes.

Ten minutes later the young man from Tupelo, wearing black slacks and a pink shirt, sauntered onto the stage. He stepped in front of the microphone, legs spread wide apart, and smiled out at his audience. Slinging his guitar around to the front, he launched into "Blue Moon of Kentucky."

"It's *him*!" Jessie's eyes lighted with recognition as she leaned forward in her chair.

"Him *who*?"

"It's the same boy who beat me in that talent contest years ago in Mississippi!"

"C'mon, Jess."

"No, I really mean it," Jessie insisted, her face aglow with the memory. "He was from Tupelo and he was only eleven years old—two years younger than I was. I thought his name was Melvin or something like that."

Austin glanced up at the energetic performer in the spotlight. "He sure doesn't *act* like a Melvin."

"Elvis. I remember now."

"Eleven years old and he beat you, huh?"

Jessie nodded her head, her eyes still turned toward the stage. "He sang 'Old Shep.' I don't think there was a dry eye in the auditorium when he finished."

"He sure picked the right song. Everybody knows how you *rednecks* are about your dogs."

But Jessie was lost in the music and the spell of the young singer's voice.

Halfway though the song most of the people in the audience were on their feet, clapping along to the driving rhythm of the beat. Seeing the reactions of their girlfriends, some of the men scowled at the young singer, but by the time the next song was over he had even won most of the men over.

Jessie thought of her time in Hollywood, remembering the effect that Tony Vale's smooth, polished style had on an audience—especially the female members. But Tony's charisma paled in comparison to what she was seeing now. Leaning over the table toward Austin, she held one cupped hand next to her mouth. "A performer like him comes along once in a lifetime."

"Thank goodness for that!"

Jessie squeezed Austin's hand. "Be honest, now!"

Gazing across the backs of the patrons, most of

whom were now seated, Austin listened to Presley's almost haunting version of "That's When Your Heartaches Begin."

"I have to admit, he does have . . . something."

THREE

THE FIG TREE

★ ★ ★

Wearing faded jeans and one of her father's old khaki shirts, Jessie watched the water run into the teakettle and listened to it flowing through the pipes. When she turned the faucet off, the pipes sang and stopped with a knock—sounds she remembered as a thirteen-year-old when her family, all six of them, had lived in the little two-bedroom rented garage apartment behind the big house that her father later bought. Since returning from her Hollywood adventures, she had been its sole occupant.

Taking a kitchen match from a box on a shelf above the sink, Jessie held it above the burner on the stove and turned the gas on. With a popping sound flames glowed in a blue circle. Setting the kettle on the stove, she pushed aside the red-and-white checkered curtains and gazed down into the small area of backyard between the garage apartment and a red brick wall at the rear of their property. A willow and a fig tree leaned toward each other like old friends having a talk.

Smiling, Jessie could almost see Cassidy as a five-year-old climbing the forbidden fig tree and an irate Dalton sent by his mother to fetch his little brother down, out of danger. For nine straight years without fail the tree had provided figs for her mother to make preserves for their family.

She remembered the family's first Christmas in their new home and walking along the streets in the chill night air past the old houses with their dry winter lawns and leafless trees, whose branches had formed stark and elegant sculptures in the warm glow of the lights.

The whistling of the teakettle drew Jessie back to the present just as a soft knocking sounded at the door. She turned the burner off and waved through the half-glass door for her mother to come inside.

"I'm not interrupting you, am I, sweetheart?" Catherine wore a print housedress and a smile that, although most people would never have suspected it, hid an approaching sadness.

"No, Mama, you're not interrupting anything," Jessie replied, taking two cups down from a shelf above the stove. "You're just in time for tea."

"Let me do it." Catherine took two tea bags from a tin on the shelf, dropped them into the cups, and filled the cups with steaming water from the teakettle.

Jessie sat down, watching her mother's practiced and precise movements about the tiny kitchen. "You know, you make me so mad sometimes!"

Catherine stopped, her hand on the sugar bowl. "Goodness, what have I done *now*?"

"It's not what you've *done*," Jessie teased. "It's what you *haven't* done."

Catherine sat down across from her daughter, noticing the mischievous gleam in her brown eyes. "And just what is *that* supposed to mean?"

"You haven't gotten any older!" Jessie rolled her eyes toward the ceiling. "Everywhere we go together, people think I'm your *sister*—not your daughter." She knew her mother, having turned forty, needed to hear things like this, and it was true—they had, in fact, been mistaken many times for sisters.

Catherine laughed softly, knowing that Jessie was trying to make the situation more pleasant for her. "I sure will miss your being back here. It's almost the same as when you were living in the house with us."

Jessie noticed a single tear glistening at the corner of her mother's eye.

"And our little chats every afternoon when you'd come home from class."

"Mama, I'm just going to Memphis—not the other side of the world!"

Catherine lifted her tea bag from the cup, squeezed it against her spoon, then poured cream from a delicate porcelain pitcher into the steaming liquid. Adding a spoonful of sugar, she held the cup with both hands, sipping slowly. "I know. It's just that your daddy and I wanted you to finish your education."

"We've been through this." Jessie reached over and laid her hand on top of her mother's. "I've only got one more semester. That's nothing."

"Do it this fall, then."

Jessie stood up and dropped the two tea bags into the trash can beneath the sink. Glancing through the window, she noticed a mockingbird pecking greedily at a half-ripe fig. "I need to do this *now*."

"Why?"

"There's a lot happening right now with this new kind of music in Memphis."

"Rock and roll." Catherine thought she sounded like a doctor giving a patient bad news. *I'm sorry, Mrs. Jones, but all the test results show that you've got 'rock and roll.'*

"That's what they're calling it, yes."

"But you don't sing that kind of stuff," Catherine protested. "You've got too much talent to waste yourself on that dreadful, noisy *not-music*. I don't know what to call it, but in my estimation it's certainly not music, so I'll just call it *not-music*."

"Some of it's okay." Jessie found it very difficult to defend her position against her mother's logic regarding her education. She also had to admit that much of this new music was composed of thumping rhythms, howling singers, and little else. She didn't truly understand why she felt so drawn to Memphis. But one thing she was sure of—listening to the young singer from Tupelo had stirred something inside her, and she wanted very much to be a part of this new movement.

"And I'm told Adolf Hitler was very kind to his dogs," Catherine said softly.

Noticing Sharon's face at the glass door, Jessie let out a sigh of relief and waved her inside.

"Is this one of those private mother-daughter talks?" Sharon asked, pausing just inside the threshold. She wore white shorts and one of Dalton's maroon football jerseys.

"Not at all, baby. Come on in and have some tea with us." Catherine got up, fixed another cup, and set it on the white enameled table.

Sitting down, Sharon smiled at her sister. "I just thought you could use a hand with your packing."

Jessie glanced at Catherine. "Not much left to do, really, and I'm not leaving till next week. I probably won't even be gone long enough to need my winter clothes."

"Now, that's a *real* positive attitude," Sharon said as she sat down, noticing the slight tension between her sister and mother. "If Bob Hope thinks you can make it, that ought to fill you up to the brim with confidence."

"Mama thinks it's the wrong kind of music for me—"

"For *anyone*," Catherine corrected. "Some people are saying that it's undermining our country's values. I've even heard that it's called the devil's music." Having given her pronouncement, she punctuated it with a swallow of tea.

Jessie cut her eyes discreetly in Sharon's direction, then rolled them at the ceiling.

"Well, let's just talk about something else, why don't we," Sharon suggested diplomatically.

"I hear your article about the little dog over on Longfellow Street was a big hit down at the *Morning Advocate*." Jessie beamed proudly at her little sister.

Sharon's cheeks colored slightly. "Oh, it wasn't so much. They got a few letters from people wanting me to do some more—that's about all."

"That's *not* all, either." Catherine glanced at Jessie, then at Sharon. "You mean you haven't told your sister?"

"I haven't told *anyone*, Mother."

Jessie shrugged. "Told *what*?"

"The city editor wants Sharon to do a regular column for the newspaper. It'll come out twice a week."

"Just for a little while—to see how it does," Sharon added.

"I can see it all now." Jessie spread her hands in the air, slowly moving them apart as though unveiling some marvelous truth. "Sharon Temple wins Pulitzer Prize. Fifteen-year-old high-school student, when questioned by this reporter, said, 'My sister taught me everything I know.' "

Sharon laughed, glad that the tension in the room was lifting. "Well, you *did* teach me how to put on makeup. I guess that's *something*."

"I didn't do a very good job, from the looks of you," Jessie commented, tilting Sharon's chin with the tips of her fingers. "You could certainly use some lipstick. A little blush on those pale cheeks of yours wouldn't hurt either."

"I don't have time for such mundane affairs." Sharon closed her eyes dreamily, tilting her head and brushing her hair back from her face. "The literary mind must occupy itself with universal truths, matters of cosmic consequence!"

Catherine relished the time with her two daughters. All differences forgotten for the present, they lost themselves in the joy of each other's company. More tea and more talk swallowed up the hours until a voice cried from downstairs: "Hey, Mama, what's for supper? We're gettin' hungry down here."

"I believe that's my youngest," Catherine said with a smile. "Well, it's been nice, ladies, but duty calls."

"I'll come help with supper, Mother," Sharon offered as she pushed her chair back.

"No, no. You two enjoy yourselves," Catherine insisted. "Everything's almost done, anyway."

Watching her mother close the door behind her, Sharon leaned across the table, speaking in a conspiratorial whisper. "How's Austin taking it?"

"Nobody's here, Sharon. You don't have to talk like Peter Lorre."

Sharon smiled and sat up straight. "Well, what's going on between you two, then?"

Jessie shrugged.

"I take that to mean that he's not especially happy with your rock-and-roll flight of fancy."

"Austin loves me!" Jessie immediately went on the defensive. "And I love him."

"I'm seven years younger than you, Jess," Sharon confessed forthrightly. "And maybe I don't know very much about men." She traced the edge of her cup with the tip of her little finger. "But I think you're getting awfully close to the edge with this latest little adventure of yours."

"The edge of *what*?"

"Of Austin's . . . forbearance."

"Oh, don't be so silly. He's got another whole year of law school anyway."

"I don't think you'll ever find anybody else like Austin. He's so . . . patient with you."

Jessie collected the cups and placed them in the sink. "Well, that's certainly a strange thing to say."

"Why?"

Sitting back down, Jessie enumerated Austin's qualities on her fingers. "Everybody says he's handsome or smart or funny, even rich . . . and all you talk about is his patience."

"Believe me, big sister," Sharon said with the authority of someone who had lived all her life with Jessie, "whoever marries *you* is going to need more *patience* than anything else."

Jessie opened her mouth to reply, closed it in a pout, then began a smile that turned into laughter. Images flashed through her mind of the times when she had sorely tried the patience of her parents. "I guess you know me as well as Mama does. Maybe better."

"I'd just hate to see you mess things up with Austin, Jess. He's so good to you—and good *for* you."

"I know that better than anyone." Jessie pushed her chair back. "Let's go help Mama feed the men in our family."

"That's a job for three, all right."

When Sharon got up, Jessie gave her a big hug. "I'm so glad you're my sister! Sometimes, though, I feel like *you're* the big sister instead of me."

★ ★ ★

Caffey Sams, the biggest and most feared boy in the eighth grade, stood in the shade of a sycamore tree just off the schoolground. He had wiry red hair and a dark gap where his left eyetooth once had been. Mud caked the bottoms of his frayed overalls.

As a child, someone had nicknamed Caffey "Pancake" because the back of his head was so flat, and the name had stuck. No one called him that to his face but Cassidy Temple. Few of his classmates spoke to him as they passed by on their way home.

Afternoon sunlight flashed on the heavy glass door of the school building as it swung outward. Cassidy turned his head, spoke to someone behind him in the shadowed interior, then sauntered down the sidewalk toward the sycamore.

Caffey's face brightened. He admired Cassidy's shiny brown penny loafers and spanking-new Levi's. He had clung to a secret dream for as long as he could remember—that just once, his father would take him shopping for new school clothes. "What'd he do to you?"

"Who? Ol' man Day?"

"No, President Eisenhower," Caffey joked. "Yeah, ol' man Day. You know, the principal of this school. There's only one, and you was in his office."

Cassidy brushed the question aside with a flick of his wrist. "Aw, he didn't do nothin'."

"You get in a fight the first day of school and ol' man Day just lets you walk out?"

"I gotta come over here on Saturday morning and help the custodian." Cassidy squinted at his friend. "Don't you tell my daddy. I'm gonna tell him you and me are going somewhere. Okay?"

"Fine with me." Caffey glanced toward the main entrance of the school building. "You mean he ain't gonna call your daddy hisself and tell on you?"

"Not this time. We made a deal."

"Whew! You're lucky." Caffey wiped the back of his hand across his narrow brow. "When I was in fourth grade the principal called my daddy on me." He pointed to the missing tooth. "I tell 'em I'll do anything now if they just don't call *him*."

"Yeah," Cassidy mumbled, "I heard that story fifteen or twenty times already."

"Sorry, I guess I forgot."

"I need a cigarette."

Caffey grinned, turning the pockets of his overalls inside out. "Take all the money you need."

"Ain't your ol' man got any?"

"Maybe."

Cassidy turned and walked briskly down the sidewalk. "He's *always* got cigarettes. C'mon."

The two boys walked along the sidewalks, some cracked and tilted by the roots from the old trees that grew in the yards of the neat frame houses. Farther on they walked past a barbershop, a pool hall, and two bars with their doors open spilling out hillbilly music and coarse laughter onto the street.

Next to a ramshackle mechanic shop that was no more than a single garage with a hand-painted sign tacked to the front stood Caffey's house. Built of unpainted clapboard with scraps of tarpaper clinging to the roofing tacks it had been nailed with long ago, the little shack had a rusted tin roof and a front porch whose sill had rotted on one end, causing it to slant almost down to the bare earth of the front yard. Between the house and the garage, an ancient Plymouth rusted into the weeds.

In a rickety swing on the porch, Caffey's father snored loudly. Even in sleep, he looked like a giant, bearded version of his son . . . that someone had smeared with grease. Empty Dixie Beer bottles and Picayune cigarette butts littered the floor beneath him. He moaned, turned on one side with the swing creaking and popping beneath his ponderous weight, then lapsed into silence.

Caffey held his forefinger up to his lips, motioning for Cassidy to follow him around the side of the house. In back, the weeds had grown almost as high as the eaves of the house except for the narrow path Caffey had made. There was also an open area around the back door where car parts, an assortment of old tools, and trash littered the bare ground.

Carefully opening the screen door that hung drunkenly by one hinge, Caffey stepped on a grease-caked twelve-by-twelve block and up into the kitchen. Cassidy followed soundlessly behind.

Once inside, Cassidy let his eyes become accustomed to the gloom, but he could not make himself get used to the smell. Chicken bones, crusts of bread, and scraps of food lay on the table, cabinets, and floor.

The stench of rotten food was unmistakable. "How do you *stand* this place?"

Caffey's big face colored slightly. He glanced away and shrugged.

"Where's the smokes?"

Using a chair, Caffey climbed onto the counter, opened a cabinet door, and reached back on a top shelf. Producing a carton of Picayunes, he took one pack out, tossed it to Cassidy, and replaced the carton.

"Where?" Cassidy glanced through the dim front room at the porch where Caffey's father had begun snoring again.

Grabbing a box of kitchen matches from the stove, Caffey motioned for Cassidy to follow him. He jumped into the yard, walked three paces to his right, and entered a tunnel-like path which led deep into the weeds.

Following closely behind his bulky friend, Cassidy found himself strangely elated by the whole experience: the big brute of a man—if he could believe half of what Caffey said about his father—who could awaken and bring drunken mayhem down on them at any moment; the thrill of not only forbidden but *stolen* cigarettes; and this mysterious path leading through a wilderness of weeds.

Caffey slipped through a wire fence, its posts long rotted and held up now by only a tangle of underbrush and saplings. Coming out on the bank of a canal, he pointed to a small shelter made of stakes hammered into the spongy ground and covered with a remnant of canvas.

"Made it myself," Caffey boasted.

Cassidy stared at the crude structure. "I never would have guessed."

"C'mon." Caffey sat down beneath the canvas on a

61

flattened cardboard box marked "Frigidaire."

Sitting down next to him, Cassidy peeled the wrapper back on the Picayune pack and tapped a cigarette out. Then he took a kitchen match from the box Caffey had dropped next to him, flipped it into flame with his thumbnail, and touched it to the tip of the cigarette. Taking a long pull on the cigarette, he lapsed immediately into a coughing spasm.

"I thought you was supposed to be hooked on these things." Caffey lit one for himself, inhaled and let the smoke trail out of his nostrils like a pro.

"I just haven't done it for so long, I guess I forgot how." Cassidy smiled sheepishly, his eyes watering. Taking another drag, he inhaled and blew the smoke out, this time coughing only twice.

The boys smoked in silence, practicing expressions and mannerisms they had seen used by Humphrey Bogart, Gary Cooper, and Alan Ladd on their Friday-night trips to the movies. Below them, the water in the canal gurgled around a partially submerged washing machine.

Stubbing his cigarette out in the dirt next to the box, Caffey nodded behind him. "Now you know why I never asked you to come over to my house."

"Don't bother *me* none." Cassidy found himself using poor grammar whenever he was in Caffey's company. It began as an unconscious act and he continued it because it seemed to make him become part of a life so totally different from the one he had with his own family.

"Why do you hang around with me, anyway?" Caffey blurted out as though reading Cassidy's mind. "You got a nice family and money and that big ol' house—and I got," he jerked his thumb behind him, "*this!*"

Cassidy squinted at his friend through the stream of blue-white smoke trailing from his lips. "I like to keep up with the latest fashions in clothes."

A puzzled look crossed Caffey's face. He glanced down at his tattered overalls, then began to chuckle. "Yeah. I'm a regular Cary Grant, ain't I?"

Cassidy smoked the last of his cigarette, trying to look like Cary Grant himself.

Caffey crossed his thick legs and leaned his elbows on them. "You really hurt that guy today, Cass."

"Nah, he's all right."

"You bloodied his nose."

Cassidy held his cigarette between thumb and middle finger, watching the ash burn down almost to his flesh. "Look, he's in the ninth grade; he's bigger than me, and he's got a big mouth. What did you expect me to do?" He flicked the butt out into the canal. "Let him call us names?"

"I coulda handled it."

"But you didn't." Cassidy leaned over the bank and watched a crawfish backing along the bottom in the shallow water, a tiny cloud of mud trailing behind. "Let me give you some advice." He lay back and stared at the canvas stretched above them. "When a guy wants to fight, you don't mess around—you bust him one right in the nose while he's bragging to everybody about how bad he's gonna beat you up."

"That's what you done, all right."

"Yeah," Cassidy grinned. "All that big-mouth talk didn't help him much after that."

Caffey turned his broad and bland face on Cassidy. "You really like it, don't you?"

"You know anybody who likes to *lose* a fight?"

"I mean hurting people."

Cassidy, a hard glint in his eyes, sat up quickly,

63

staring at Caffey. "What's *that* supposed to mean?" He knew exactly what it meant, but it never occurred to him that someone like Caffey would find him out. He had always consoled himself with the idea that the boys he fought were mostly bigger and older than himself and had done something to start the fight. He reasoned that they had it coming. But in the deepest part of him, he knew that he was different—different in a way that he didn't want to find out about.

"Nothin'. It don't mean nothin'."

"Look, you'd get in as many fights as me if you wasn't so big," Cassidy insisted. "Everybody takes one look at you and heads for the hills."

Caffey grinned. "There ain't a lot of guys left in junior high that ain't heard about you, either. I don't think you'll find many more that'll be willing to take you on."

Cassidy's blue eyes gleamed in the shadowy half-light. "There's always high school, ain't there?"

FOUR

DAFFODILS

★ ★ ★

"I hate this!" Aaron Walters, his scalp gleaming beneath the short brown crewcut, mumbled to himself as he stood in line at the concession stand located next to a massive concrete pillar of the towering understructure of Memorial Stadium. At five-eight with slightly bowed legs—"Just enough for good balance when you run," his coach had told him—he played second-string halfback for the varsity squad.

Sharon had several classes with Aaron but could never bring herself to talk to him until now. Tonight she wore her shiny brown hair in a ponytail and had chosen her newest skirt and matching sweater for this first game of the season. *"What* do you hate so much, Aaron?"

Aaron turned around to face Sharon who stood behind him. "Oh—it's you."

His words made Sharon feel like an old stray cat someone was shooing away.

"I mean—" Aaron tried to redeem himself, "I guess

I just mean . . . hi." He had never been able to say what he really meant around girls he liked. Sometimes, however, he amazed himself at how confident and witty he could be when he was with girls that he really didn't care about.

"Aren't you going to tell me what you hate so much?"

"Oh, yeah," Aaron muttered. "I hate missing the first game of the season."

"Why?" Sharon corrected herself. "I mean, why aren't you playing?"

"I twisted my ankle at practice and Coach said I had to rest it till next week."

Sharon glanced down at the ankle Aaron was still favoring. "Don't you have to use a crutch or something?"

"Nah," Aaron replied casually, using his best John Wayne bravado. "That's for sissies. Besides, it's wrapped up real good with an Ace bandage."

"You want this stuff, buddy?" The boy wearing a white paper cap pressed down above his pimply forehead shoved a Coke and a hot dog across the counter toward Aaron.

"Oh—uh, yeah, I guess so," Aaron stammered, turning back around. He handed the boy two quarters, then glancing down at his change, asked Sharon, "You want somethin'?"

Sharon had seen the three nickels in Aaron's hand. "Just a Seven-up, please."

Aaron dropped two nickels on the counter. "The lady'll have a Seven-up."

"I heard, big shot."

Sharon sipped her drink from its paper cup as they walked away from the concession stand. As they made their way through the crowd toward the ramp that led

66

out into the stadium, she winced inwardly each time Aaron gingerly put weight on his injured ankle. "I don't think that boy likes his job very much."

"I know him from school." Aaron took a bite of his hot dog. Mustard ran down the corner of his mouth. "That boy don't like much of nothin'."

Holding to the front of Aaron's junior-high letter jacket, Sharon wiped the mustard from his mouth with a paper napkin. "Well, maybe he's having trouble at home or something."

"Maybe," Aaron shrugged, "or maybe he was just born with a rotten disposition."

As they walked out into the stadium, the Istrouma Marching Band was well into its halftime show. The brass section and drums thundered out across the field. The drum major strutted out front while the majorettes twirled their batons high into the air, caught them with practiced ease, and followed up with cartwheels. A senior wearing buckskins and feathers and carrying a lance above his head rode a paint pony around the perimeter of the stadium as the fans stood to their feet, cheering wildly.

Sharon glanced up and behind her where her family was seated. Catherine waved permission for her to stay with Aaron. A warm smile crossed her face as she took his arm, allowing him to lead her to a seat next to the aisle.

As they watched the rest of the performance, Aaron ate his hot dog, managing to keep his mouth clean, while Sharon sipped her Seven-up.

Aaron swallowed the last of his Coke and set the cup between his feet. "That was good!"

"Umm." Sharon hummed noncommittally, holding her drink with both hands.

Shifting uneasily in his seat, Aaron ran his hand

across the top of his closely cropped hair. "I read some of your stuff in the paper this summer."

"Did you like it?"

"Oh, yeah—especially that story about the little dog. I've seen him out in front of that house a lot of times, but I never thought much about him till I read your article."

Sharon sipped her Seven-up. She felt content even without conversation.

Aaron watched the band, their halftime show finished, filing back up into the stands. "How do you think up stuff like that to write about?"

As no one had ever asked her that question before, Sharon found herself considering a new possibility—that she was different from most people in this particular respect. "I—I don't really know. I guess I always thought that everybody came up with ideas like that."

"Well, I never did," Aaron said emphatically. "Nobody else I know of either."

Sharon turned this new mystery over in her mind. "When you see someone just passing by on the street, don't you ever wonder what kind of house they live in or who they fell in love with and married, or if they might have had their heart broken and stayed single—things like that?"

Aaron's brow furrowed and he bit the corner of his bottom lip, before saying, "Nah."

"Oh, I see." Sharon thought briefly about his reply. "Maybe I'm just strange, then."

"No, no, I don't mean that at all!" Aaron hoped he hadn't hurt Sharon's feelings and quickly tried to make amends. "I think somebody who can write stuff like that is . . . special. I wish I could do something like that."

"I wish I could run the hundred in ten seconds flat too," Sharon smiled.

"Huh?" Aaron found his brain muddled at the thought of someone as feminine and fragile-looking as Sharon flying down the track.

"*You* can do that, can't you?"

"Yeah . . . almost, but . . . aw, you're pulling my leg, ain't you?"

"Yes, Aaron, I'm pulling your leg," Sharon admitted. "But I only do that with people I like."

"Me too. I—I mean I really wouldn't pull your—"

"I know what you mean, Aaron." Sharon placed her hand on top of his. "That was awfully sweet, what you said about my being special."

Aaron trembled slightly at the touch of Sharon's hand on his. "Well, you *are*. I really mean that!"

"Thanks."

Out on the field the teams were taking their formations for the second half kickoff. On the sidelines, Coach Ellis A. "Big Fuzz" Brown, with a fedora jammed down above his round face and a cigarette dangling from his lips, gave last-minute instructions to his quarterback.

"See, they got your brother and Billy both playing deep," Aaron instructed Sharon. "It don't give the other team much choice where to kick the ball."

"Why's that?"

"'Cause both of them are such good runners, there *ain't* no good place to kick it."

"Oh, I see."

"That's why I had such a good chance to play tonight if I hadn't been hurt."

"But if they're both so good, how—"

"Because Billy and Dalton are gonna put us so far ahead that Coach'll let the second-string boys like me have a chance to play." Aaron had begun to enjoy his role as instructor.

"I just can't wait until the next game!" Sharon exclaimed, clasping her hands together and smiling.

"Why's that?"

"Then I get to see *you* play."

"I ain't much next to *them* two," Aaron said, grinning, but he sat up a little straighter when he said it.

Then the crowd rose to its feet for the kickoff, and Sharon lost Aaron's attention to the game. She glanced back over her shoulder. Catherine nodded toward her and Aaron, then leaned over, whispering something in Jessie's ear.

Sharon turned to the game, glancing at Aaron's eager eyes. He watched every play as though it were the last he'd ever see. Having been raised by a father who had been a college quarterback, she knew that Aaron considered the game of football a sort of classroom activity and he, a dutiful student.

The evening had turned out far better than Sharon had expected. She had never been very interested in boys, except for Aaron, and then only for the last few months of the previous school year. Now she had won him over as a friend—and perhaps even more than a friend.

Sharon inched over closer to Aaron and slipped her hand over his arm. She felt warm inside and at the same time a slight chill seemed to run across her arms and back. It proved to be a pleasurable sensation. She gazed out at the field, watching the players moving in their choreographed and erratic rhythms. But her mind had taken her to a far-off day of sunshine and blue sky. She could feel Aaron's hand clasping hers as they walked through a rolling, waving field of daffodils.

★ ★ ★

"Maybe I won't go to Memphis after all." Jessie, her eyes still puffy from sleep, sat at the kitchen table, holding a cup of steaming coffee in both hands. She wore a charcoal skirt, black pumps, and a rose-colored sweater, but had yet to put on any makeup or comb her hair.

"Good," Catherine agreed quickly. "I'll just run and put your suitcase away."

Jessie glanced at her mother, then stared out the kitchen window at the yellow sunshine pouring down through the trees into the backyard. A bluebird hopped about on the brick ledge of the fountain next to the splashing water. "I'll be okay in a second," she muttered, "just as soon as this coffee gets my heart going again."

"You sure this is what you want, Jess?" Wearing Aaron's letter jacket in spite of the warm September weather, Sharon sat across from her big sister, watching her push soggy Rice Krispies back and forth in a bowl of milk. "Last chance to change your mind."

"I'm sure."

Willing a pained expression off her face at Jessie's reply, Catherine glanced at her watch, stepped to the kitchen door, and called, "Get a move on, Cassidy Temple! You'll make your sister late for her bus."

Cassidy, wearing jeans but still barefoot and shirtless, stepped out onto the second-floor landing and peered over the rail. A look of irritation crossed his face. "Mama, do I have to go? I can tell her good-bye right here."

"Your father's out of town on business, and Dalton had to go to an early practice," Catherine said firmly.

"The rest of us will see Jessie off at the station—and that includes *you!*"

"Yes, ma'am." The weak reply floated downstairs as Cassidy trudged back to his room.

Catherine walked over to the stove and broke two eggs into a cast-iron frying pan of hot grease. "I declare, that boy won't budge unless he's threatened."

"He's not so bad, Mama." Sharon could always be counted on to come to the defense of her little brother.

"Just give him time," Jessie mumbled into her coffee cup, pushing her hair back from her face as she drank. "Just give him time."

Frowning, Catherine splashed grease onto the eggs with a spatula. "You're right, Sharon. He's not so *bad*."

Right on cue, Cassidy bounded down the stairs and stepped into the kitchen. His face shone from a brief stint with soap and water, and his hair had been raked through once or twice with a comb. "I thought I heard my name being taken in vain down here."

Catherine lifted the eggs onto a plate, spooned on a pile of grits, and added two biscuits to it before placing it in front of Cassidy. "Hurry and eat. It's almost time to leave."

"I'll get indigestion if I do."

Catherine waved the shiny spatula back and forth. "You'll get *this* on your rear if you don't."

Cassidy grinned and obediently dug into his breakfast.

"So glad you could join us, Cass," Jessie teased. "Hope I didn't ruin any of your plans."

"Oh, yeah!" Cassidy dotted the air with a forefinger. "Mama, how 'bout calling Grace Kelly and telling her I'll have to take a rain check on our lunch date."

Jessie rested her chin on the palm of her hand.

"Leave the jokes to Groucho Marx, little brother."

Cassidy's eyes flashed with sudden anger. "*You* leave the singing to Patti Page, *big* sister!"

"Be nice to your sister, young man!" Catherine intervened. "You may not see her for two or three months."

"Sorry," Cassidy mumbled as he bit a chunk out of a biscuit dripping with butter.

Lapsing into silence, Jessie sipped her coffee and stared out the window at the play of light in the trees and the early shadows slanting across their clipped lawn. The sound of her brother eating breakfast and the soft conversation of her mother and sister about grades and colleges faded into a familiar and not at all unpleasant drone.

Jessie summoned up an image of her first day in Memphis. She saw herself walking into a recording studio. The producer, hesitant at first, relents and allows her two minutes' time in the sound studio. After the first eight bars of her song, his expression of total surprise breaks into a smile. After that, things become a dazzling cavalcade of hours standing in front of a microphone until the song is perfected, bursting flashbulbs, press releases, and her pictures on the covers of an endless array of album and magazine covers.

"Jess, aren't you going to eat something?" Catherine stood next to the table, her hand gently resting on her daughter's shoulder. "It's a long ride."

"No, thanks anyway." Jessie gulped the last of her coffee. "I'm too jittery to eat now."

"I fixed you a little something for the road." Catherine set a brown paper bag on the table.

Jessie wondered why she felt so driven to leave her home and family once more. Then there was Austin, who meant more to her than anyone. Still, there would be time for all that later. The inexorable tug of glitter and bright lights would not be denied.

"I guess we'd better be leaving," Catherine sighed. "Cass, you take Jess's suitcase. Sharon, why don't you go back the car out of the garage?"

"Gee, thanks, Mom." Sharon took the keys from Catherine and raced out the back door.

"Jess, do you have Mrs. McLin's address and phone number?" Catherine asked for the second time that morning.

"Yes, ma'am."

Taking hold of the suitcase resting against the wall, Cassidy groaned, "What you got in this thing, lead pipes?" He gave his sister a crooked grin. "That's it! Jess has always harbored this secret wish to be a plumber, and now she's going to Memphis to open up a business!"

Ignoring her younger brother, Jessie put her arm around Catherine's shoulders, kissed her on the cheek, and walked with her out the back door.

The coolness of night still lingered on the morning. Dew sparkled on Catherine's roses like beads of clear glass and the smell of freshly turned earth drifted through the damp air.

Jessie gazed up at the little garage apartment that had been her home for the last two years. Catherine had kept her room upstairs in the big house just as it had been when she moved out. She thought of the backyard gatherings of friends and family: Fourth-of-July barbecues; birthday parties with balloons and bunting strung in the trees; campaign parties with women in silks and satins and pearls and their men standing about stiffly in frosty white shirts and dark ties. The past flooded over her as Jessie watched

Sharon carefully backing the big Chrysler out of the garage.

Why am I calling back all these silly memories? Jessie saw Sharon come around to the back of the car and open the trunk. *Maybe that's why I look for a reason to leave like this, just so I can stir up these feelings in myself—and my family.*

On the edge of her vision, Jessie saw Cassidy heave the brown suitcase into the trunk and slam the lid. *Am I really so insecure that I do things like this just to get attention—just to have people ask me not to leave them—to make them show me how much they care about me? Does trying to make it as a singer really have nothing at all to do with singing?*

"Jess, are you all right?" Catherine stepped in front of her, a look of concern on her face.

"Huh? Oh, sure, Mama." Jessie brightened. "I was just thinking of all the fun I'm going to have in Memphis."

★ ★ ★

Not quite as wide, but it's just as muddy as it is in Baton Rouge. Jessie glanced down through the bus window at the roiling, brown water of the Mississippi. Ahead of her, she could see the downtown business district of Memphis. Perched high above the river on a bluff, its stores and office buildings glinted in the slanting amber light from the sun going down behind her.

As the bus made the long, gradual descent down the eastern slope of the bridge and on into the city, Jessie thought it not much different from her own home or any other southern city she had visited—except New Orleans, which looked as though it belonged in Europe instead of America.

People thronged the sidewalks, rush-hour traffic backed up at intersections, and the sounds of honking horns, squealing brakes, and the insistent drone of hundreds of voices lay a blanket of sound over the city. Car and truck exhausts, warehouses filled with fresh produce from the countryside, and food cooking in the restaurants spilled their smells out into the streets.

Some of the businesses Jessie recognized as common to most moderate-sized and larger cities; some of them she had never heard of before. Glimpsing the Woolworth's five-and-ten-cent store and later the huge, familiar sign in front of the Sears building, she felt a sense of instant belonging.

The bus glided up a low concrete ramp and around to the parking area behind the terminal, coming to a stop with a dull whooshing of its air brakes in one of the yellow-lined parking spots. Jessie climbed down out of the bus along with the other passengers and waited for her bag to be unloaded from the luggage compartment.

Inside the crowded terminal, Jessie set her suitcase down next to a phone booth, stepped in, and shut the door against the babble of voices and the echoing sound of the PA system announcing arrivals and departures. Taking a slip of paper out of her purse and dropping a nickel into the phone, Jessie dialed the number while keeping an eye on her suitcase.

The telephone rang four times before a soft voice answered it.

"Hello."

"Mrs. McLin?"

"Yes."

"Hi. This is Jessie Temple."

"Jessie who?"

76

Jessie's heart sank. She could see herself with no reservation being turned away from hotel after hotel, wandering the darkened streets of Memphis, looking for someplace to spend the night. "Temple. Jessie Temple. My mother was Catherine Taylor Temple. She and your daughter were friends at Ol' Miss back—"

"Land sakes, yes!"

The voice at the other end of the telephone line brightened almost visibly for Jessie.

"Your mother was the sweetest little thing! She and my Patsy were such good friends back in those days."

"Yes, ma'am."

"Both of their husbands played football for Ol' Miss, you know. Well, of course you know—one of them was your own daddy, wasn't he?"

"Yes, ma'am."

"Catherine and my Patsy used to come up here and stay for the weekend once in awhile when your daddy and Patsy's husband—he played right guard on offense, I believe—were out of town on a road trip and—"

"Mrs. McLin?" Jessie hated to be impolite but she didn't hear any indication that this nice lady on the other end of the telephone line would stop talking otherwise.

"Oh, I'm sorry, child! I do tend to get carried away sometimes, don't I?"

"Is the room still available?"

"Why, certainly! I don't rent to just anybody, you know. If you're anything like your mother—she was the sweetest little thing you ever saw. . . ."

Ten minutes later, Jessie had managed to get directions to Mrs. McLin's home. After speaking to a uniformed ticket agent behind the long counter, she picked up her suitcase and walked two blocks to the bus stop.

Travel-worn and hungry, Jessie rode a local bus through the copper-colored Memphis twilight toward her new home. Leaving the business district, the bus headed east. Jessie stared out the window as the stores and office buildings gave way to white-painted houses with wide front porches and sprawling lawns landscaped with pretty flower beds and shrubbery. Old and stately trees—oaks and elms and maples—grew along the wide avenues and side streets, shading the houses. Children rode bicycles along the sidewalks or ran across yards, summoned by mothers at front doors calling them in for supper.

As she took in the sights of residential Memphis, Jessie saw a black-and-white cat perched in the lower branches of a sweet gum tree. Beneath the tree, next to a fire hydrant, sat a shaggy black mutt staring patiently upward.

Pulling the cord above the window, Jessie rang a bell and stopped the bus in a quiet neighborhood where she had spotted a small corner grocery. Hauling her suitcase off, she ambled along the sidewalk checking addresses. Halfway down the block, the yellow glow from a wrought-iron fixture hanging down from a high porch ceiling illuminated the correct numbers.

Jessie gazed at the two-story frame house surrounded by a white picket fence and flanked by ancient elms. Low, clipped hedges bordered a stone walkway leading up to the front door. With the fragrance of night-blooming jasmine floating on the air, she walked up onto the porch and rang the bell.

A shadowy figure moved behind the leaded glass of the front door. When it opened, a delicate, elfin face appeared through the screen. "Jessie Temple?" As soft as thistledown, Velma McLin's words held a tone of uncertainty.

Without the burden of harshness imparted by the telephone lines, Jessie felt immediately comforted by the sound of the soft voice. "Yes, ma'am."

"Come in, child. Come in." Velma McLin opened the screen door and ushered her guest inside.

Jessie set her suitcase down just inside a high-ceilinged hallway. Hardwood floors gleamed in the light cast from a crystal chandelier. Against the patterned wallpaper hung portraits and faded prints of family members in the stiff and formal poses of the past century. "It's so nice to meet you. My mother has told me for years how much you've meant to her."

"She was always such a sweet little thing," Velma repeated. "Follow me. You must be famished." She tilted her head to one side, her eyes staring for a moment at the reflected light off the floor. "Oh, would you like to freshen up first?"

"Yes, ma'am." After washing up in the hall bathroom, Jessie followed Velma, who smelled of lilacs and wore a green print dress of soft cotton with high-topped black shoes. They followed the hall into a black-and-white tiled kitchen with pale yellow curtains and outdated appliances. The white enameled table was set for one. Pots sat warming on the stove.

"Now, you just sit right down and I'll have your supper in no time at all."

As Jessie ate, she listened to Velma recount the days when Catherine and her daughter would visit her and the times she went down to Oxford for the Ol' Miss home games. When Jessie had finished her fried chicken, field peas, and cornbread and had eaten a second helping of peach cobbler, Velma told other stories from her past. Without fail, she provided biographies of each character as they played out their parts.

Then Jessie followed the tiny gray-haired lady upstairs to her bedroom, which was located at the back corner of the house. It held a matching dresser and wardrobe and a poster bed. An antique secretary sat in the center of a braided rug next to a span of tall windows.

Velma had two more stories for Jessie that just couldn't wait until morning. Then, after bidding her good-night, Velma went along the upstairs hallway to her own room. Ten minutes later, she returned, reminding Jessie that breakfast was at seven.

After bathing and putting on a fresh nightgown, Jessie glanced down into the backyard. In the pale light, she saw a fig tree standing next to a drooping clothesline. Laden with fruit, it seemed to welcome her like an old friend.

Jessie turned back the homemade quilt and slipped between the cool sheets still carrying the smell of the sunshine that had dried them. Just before she fell asleep, a childlike smile touched her face.

PART TWO

★ ★ ★

ALL OUR
GOLDEN DREAMS

FIVE

A Disarming Smile

★ ★ ★

"From the looks of you, things aren't going too well in the singing business." Velma poured hot water into cups from the kettle while the coffee perked.

Jessie, immersed in her customary morning frowziness, sat with her elbows on the table, her chin propped on both hands. "Umm." She lifted her eyes slightly, squinting at the golden light streaming in the windows.

Velma smiled, remembering her own Patsy's breakfast demeanor as much the same. "Well, *I* got a singing job for you, Miss Temple."

Immediately brightening, Jessie sat up straight, rubbing the fog of sleep from her eyes. "Really!"

"Yes, indeed!"

"How did you ever manage"—the corners of Jessie's mouth reversed themselves. "I've been walking these streets for a whole week and—"

"Nothing to it," Velma smiled. "All I did was make one little phone call."

Staring at the tiny gleam in Velma's eyes, Jessie began to suspect that all was not as it appeared. "Velma, are you pulling another one of your pranks?"

"Oh, this is for real," Velma insisted with a grin. "My pastor was just delighted to find out that you'll be singing a solo tomorrow morning."

"Velma! How could you?"

"It was just my little joke. I'm sorry if you thought it was one of those record jobs."

"Oh, I don't mind about that, but now I won't have time to practice the song."

"Sure, you will. The piano player is going to meet us in the music room a half hour before church starts."

Jessie had almost gotten used to Velma's surprises. Looking at the joy on her powdered face, she couldn't imagine ever getting mad at this sweet soul who had taken her in and treated her like a daughter.

"You can practice your song," Velma continued, "and we'll still have time for a nice cup of tea before service. The kitchen's just down the hall."

Jessie folded her arms, giving Velma a stern look. "I assume that *you've* picked out a song for me."

"No," Velma replied innocently.

"How'd you miss out on that?"

"Well, I *did* help the pastor pick one out."

Jessie turned her head toward the ceiling, a gasp of exasperation escaping her lips. She pictured Velma dragging her out onto the platform in front of the whole church to do a song she couldn't possibly sing.

"I think you'll like it."

"What if I don't even *know* it?"

"I talked to your mama on the telephone for a long time, Jess." Velma took their cups from the stove and poured the hot water into the sink, then filled them with fresh coffee from the pot before placing them on the table.

Spooning sugar into her coffee, Jessie waited for Velma to finish her explanation.

"She told me a lot about you." Velma sat down across from Jessie. "How you've been singing in church most all your life and how you'll practice and practice till the song's just perfect before you'll even consider singing it."

"I hope she told you what songs I know."

Velma nodded. " 'How Great Thou Art.' Think you can sing that one?"

Jessie felt a sense of relief wash over her. "*That* one I can do." She had never given any performance without believing that every note was as perfect as she could make it, and she had accomplished that with "How Great Thou Art" long ago.

"You sure you don't want some breakfast, sugar? I told your mama I'd see that you ate properly."

"Well, you've certainly been true to your word." Jessie placed her hand on her stomach. "I haven't eaten this much in years. You'll have me ruining my figure."

Velma shook her head seemingly for no reason. "I just don't understand it."

"Understand what?"

"Why someone hasn't hired you to make a record or sing on the radio, or whatever it is that you want to do." Velma made a clicking sound with her tongue.

Jessie held her cup in both hands, enjoying the rich aroma of the coffee. "I'm finding out that it's pretty tough to break into the record business, Velma. I could pay a studio to have a recording made—I guess."

"They're supposed to pay *you*. That's no way to get started in a new career."

"Elvis did."

"Who?"

Jessie started to explain, then muttered, "Just a singer."

"Oh. But you've got such a wonderful voice, child. I've never heard *anyone* sing better." Velma's eyes drifted out of focus as she looked back into the past. "There was this *one* singer from back in the twenties. What was her name?" She tugged her earlobe between thumb and forefinger. "Helen Morgan—that's it! She sang 'Don't Ever Leave Me.' "

Jessie noticed Velma's faded eyes grow bright from some half-forgotten pain that had crept in from her past. "Velma, are you all right?"

"What? Oh yes—yes!" Velma quickly dabbed the corners of her eyes with the tip of her ring finger.

Feeling that Velma needed a change of decade, Jessie pushed ahead. "It's a shame *you* don't own a recording studio. I'd have it *made*."

Velma gave her a tired smile. "You surely would, wouldn't you?" She lapsed into silence, her eyes staring at something only she could see, a sad smile still on her lips.

Waiting for Velma to pull herself free from the bittersweet embrace of her past, Jessie sipped her coffee and wondered what Austin would be doing at this hour of the morning. *It's an hour later in Boston, so he's probably sitting in an eight o'clock class—business contracts or something—bored to death. Maybe I'll just catch a bus and go on back home. I couldn't leave until Monday. Velma's got her heart set on my singing Sunday morning.*

"Maybe you should go on back home, child." Velma's powdered brow furrowed with concern. "I hate to see you come in every day so discouraged."

"That's just part of the business," Jessie assured her. "Sometimes it takes years to get a break—most of the time, it never happens at all."

Velma nodded sympathetically.

"But you could be right. I don't know if I really have my heart in this." Jessie surprised herself with her own words. She had never even let a thought like that rise to the surface before this moment. "Or maybe I'll try just a little while longer. After all, this could be my last chance."

"You're too good for the business anyway," Velma stated emphatically.

"Apparently 'the business' doesn't share your opinion of my talent."

But Velma's mind had already fastened on more important matters. "You're going to be such a blessing to our congregation Sunday morning."

"I certainly hope so." Jessie felt torn between Memphis and Baton Rouge. She hated to admit defeat so soon and go back home to her family with nothing to show for her trip but a Greyhound ticket stub. Her experience with Hollywood and the USO had gone so smoothly that she hadn't been prepared for even a few days of "Don't call us; we'll call you." *I'll try it just a little while longer. Then at least I won't look like some starry-eyed adolescent giving up before even getting started.*

"I sure will miss you when you leave, Jess." Velma's eyes stared at something far away. "It's been like having my own Patsy back home."

"I'm staying, Velma." The words seemed to leap from Jessie's lips before she could think them into existence. "I got a job today."

Velma appeared stunned at the sudden turnaround the conversation had taken.

"Oh, it's not *much* of a job. I can quit anytime I want to. But as long as I'm going to be here for a while anyway, I might as well make some money."

"Job?" Velma found herself unable to adapt to Jessie's abrupt swings.

"As a waitress."

"A college girl like you?" Velma seemed to find Jessie taking such a position unthinkable.

"Just for a little while."

"My goodness! What would your mother think? She might blame *me*."

Jessie laughed out loud at Velma's reaction. "It's not like I'm going to work in one of those dime-a-dance honky-tonks, Velma."

"I should hope not!" Velma remembered those seedy establishments that had gained some popularity during the years of her youth.

"It's at Taylor's Café," Jessie explained, determined to set Velma's mind at ease. "It's a family place. The strongest thing they sell is root beer floats."

Feeling better, Velma managed a smile.

"And," Jessie continued with the most important reason of all for taking the job, "it's right next door to Sun."

"Am I supposed to know what that is?"

"I guess not. Hardly anyone else does."

★ ★ ★

"Hey, Jess! How 'bout shaking a leg with that blue-plate Special?" A burly man with long, greasy hair waved in her direction.

Wearing a white uniform and carrying a tray laden with food, Jessie shoved her way through the lunchtime crowd of Taylor's Café toward the row of booths located against the far wall. Three men, all truck drivers for Crown Electric, sat waiting impatiently for their noon meals.

As Jessie served the three men, she prepared her verbal defenses.

"What's a pretty little thing like you doing in a job like this?" the burly man asked.

"What kind of job *should* I have?" Jessie glanced at the name *Spike* stitched on his coveralls.

"Oh, I don't know." Spike shifted positions on the red leatherette seat, making a tearing sound. "You look kinda like one of them stars in *Silver Screen* magazine to me. I jes' might have some contacts in the business."

Jessie poked the Crown Electric tag above Spike's name. "You mean down at *Crown* studios?"

Color rose in Spike's neck as his two friends laughed at Jessie's comeback.

"Yeah," Dudley, a hatchet-faced driver with a cast in his left eye, grinned. "You could *wire* one of them studio big-shots about how pretty Jessie is. Get it? Electrician . . . wire?"

"That's real funny," Spike groaned, watching Jessie thread her way through the crowd and back over to the kitchen. "You're almost as funny as that smart-aleck waitress."

As Jessie waited for her next order, she glanced toward a slim man in gray pleated slacks and a red shirt who stepped in off the street. He checked his reflection in the glass of the door, then ran a comb through his thick, dark hair. The last time she had seen him, he had been on the stage of that rollerrink-turned-nightclub down in Plaquemine, Louisiana.

"Hey, Elvis!" Dudley stood up and yelled across the

restaurant. "Come on over."

Jessie remembered reading in a newspaper article that Presley had worked at Crown Electric until his smash success on the Louisiana Hayride in November of the previous year. She edged closer to listen in.

Presley wandered over toward the booth, waving greetings to a few of the regulars, stopping to talk with others at a table or two along the way.

Jessie noticed that Presley's smile, relaxed and genuine, seemed to have an infectious quality about it. The faces of his friends brightened as he spoke with them.

When Elvis finally managed to make his way over to the booth, Dudley stood up and shook hands with the young singer. "How's it feel to be famous?"

"The Louisiana Hayride and a song or two on the radio don't make me famous."

"Maybe not, boy. But it ain't gonna *hurt* you none." Dudley grinned. "I heard ol' Webb Pierce got madder'n a wet hen at that Overton Park concert last month when you got more applause than *he* did."

Elvis shrugged and slid into the booth with the three truck drivers.

Having seen him in Taylor's Café many times before, a waitress with short hair and a boyish face hurried over to the booth carrying a Seven-up for Presley.

Trying to look casually disinterested, Jessie kept one eye on her tables while she listened. Talking about himself apparently made Presley uncomfortable. He changed the subject as quickly as he could, preferring instead to talk about the days when he, like the three men in coveralls, had driven a truck for a living.

People finished their meals and hurried back to their jobs, leaving Taylor's deserted except for Presley and the Crown Electric boys. In a few more minutes the drivers got up to pay their checks, leaving Presley alone with his Seven-up.

With the lunch rush over for another day, Jessie summoned up the courage to go over and tell the young singer how much she enjoyed his music. When the Crown Electric boys opened the door to leave, the sound of guitar music and a man's voice raised in song rang out from the street.

"It's *him* again." The other waitress collected the dishes off the last table, shaking her head in disgust.

"Him *who*?" Jessie asked.

"That nutty preacher!"

"Preacher?"

"He's been preaching on and off out there for a year or more. I thought he was gone for good this time"—she lifted her tray and moaned—"but he's back."

Intrigued by someone who would preach on a downtown street corner, Jessie dropped her dishcloth on the counter and walked to the front. Peering though the door built into the corner of the building, she saw a man about her own age standing on the sidewalk. An inch or two under six feet tall, he had light brown hair combed straight back from his forehead. His dark blue suit needed pressing. Jessie noticed that his left shoe had a built-up sole; the foot turned slightly inward.

With the guitar hanging by a strap around his shoulder, the preacher played and sang to his tiny, temporary congregation: a red-haired ten-year-old on his bicycle, left foot on the sidewalk for balance; a white-haired lady holding a bag of groceries; and a bleary-eyed man wearing filthy khakis who could have been in his late teens or early twenties.

Across the street, two very large men in business

suits glared at the impromptu church service. They spoke together with animated gestures.

Jessie turned her attention to the obviously drunk man, his clothes in rags, still clinging to his empty bottle in its brown paper bag. She noticed that the little finger and the ring finger of his left hand were missing. She couldn't decide who she felt sorrier for—the preacher or the drunk.

Through the glass of the door, Jessie could hear the preacher's voice straining at the song as though he had been hoarse for a long time:

> I love to tell the story,
> 'Twill be my theme in glory
> To tell the old, old story
> Of Jesus and His love.

"Excuse me."

Jessie stepped back, turned, and stared directly into Elvis Presley's disarming smile. "Oh, uh—sure."

"I think I know that preacher," Presley said in his Mississippi drawl. "His name's Billy Pilgrim. He's a good ol' boy, but he never *could* sing much."

Jessie watched Presley push by her, joining Pilgrim on the sidewalk in singing the last verse. She held the door open so she could hear them better. The song seemed to come alive. There was no mistaking that old-fashioned sound distinctive to Southern gospel music.

Jessie tried to imagine Elvis Presley as a boy, singing in the choir on Sunday mornings or rising from a hard wooden pew and joining in with the congregation as they lifted their voices during Wednesday night prayer meetings.

> I love to tell the story,

More wonderful it seems
Than all the golden fancies
Of all our golden dreams.

When the song was over, a smattering of applause rose from the gathered few. Jessie watched Pilgrim turn and shake Presley's hand. She thought Presley's smile looked like that of a child—open and warm and without guile.

"You oughta come back to gospel music, Elvis." Pilgrim's voice was softly hoarse as he spoke. "I don't think you'll ever really be happy till you do."

"I tried, Billy," Presley nodded. "The Blackwood Brothers turned me down."

"You're a lot better now."

"Maybe. But I think it's too late." Presley waved and turned away.

Pilgrim placed his guitar in a battered cardboard case on the sidewalk. Picking up a brown Bible, he gazed at each person around him in turn. "God is not willing that *any* person here should perish, but that *all* of you should come to repentance." He opened the Bible, thumbed through a few pages, and began to read. "For God so loved the world, that he gave his only begotten Son, that whosoever believeth in him should not perish, but have everlasting life."

Suddenly the men from across the street appeared as though from nowhere, their voices loud and harsh in the silence that fell after the song had ended. Startled, Jessie stepped back, letting the door shut. One of the men stepped close to Billy, shouting and brandishing his fist. She couldn't make out the words, but the man's twisted face mirrored their meaning. The other man stood with his arms folded across his chest.

Closing his Bible, Billy stood his ground, looking

as though the two men had come to present him with an award rather than to berate him in public.

Jessie noticed Presley casually strolling back along the sidewalk toward Billy. He appeared to have no interest in the disturbance going on.

Incensed by the preacher's refusal to respond to his threats, the big man drew back his fist. Presley grabbed the man's wrist and spun him around. Then with a word or two he pointed at Billy and directed the man to leave him alone.

Jessie saw what happened next as little more than a blur: the man's arm sweeping toward Presley, who brushed it aside, spun around, and buried his right elbow into the man's stomach.

The big man dropped to his knees, his face pale, his mouth wide, gasping for air. His friend was already walking briskly back in the direction he had come from. With an effort, the first man struggled to his feet, both hands holding his stomach, and followed at a much slower pace.

During this time, Billy Pilgrim had never moved, observing the brief struggle as though it was a rehearsal for a play.

Presley watched the two men disappear around the corner of a building, then turned Billy's street-corner pew back over to him with a wave. "Good thing for you I got a soft spot in my heart for preachers—or maybe it's in my head."

Billy smiled, nodded his thanks as Presley turned to leave, and opened his Bible.

"Hey, Jessie! We got work to do in here."

Reluctantly, Jessie turned away and began to help the other waitress fill sugar bowls and salt shakers, getting the tables set up for the supper crowd. Hurrying through her chores, she returned to the front door just in time to see the little church service breaking up.

The red-haired boy peddled away on his bicycle, while the white-haired lady tottered across the street with her groceries. Standing at the edge of the sidewalk, the young man with the old face let his bottle drop into the gutter. He stared across the twenty feet that separated him and the preacher as though it were a great gulf.

Pilgrim smiled and said something that Jessie couldn't understand. She glanced back at the young man just as he began to shuffle unsteadily across the sidewalk toward Pilgrim. Stopping before the preacher, he fell to his knees. Pilgrim then knelt down, laying his hand on the young man's shoulder. Bowing his head, he began to pray.

Jessie could see the young man's body shaking, wracked with sobs as Pilgrim now lay his hand on the man's head, his voice rising in prayer. She could understand none of his words.

As she watched the two young men kneeling together, people walking by ignoring them or pointing in jest, Jessie felt suddenly ashamed of herself. She thought back to the girl of eighteen who had sat next to her on the bus. Alone and lost in the world, she had poured out her troubles. Jessie had listened with a sympathetic ear, but had let the girl get off at Helena, Arkansas, without telling her about the One who was the answer to all her troubles.

Jessie remembered other opportunities she had had to share her faith with someone—and didn't. *If you're ashamed of Me before men, I'll be ashamed of you before the Father in heaven.* The words pierced her like a blade.

Staring through the glass door, Jessie felt as

though nothing could tear her eyes from the scene playing out before her. Finally, the young man rose to his feet. She would never forget what she saw. His face looked transformed, as though the years had been washed away. Tears still streaked the grime and the dirt and the stubble, but his eyes shone with a new light. *Joy! Glory!* The words leapt into Jessie's mind.

Pilgrim spoke a while longer with the young man, the joy on his own face shining just as bright. Then he took a New Testament from his pocket and pressed it into the man's hands. With a final word, he turned and picked up his guitar.

The man in khakis took the little black-covered book, opened it, and began to read something on one of the pages near the front. With a last look at Pilgrim, he turned and walked away. The weight of his past no longer bowed his back or forced his legs into an old man's sluggish gait.

SIX

BILLY

★ ★ ★

"Hello." As soon as she spoke, Jessie thought it a dumb way to start a conversation with a complete stranger. *You've really got a way with words, Jess!*

Billy Pilgrim had been walking away from his impromptu podium, his left foot slapping the sidewalk lightly as it turned inward with each stride. He turned around slowly, his guitar case slung on his right shoulder, and his Bible clutched in his left hand. An odd expression, confusion mixed with curiosity, crossed his face. "Well, hello to you too. Do I know you?"

"No." Jessie couldn't seem to think of a way to keep the conversation going. She couldn't understand why this average-looking, average-sized street preacher in his mail-order suit of clothes would affect her the way he did. Elvis—that she could understand.

"Well, I guess I'll just wish you a pleasant day, then." Billy turned to walk away.

"Have you eaten yet?"

Turning back around, Billy smiled. "If we're going to talk, I'm putting this thing down." He eased the sling off his shoulder and set the guitar case on the sidewalk. "This guitar's bothersome to haul around all the time. I should have taken up the piccolo."

The remark was so unexpected, Jessie laughed out loud. "I'm sorry. You just looked so funny when you said it." Jessie noticed an L-shaped scar an inch long above Billy's left eyebrow. His slim nose was slightly crooked as though it had been broken and hadn't received medical attention. Another scar, white with age, ran two inches in an upward curve from the left corner of his mouth, giving that half of his face a perpetual expression of humor.

"Some people say I look funny even when I *don't* say anything."

"I think you look nice." Jessie regretted saying the words before she had finished speaking, although she realized she meant them. In spite of the shabby clothes, his hair looked freshly washed, shining like a girl's in the afternoon sunlight. But it was his eyes that she was most taken with—sea green with long lashes, they held a special kind of light that Jessie thought must be reserved for all saints and some preachers.

"Thanks." Billy cleared his throat and glanced at the redheaded boy who had been at his service. Pedaling back by them on his bicycle, he put his feet up on the handlebars and waved as he passed. Billy waved back to him, then gazed at Jessie. "I hope you don't get offended at what I'm about to say, but why did you stop me?"

Jessie suddenly realized that she didn't know why. Was it because she felt guilty because of her own shortcomings and thought she could somehow make amends by merely buying a meal for someone who was in no way ashamed of the gospel? Perhaps it was simply because this man knew Elvis, and all that that portended. As these thoughts raced through her mind she returned Billy's gaze and said, "Because you look hungry."

It was Billy's turn to laugh. "That may be the most completely honest answer I've heard in a long, long while."

In spite of the implications of Billy's words, Jessie began to feel completely at ease in the company of this unassuming street preacher with the terrible clothes and the priceless eyes. "We've got chicken-and-dumplings, squash, fried okra, and for dessert, homemade blackberry cobbler."

Billy patted his pockets. "I'm afraid all I've got is some loose change."

"Oh, don't worry about that," Jessie assured him. "We get the leftovers from lunch and there's always plenty. Besides, my mama always taught me that feeding a preacher was right up there with 'entertaining angels unawares.'"

"Well, since you put it that way"—Billy picked his guitar up and slung it heavily over his shoulder—"let's get going before an angel shows up and takes my place at the dinner table."

★ ★ ★

The afternoon sunlight filtering through the closed venetian blinds on the windows filled the almost-deserted restaurant with pale light and murky shadows. One lone customer, a balding man in overalls, sat at the far end of the long counter, nursing a fountain Coke. From the kitchen came the muted sounds of dishes clattering and pots banging against one another.

"You really think you can make it in the music business?" Billy pushed his empty dessert bowl aside and picked up a cup of steaming coffee.

"I don't really think it matters very much what *I* think," Jessie shrugged.

Billy set his coffee cup down. "I'm afraid I don't understand that at all."

"What matters is what the record producers and the disc jockeys think."

"And?"

"And nobody thinks I can do it."

"Have you tried next door?"

"Sun?" Jessie glanced in the direction of the studios located next door. "First place I went."

"No luck, huh?"

"Sam Phillips said I had the wrong kind of voice."

Billy remembered bits and pieces of the rock-and-roll songs he had heard. "I think that's probably another way of saying that you've got talent."

"Probably just his way of letting me down easy," Jessie mumbled. She found herself becoming discouraged, just mentioning the audition.

"He tell you anything else?"

Jessie gave him a sad smile. "Just that I should be singing 'Hey There' on the Hit Parade—you know, kind of like another Rosemary Clooney."

"I think he meant it."

Jessie felt no need to reply to Billy's opinion as she would have most other people she had just met.

Billy watched the sunlight play in Jessie's pale hair as she tilted her head. Sipping his coffee, he found himself content to enjoy the feeling of the good food inside him and the good company of his new friend.

Weary with discussing her failures in the music

business, Jessie took another track. "You really know Elvis Presley?"

"Yep."

Jessie looked up, waiting for Billy to follow up on his cryptic reply.

Billy set his cup on the table. "I can't thank you enough for this meal, Jessie. I haven't eaten cooking this good since the last time I visited my grandmother."

"Well?"

"Well?" Billy looked puzzled. "Oh, you want to know about my grandmother. Well, she—"

"No, silly." Seeing the smile only in Billy's eyes, Jessie knew she had been had. It reminded her of the little word-games Velma played with her.

"Guess you'd rather hear about Elvis, huh?" Billy nodded. "We went to school together in Tupelo. Both of us from families as poor as Job's turkey."

Jessie's eyes shone with excitement. "Were you best friends or anything like that?"

"Uh-uh. Just two boys growing up in the same little town." Billy shook his head. "We weren't even in the same grade. I'm two years older than he is."

That makes you the same age as me. Jessie wondered what importance that had for her. "What was he like?"

Billy shrugged. "He always loved to sing—ever since *I* can remember, anyway. Used to sing at the Tupelo courthouse on Saturday afternoons."

"The courthouse?"

"Yep." Billy stared at Jessie across his coffee cup, holding it with both hands. A faint smile crossed his face as he remembered the days from his past. "WELO radio broadcast the 'Saturday Jamboree' from there."

Jessie pictured Elvis lined up on the courthouse grounds waiting his turn to go on. "How did the station decide who got to sing?"

"First come, first served. It was all very professional," Billy smiled. "Ol' Elvis, he'd get there real early. Usually managed to get on the air about twice a month."

"Did you ever try it?" Jessie noticed for the first time a small dimple on Billy's left cheek as he smiled. It gave his face the appearance of a cherub grown gladly older.

Billy shook his head. "I used to go down to watch, though. Not much else to do on Saturdays in Tupelo."

"What kind of songs did he sing?" Without knowing why, Jessie found herself wanting to find out about the smallest details of Presley's boyhood.

"He'd do some Gene Autry songs, a little gospel, and when the war started, I remember he sang one called 'God Bless My Daddy, He's Over There.' "

"Did his daddy go off to the war?" As always when the war was mentioned, Jessie pictured her daddy at the train station the day he returned home from the South Pacific after World War II.

Shaking his head, Billy glanced across tables reflected in the parquet linoleum floor toward the counter. An ice-cream sundae sign proclaimed that Borden's was the house brand. "No. The army didn't take ex-cons."

It was obvious to Jessie that Billy felt an aversion to talking about the shortcomings of others. She quickly changed the subject. "I'll bet he sang 'Ol' Shep,' didn't he?"

"How'd you know that?" The dimple reappeared on Billy's cheek. "That was *always* his favorite."

"I was in a talent contest before we moved to Louisiana," Jessie frowned. "Elvis beat me out for first prize, singing about that stupid dog saving a boy from drowning."

"You must have been singing a long time."

Jessie thought back on the Sunday mornings in the church choir and the all choruses, duets, and ensembles at school. "All my life! At least, it seems that way."

Billy rubbed his chin between thumb and forefinger. "How'd you like to sing for me?"

Jessie immediately pictured herself on some downtown corner in front of a street urchin, an irate businessman, and a drunk thrown in for good measure.

As though he had read her mind, Billy explained, "It won't be on some street corner. I'm preaching mostly in churches now, believe it or not."

"I didn't mean—"

"It's all right. God doesn't call most people to preach in the streets." Billy rested his chin on his folded hands, leaning forward to look directly into Jessie's cornflower blue eyes. "I have an idea that our meeting today wasn't by accident."

"Well, I certainly didn't—"

"I know that," Billy smiled and let his suggestion drop. "Well, what do you think?"

Confused by the sudden change in the conversation that ended in Billy's offer, Jessie found herself unable to think clearly. "I—I don't know."

"Well, why don't you just think it over," Billy suggested. "You don't have to give me an answer right now."

"Where is it?"

"One of the big churches right here in Memphis." A faraway look flickered in Billy's eyes. "I guess I

thought I'd always be on the streets or in a tent with
a sawdust floor"—he nodded his head slowly in
thought—"or in those little brush-arbor meetings
back in the hills. I always liked them best."

Jessie felt herself being drawn into the life of this
unassuming young preacher with his guileless eyes
and warm smile. She felt almost as though she had
little choice in the matter—that it was all set. But the
now-distant glitter of show business still whispered
its shining promise in her ear.

Jessie's apparent disinterest in Billy's offer in-
stilled his voice with a tone of defeat. "You don't have
another singing job somewhere, do you?"

Jessie glanced around the restaurant, noticing the
man in overalls walking toward the front door. "Dozens," she smiled, tapping her name tag with her forefinger. "I just do this because I'm so eccentric."

Laughing softly, Billy pressed his offer, "Well, why
don't you just go ahead and do it?" Billy noticed that
Jessie's nails were manicured, but that she wore no
polish.

"Just exactly what is this *it*?"

"Lead the worship service, sing a couple of songs
right before I preach, and then sing during the invitation." Billy held his hands out palms up. "Just like
eating lettuce . . . nothing to it."

"You don't even know if I can sing."

"I know."

★   ★   ★

"I just don't think it's proper for a girl of your background." Tapping her high-topped shoe nervously on
the ceramic tile of the bathroom floor, Velma sat on
the edge of the bathtub, her hands clutched together

in her lap. "There's something so . . . so *unseemly* about it."

"About singing in church on Sunday morning?" Jessie stopped brushing her hair, turning to face Velma. "How could that be *unseemly*?"

"I mean the way you met this . . . this *man*." Velma clicked her tongue. "A complete stranger preaching on a street corner. What would your mother think?"

Jessie turned back to the mirror, brushing her shiny-clean hair with long strokes. "She'd like him."

Velma couldn't seem to come up with an argument against Jessie's simple reply. "Well, I *still* think you should just come to church with me. I can't count the number of people who told me how much they enjoyed your singing last Sunday. And the pastor—why, I think he's about ready to hire you as music director."

"Can't. I've already promised."

Velma stood up and walked over to the lavatory. Straightening the collar of Jessie's orchid-print dress, she relented. "Well, it looks to me like you've got your mind made up. Are you coming home right after the service?"

"We may get something to eat first." Jessie opened a tube of lipstick and began applying it carefully, pressing her lips together to blot it. "Sometimes the pastor or one of the deacons asks Billy out for dinner."

"Do you even know *how* he's taking you to the church?" Velma seemed determined again to find something that would prevent Jessie's going.

"A taxi, I guess. Or maybe the bus."

"The bus?" Velma sighed heavily. "I just hope you know what you're doing, child."

The doorbell rang downstairs.

Velma sighed again. "Well, I suppose that's your *street preacher*."

"I'll get it," Jessie insisted as Velma turned to leave. She hurried past her and down the stairs, opening the front door before Velma could get there.

"Morning," Billy smiled through the screen. "Hope I'm not early."

Startled for a moment, Jessie hardly recognized the man who stood before her. Gone were the cheap, mail-order clothes, replaced by a well-cut charcoal-colored suit and crisp white shirt set off by a deep-red tie. His new shoes almost sparkled. "I thought you were someone else at first."

"Like my new suit?" Billy asked proudly, grinning. "The pastor bought it for me."

Jessie stared at Billy's neatly trimmed hair. It gave off a soft, healthy sheen in the early sunlight. "Oh, I'm sorry! I forgot my manners. Come on in." She lifted the latch, shoving the screen door outward.

Velma stood on the bottom stairstep, giving Billy Pilgrim the once-over.

"This is Mrs. Velma McLin, Billy." Jessie took Billy's hand, leading him over to the stairs.

"Pleased to meet you, ma'am." Billy held out his hand. "Jessie says you're like a second mother to her."

After looking Billy up and down, Velma touched his hand lightly. "Nice to meet you."

"Well, we'd better be going." Jessie sensed the tension in the air and wanted to be on her way.

"Ask your young man to come have coffee with us, Jess." Velma stepped down and walked along the gleaming hardwood floor toward the kitchen.

"We really have to—"

Billy silenced her with a finger across his lips. "We've got time for a quick visit."

After a fifteen-minute interrogation by Velma, Billy led Jessie down the front walk. Set ablaze by morning sunlight, the leaves on the oaks and elms had been painted in October shades of gold and rust and red.

"Daddy's come up for a visit!" At the end of the walk, Jessie stared at a black '39 Ford coupe. She ran to it and glanced inside as though Lane might be hiding from her.

"What are you talking about?"

"This car! It's my daddy's."

"No, it's not. It's mine."

"But you don't *have* a car."

"I do now."

Jessie opened the door. "The seat covers are different. It's *not* his."

"Didn't I just say that?"

"But it's just like the one he's had for *years*." Jessie walked around the car, taking it in. "I was only six when he bought it. It's like part of the family."

"What can I say?" Billy shrugged. "Your father's got good taste in automobiles."

"But how did you—"

"Get the money," Billy finished for her. "I've had my eye on this car for six months. Finally the ol' boy who owned it decided to buy a new one. He said he'd let me pay him twenty dollars a month and there it is—in all its glory."

"Is everything all right out there?" Velma stood on the front porch.

"Yes, ma'am," Jessie called back. "I was just admiring Billy's new car."

Billy opened the car door for Jessie. "Let's see if it rides as good as your daddy's does."

Climbing onto the front seat, Jessie glanced around at the interior of the car. "This isn't a bad car at all. Somebody's taken real good care of it."

"Yep," Billy agreed, sliding behind the steering wheel. "Just as good as new."

"Well, almost."

Billy started the engine, grinned at Jessie as it purred to life smoothly, and eased away from the curb. "Runs like a sewing machine, don't it?"

Jessie nodded, then gazed out the windshield at the light of early autumn falling like copper-colored rain on Memphis. Noticing Billy's left foot pressing loosely against the clutch as he changed gears, Jessie decided this was as good a time as any to ask, "What happened to your foot?"

"Car wreck."

From the abrupt answer and the tone of Billy's voice, Jessie could tell that she had touched a tender spot in his memory. "I'm sorry. I didn't mean to bring up anything unpleasant."

"It's okay," Billy said, cheerful once more. "It happened a long time ago." He flicked the radio on. "Guess I was lucky. Mama and Daddy were both killed."

"Oh, Billy, I didn't mean—"

"No, it's really all right." He tuned the radio to a Sunday morning gospel show. "Daddy was drunk—which was pretty much his normal state back then. Somebody told me not too long ago that they never knew ol' Henry Pilgrim drank till they saw him sober one time."

Jessie could see the shadows in Billy's eyes even though he tried to make light of the tragedy.

The Chuck Wagon Gang's unmistakable version of "I'll Fly Away" played on the radio. "That song sure reminds me of a little church back in Tupelo. Brother Ballard, the pastor, always sang the bass parts." Billy smiled at the memories. "Elvis sang there, too, when he was just a boy. I guess it's where he really fell in love with music."

Jessie felt that Billy was only putting off the telling of this painful episode of his life.

"We were on the way to some beer joint—Daddy always made me and Mama ride along with him and wait outside in the car while he was inside, drinking with his buddies—when he drove right out in front of a log truck."

Jessie found herself wanting to know more about this strange man who had come into her life so suddenly and unexpectedly, stirring emotions that she did not want to face. "You must miss them terribly . . . well, your mother anyway."

"No—I guess not," Billy admitted. "Never really knew her. I was only two when that log truck sent her right to heaven." His gaze turned inward. "Everybody says she was a good Christian woman."

Billy turned his face toward Jessie and there was nothing forced or artificial about his smile. "But what Satan intended for evil, God turned into something good for Mama—*and* me."

Jessie's expression spoke the words she seemed unable to form in response to this unique twist in Billy's sad story of drunkenness and death.

"I went to live with my grandmother in Tupelo," he explained. "If I hadn't, I know I would have ended up just like my daddy—a good-for-nothing drunk."

"So you've always been a good boy, then," Jessie said with no thought of teasing Billy, but realized he might take it the wrong way. "I don't mean that you—"

Billy turned his head toward Jessie, his eyes lighted with the happiness of a beautiful morning around him and the promise of a pulpit to preach from somewhere up ahead. "I believe you apologize more than anybody I've ever known. There's nothing wrong with growing up a 'good boy.' "

"You're right, there isn't."

"I wish *I* had."

"I believe you're the most *confusing* person *I've* ever known," Jessie used a play on Billy's opinion of her. "You said going to your grandmother's was the best thing that ever happened to you—didn't you?"

"Yep," Billy agreed simply, "but I didn't say that I took to her righteous example right away."

Jessie found herself becoming more and more intrigued by Billy's life. "Well, tell me, then."

"Can't do it."

"Why not?"

Billy pointed down the street. "We got some singing and preaching to do."

Jessie gazed out the window at the church, one of the oldest and most beautiful in Memphis. Constructed of stone and masonry, its Gothic architecture suggested a somber congregation whose services would be formally structured down to the last *Amen*. Jessie couldn't imagine why the pastor had asked someone like Billy to preach.

"Pretty, isn't it?" Billy pulled into the blacktopped lot, parking in a slot marked *Visitor*.

"Are you sure this is the right place?"

Laughing, Billy cut the engine and pulled the parking brake. "You're wondering why an itinerant preacher like me with no obvious exposure to the social graces would get asked to speak in a swanky place like this?"

"No," Jessie said without even a rumor of conviction in her voice. "Well—yes."

Billy laughed again. "I haven't the slightest idea."

"What?"

"It's the truth. The pastor called me one day and said he'd heard me at one of the other churches in town, and would I do him the honor of holding a service or two at his church." Billy held his hands out in front of him, palms up.

"This makes me very nervous."

His big Bible firmly clasped in his left hand, Billy got out and went around to open Jessie's door. "You? *Everybody's* going to like your singing. But you *never* know how a church will take to an outside preacher—especially one like me."

Although Jessie had no idea how it could have happened, Billy's simple words seemed to siphon away her anxiety. She knew somehow that these people would indeed love her singing. "Let's get on with it, then."

Billy took her hand and helped her out of the car. "We'll go right down to the basement."

"Are you sure the music director and the whole choir's going to be there just for me to practice?"

"Yes, ma'am. They're just thrilled that you're going to sing for them today."

"I bet."

"It's not every day they get to hear somebody who sang with Bob Hope."

Jessie stopped, feeling a sudden chill in the shadow of the towering spires. "How'd you know that?"

"Sam Phillips told me."

"Phillips? You know him?"

"Nope."

"Well, how did—"

"I stopped by Sun Records when I left Taylor's the day we met," Billy said casually, directing Jessie down a flight of stone steps. "I knew you could sing, but I had to find out how good you really were. Phillips said you're as good as anybody who's ever walked in that recording studio."

"You're really something—you know that, Billy Pilgrim?" Jessie scolded, but her face gave her away. As was the case with Velma, she found it almost impossible to work up any real anger toward Billy.

"We can't have just *any* old nightingale singing for the likes of these fine folks—now, can we?"

"They can't be *too* picky," Jessie glanced over her shoulder as she started down the steps, "not if they let *you* preach for them."

Chuckling softly, Billy followed after her. "I can see we're gonna get along just fine, Miss Jessie Temple."

SEVEN

HE-MAN HILL

★ ★ ★

"I haven't seen an altar call like this since I was a young preacher." The pastor, whose name Jessie had forgotten in the nearly constant press of people she had met that morning, sat next to her on a front pew. Tall and angular, he wore a charcoal gray suit. His thin hair approximated the color of tree bark.

Watching a large part of the congregation as they returned to their seats, Jessie nodded in reply. Billy's message had been a call for the church to return to holiness—to awake out of sleep; to walk upright before God.

Jessie opened her Bible and read again in First John the passages that Billy had based his sermon on. "And hereby we do know that we know him, if we keep his commandments. He that saith, I know him, and keepeth not his commandments, is a liar, and the truth is not in him. . . . He that saith he abideth in him ought himself also so to walk, even as he walked."

The faces and the actions of the people revealed

the life-changing effect of Billy's message. Jessie felt it in her heart. She knew that her Christian life required more than merely walking down an aisle and getting her name added to a church roll. It required that she walk as Jesus had walked when He was on the earth. And when she stumbled in that walk—she comforted herself with the assurance—she had an *Advocate* with the Father.

"Brothers and sisters," Billy began as soon as everyone had found their seats. He stepped down off the platform and stood in front of a long, elaborately carved table. "We're going to close this service by sharing the Lord's Supper. I know it's not your traditional communion time, but your pastor has graciously given permission for us to do this."

Jessie could almost feel the warmth radiating from Billy's smile as he gazed out on the congregation. Glancing around, she noticed that same glow on the faces of many members of the congregation.

"Turn with me, if you will, to the sixth chapter of the Book of John." Opening his Bible, Billy spoke as he turned through the pages, locating the scripture he wanted. "In the second chapter of Acts, we're told of four things that the early church held to steadfastly: the apostles' doctrine, fellowship, prayers, and the breaking of bread—which refers to the Lord's Supper.

"In John six, verse forty-eight, Jesus says—and He is talking not only to the multitude in Capernaum but to His disciples—'I am that bread of life.'

"Now, let's go down to verse fifty-one. 'I am the living bread which came down from heaven: if any man eat of this bread, he shall live for ever: and the bread that I will give is my flesh, which I will give for the life of the world.'

"Look at verses fifty-three and -four. 'Verily, verily,

I say unto you, Except ye eat the flesh of the Son of man, and drink his blood, ye have no life in you. Whoso eateth my flesh, and drinketh my blood, hath eternal life; and I will raise him up at the last day.' "

Billy closed his Bible, holding his place with his forefinger, and began pacing slowly back and forth as he spoke.

Jessie thought that his step seemed sure and steady, his crippled left foot holding firmer as he walked.

"Some of you may think these are pretty strong words that Jesus spoke. Well, you're not alone." Billy opened his Bible again. "In verse sixty Jesus' own disciples said, 'This is an hard saying; who can hear it?'

"It *is* a hard saying, so Jesus explains it in verse sixty-three. 'It is the *spirit* that quickeneth; the *flesh* profiteth nothing: the words that I speak unto you, they are *spirit*, and they are *life*.' "

Billy closed his Bible and dropped it on the table behind him. "Jesus always spoke words of life, but to many of the people He spoke to that day, His words were a 'hard saying' and so they left Him.

" 'Then said Jesus unto the twelve, Will ye also go away?' " Billy gazed out at the people, most of whom—caught up in his simple, straightforward message—paid him rapt attention. "And who do you think answered for the disciples?"

In the third row, a stout man with white hair called out, "Peter. Who else?"

"Who else, indeed," Billy smiled. "He was *always* the one opening his mouth, wasn't he? But this time Peter knew what he was talking about. 'Lord,' Peter said, 'to whom shall we go? thou hast the words of eternal life. And we believe and are sure that thou art that Christ, the Son of the living God.' "

Billy motioned for the ushers to come forward and as they began to prepare to serve communion, he took his Bible again and read to the people.

"The cup of blessing which we bless, is it not the communion of the blood of Christ? The bread which we break, is it not the communion of the body of Christ? Ye cannot drink the cup of the Lord, and the cup of devils: ye cannot be partakers of the Lord's table, and of the table of devils.

"On that last night Jesus spent with His disciples He took the bread, blessed it, and gave it to them; He took the cup, gave thanks, and gave it to them. And then He told them, 'I will not drink henceforth of this fruit of the vine, until that day when I drink it new with you in My Father's kingdom.'"

Laying his Bible aside once more, Billy spoke in a voice as soft as the autumn light falling through the high windows. "This may be the last time that some of us will drink of this fruit of the vine until that day when we drink it with Jesus in the Father's kingdom."

★ ★ ★

"How'd you like the food?"

Jessie watched the play of light in the trees as she rode with Billy through the autumn afternoon. "It was awfully nice of them to treat us to lunch. I heard it's the best restaurant in Memphis."

"That's not what I asked you."

"I think the cooking at Taylor's is better."

"What a commoner!"

Glancing at the boyish expression on Billy's face, Jessie wondered how he could hold an audience like this morning's spellbound with his preaching. Unsophisticated and with no formal training as a minister, he seemed to undergo a transformation when he stepped into the pulpit. "What were you and the pastor talking about so long in his study after we got back to the church?"

"My, my," Billy grinned, watching the leaves tumbling through the pale gold light, "aren't you the little 'Nosy Nellie'? That's what my grandmother used to say."

"Can you be sensible for just one moment?" Jessie found it hard to adapt to Billy's behavior swings. One moment the consummate evangelist, rubbing elbows with Memphis' elite and then thirty minutes later acting like a silly little boy.

"I reckon I could." Billy spread his arms, taking both hands off the steering wheel. "But it's such a beautiful day and the service was such a blessing that I feel like I'm in the third grade again and it's the day before Christmas."

"I don't think you'll ever grow up, will you?"

"I certainly hope not."

"Well—"

"Radio."

"Radio—what?"

"They want me to go on radio on Sunday mornings."

A shadow crossed Jessie's brow. "But you've been preaching every Sunday. You can't give that up just to go on some radio program."

"It's at eight o'clock. Two opening songs—which you'll sing, of course—and a twenty-minute sermon," Billy said as though Jessie had already agreed.

"Wait a minute!" Jessie insisted. "Don't I have some say-so about all this?"

"Nope." Billy swung the Ford into a sharp turn, gliding smoothly down a gentle slope in the road. "Of course, you do. But how could you possibly turn me down?" He gave her his brightest smile, punching a dimple in his cheek with one forefinger. "You can't, can you?"

Jessie laughed in spite of herself. "When does this new career of yours—ours—begin?"

"Next Sunday."

Jessie felt herself being swept away by Billy's enthusiasm and the joy he seemed to find in every part of the work he had obviously been called to. Changes had begun taking place so fast that life hardly seemed real to her.

"That all right with you?"

"Huh? Oh, sure."

"Good. You're going to draw the sinners in close with that sweet voice of yours and I'll drop the gospel net around them before they know what hit 'em."

"Sounds like I'm the bait."

Billy pinched the bridge of his nose, his eyes going out of focus with thought. "Never considered it that way before, but I guess that's one way of looking at it. Anyhow," he shrugged, "whatever it takes to make all them lost souls out there in radioland listen to the gospel, I'm for it."

Jessie settled back against the seat, the cool autumn breeze like a refreshing balm against her skin. "Billy, can I ask you a personal question?"

"Why, certainly," he answered almost distractedly, his eyes staring at something beyond the mild afternoon. "We're partners now."

"How did you go from street preaching, to this big church today, to being on the radio in such a short time?"

"Short time?"

"Well, it was just a little over a week ago that I saw you out in front of Taylor's."

"I see what you mean," Billy nodded. "Well, little girl, it wasn't as easy as all *that*."

As always, Jessie was a little surprised at how easily she got Billy to talk about himself.

"I preached on them streets for almost two years before anybody ever asked me inside a church house. The first time was a little over a year ago now, and I can tell you it wasn't like the one we went to this morning."

"How'd people find out about you?"

Billy held the steering wheel with both hands, extending his arms, stretching lazily. "Folks getting saved on street corners and such, then getting their lives cleaned up, finding churches to go to, giving their testimonies—first one thing and then another."

"But why did you go back to that corner at Taylor's when you can preach in churches now?" Jessie pictured again the boy sitting on his bicycle; the young man missing the ring finger and little finger on his left hand, his haggard face beginning to shine with hope as he listened to the simple message from a street preacher wearing a mail-order suit.

Billy's eyes filled with a soft light. "I guess my heart's out there with the ones who wouldn't exactly fit in with regular church folk." He cleared his throat. "Like that young man standing there in front of Taylor's holding on to his bottle like it was a life raft and he was about to go under."

"Maybe that's what he felt like."

Billy nodded. "I knew when he dropped that bottle in the gutter and headed across that sidewalk toward me, he meant business. He turned loose of that old life and found a new one right there on the street corner."

Jessie's experience with preachers had been with those who had churches to support them or who had large meetings with offerings taken up. Never had she met someone who stepped out with nothing but faith to lean on. "How did you survive those first two years, Billy?"

His eyes narrowed in thought. "You know, I guess it seems kind of strange, but I never thought much about it all that time. I just . . . got by somehow."

"But you must have had some kind of income."

"Well—once in a while somebody would slip some bills in my pocket after I finished preaching, or I'd get a letter at the house with some money in it." Billy shook his head slowly. "No one ever told me their name—none of the letters were signed. It was almost like getting manna from heaven."

"You've got a special kind of faith, Billy."

"Nah!"

"*I* think you do."

"No, that's not it," Billy insisted, shaking his head. "When you hit rock bottom, it's just easier to trust God—at least, that's what I think."

"You never said anything about hitting rock bottom." Jessie was about to ask Billy to explain when he seemed to read her thoughts.

"That's another story for another day." Billy swung the steering wheel to the left, turning into the narrow gravel parking lot of a neighborhood grocery.

Jessie gazed at the little frame building with its screen door hanging slightly ajar. Alongside the Chesterfield and Camel cigarette advertisements decorating the front wall of the building hung dented metal signs proclaiming the refreshing taste of Coca-Cola, Royal Crown Cola, and Orange Crush. "Why are we stopping here?"

"I got me a craving."

"You sound like a Mississippi redneck."

"And proud of it." Billy opened his door, then turned to Jessie. "You comin'?"

"I'll wait out here."

"Suit yourself. I'll be right back with something almost as good as manna."

Jessie watched Billy go inside the little store, the screen door banging shut behind him. Then, noticing a weathered bench against the wall, she got out of the car, walked over, and sat down. High above her in the crown of a sycamore tree, a dove cooed an autumn lullaby.

With a banging again of the screen door, Billy stepped outside holding two dark brown bottles, still wet from their ice-water bath. He glanced over at the car, then noticed Jessie sitting on the bench next to him. "Oh, there you are! You're in for a real treat." He handed her one of the bottles.

Taking the cold bottle from Billy, Jessie held it up to the sunlight. "This is my sister's all-time favorite drink. She'd rather have one of these than a new dress—well, almost."

"I know exactly how she feels. We Orange Crush fans are a loyal breed." Billy sat next to Jessie on the bench and leaned back against the rough boards of the storefront. "When I was growing up my grandmother would buy me one every Saturday afternoon when we'd go to the store for groceries. I looked forward to it all week long."

As she sat next to Billy on the bench in front of the little store sipping her Orange Crush, Jessie's mind turned toward Sharon. Being seven years older, it seemed that Jessie hardly noticed her little sister when she was growing up. Only in the last two years had they grown close.

Jessie recalled their talks in the little garage apartment behind her family's home and the times when Sharon had spent the night with her on Fridays. It was as though they were schoolmates sleeping over at each other's houses.

Sharon would talk of wanting to become a great writer or of Aaron Walters, her recent and only boyfriend. Jessie would confide in her younger sister about all the years she had dreamed of becoming a singing star and of how she had now become torn between a career that seemed as insubstantial as smoke and the very real and attractive alternative of settling down as the wife of Austin Youngblood.

"Penny for your thoughts."

Jessie took a swallow of her drink, savoring its cool, fruity taste. "Just thinking about home."

"So was I."

"You too?"

"Yep."

"How long since you've been home?"

"Too long," Billy replied, turning his bottle round and round where it left a dark wet stain on the rough wood of the bench. "My grandmother's getting on up in age. I need to get back there more often than I do."

"I guess I'll go down for Thanksgiving—or Christmas at the latest."

"You homesick, Jessie?"

"A little . . . maybe."

Billy snapped his fingers. "I've got it! Why don't we go on down to Tupelo to visit my grandmother? She'll make you feel like you were at your *own* home."

"I don't know, Billy," Jessie said. "Your grandmother might not want a stranger barging in on her, and besides—I've got to work tomorrow."

"She'll love you to death." Billy acted as though the decision had already been made. "And that café can get by one *day* without you. I'm pretty certain of that. Who knows—you might just be singing full-time with me before too long, anyway."

"Can we see some of the places where El—where you and Elvis ran around together?"

Billy smiled. "That boy does have a way of fascinating the womenfolk, doesn't he? Sure we can."

"Well, I'll have to check with—"

"We'll leave in the morning. Monday's kind of a slow day anyway."

★ ★ ★

Wearing gray slacks and a maroon cotton pullover, Jessie stared out the window at the banks where the roadbed had been cut through the high rolling hills of northern Mississippi. Kudzu still grew thick and green in the mild October weather, but soon the first frost of the year would wither and blacken the leaves, leaving only a network of vines like thick gray veins layered on the red-clay hillsides.

"You see this next bend in the road?" Billy pulled over to the side of the road, parking on the shoulder that angled down into a shallow ditch.

Jessie glanced over at him. He still looked somewhat out of sorts to her, dressed in faded khakis and a blue plaid shirt instead of his usual suit and tie.

"We always called this place 'He-man Hill.' "

Staring at the gravel road curving down to the left and out of sight between the green banks, Jessie noticed the steep drop-off where the right bank gradually sloped down below the level of the roadbed itself.

"Aren't you going to ask me why?"

"I figure it's got something to do with teenage boys trying to prove their manhood," Jessie replied sol-

emnly. "Probably by seeing who can be the most stupid."

"I guess that's about it," Billy shrugged. "Never had
it explained quite that way before." He opened the
door of the car and motioned for Jessie to follow.

Jessie got out and walked along the gravel shoulder to the beginning of the curve. Above her the morning wind moaned softly in the tall pines.

Billy stood at the edge of the shoulder, gazing fifty
feet below at a stream running along the base of the
hill. It meandered through the trees where it joined a
creek crossed by a bridge at the far end of the curve.
"We'd come out here on Saturday afternoons and see
who could take that curve the fastest."

"I might have guessed." Jessie stared at the sharp
precipice that fell away at the edge of the narrow
shoulder. "Surely you had more sense than to try it
yourself."

"Nope," Billy admitted readily. "I was right in there
with the stupidest of 'em."

Jessie shook her head slowly.

"I didn't have much choice. I couldn't play ball
with this bum leg." Billy gave Jessie a pleading look.
"I had to do *something*—didn't I?"

"I'm glad I was born a girl."

"Me too," Billy agreed quickly, then returned to the
remembered contest. "Ol' Jack Piker was the best of
the bunch, though." Billy smiled at the memory. "Yes-
sir, he took this curve at forty-eight miles an hour."

"Amazing."

"I thought so too."

"I mean, the things boys risk their lives for."

"Oh—that."

Jessie remained silent, refusing to become part of
something so inane.

124

"Well, anyway I was second best."

Holding to her silence, Jessie watched a fox squirrel, its deep red fur glowing in the sunlight, leap from one high branch of a white oak to another.

"Aren't you going to ask me how fast I took it?"

"No."

"Forty-five."

"Why don't we go on into town?"

"Sure thing."

Jessie climbed back into the car, next to Billy, perplexed by his leaps into and back out of boyhood. At times he seemed as wise as an Old Testament prophet. Then he would become caught up in something more suitable to a ten-year-old. *Maybe it has something to do with his growing up without a daddy. I suppose he just didn't have anyone around to show him what it was like to become a grown man.*

"I believe I could take it at fifty with this Ford. It handles like a dream."

"Don't you dare!" Jessie gave him a look of disbelief that he would even think of such a thing.

"Just kidding." Billy started the engine, slipped the car into gear, and drove carefully down the long curve of the hill, gravel crunching beneath the tires. "I guess you think I'm silly, bringing back all those old times when we did such dumb things."

"Boys will be boys." Jessie listened to the boards thrumming under the tires as they crossed a bridge. "Oh, look! What a lovely spot."

Glancing across the bridge rail, Billy saw the grassy bank of the creek beneath a spreading willow. Sunlight turned its flowing leaves into pale green showers. "Yep. That's the old swimming hole. And in the springtime it's where the boys would take their girlfriends on picnics—when they were real serious about them, that is."

"You take anybody there, Billy?"

Billy's cheeks reddened slightly. "Nah."

"I'll bet."

"Well, maybe a time or two." Billy took a deep breath. "I thought I'd forgotten about this town, but these old places are so familiar to me. It's almost like I never left."

"Sounds almost like the lyrics of a song I used to love to sing." Jessie felt the words carry her back in time. She could almost feel the bitter wind of Korea as she stood on a makeshift stage singing for several thousand marines, one of whom happened to be her own father. *"I'll be seeing you. . . ."*

"Yeah," Billy nodded. "I remember that old song. I think it was one of Mama's favorites."

"My mother always liked it too." Jessie thought again of that cold and remote country where she had come to realize how very much she loved her father. She felt it had become a sort of turning point in her life—the first time she could ever remember placing more value on someone else's life than she did her own. A prayer of thanksgiving that God had brought her father home safely rose from deep in her being.

EIGHT

TUPELO

★ ★ ★

"Mammaw, I believe your cooking's better than it was when I was growing up here." Sitting in a ladder-back chair that he had tilted against the wall, Billy placed his hands behind his head and stared at a black-and-tan terrier trotting down the gravel lane that ran in front of the little tin-roofed house.

"He says the *same* thing every time he comes home." Minnie Pilgrim smiled at Jessie, sitting next to her on the front-porch swing. A sturdy woman with white hair worn in a bun at the back of her head, Minnie stood little more than five feet tall. An embroidered apron covered her simple cotton dress.

"I didn't mean it all those other times though." Billy grinned at the terrier as it stopped, sat down, and scratched behind its right ear, then resumed its journey, disappearing behind a battered Chevrolet pickup.

"I'd never tell my mother or grandmother," Jessie offered, patting Minnie gently on the hand, "but that was the best blackberry cobbler I've ever eaten."

"Awfully nice of you to say so, child. Canned 'em myself last summer," Minnie nodded. "That fence row down at the back of the pasture was plumb covered up with the biggest, juiciest berries I b'lieve I ever saw."

"Is ol' Vester still helping you pick them?" Billy glanced over at Jessie. "That's Elvis's uncle on his daddy's side. He'd pick a bushel of berries for one of Mammaw's cobblers."

"Yes, he did," Minnie grinned, "and I baked him *two* this year 'cause he done such a good job."

Billy fastened his eyes on a gray cloud blowing in from the northwest. "I'll bet you didn't know Jessie came in second to Elvis in a talent contest back in '46, Mammaw."

"I'll bet I did."

"Really?"

"Yep," Minnie nodded, relishing her story. "I heard him telling you boys one day about that pretty little Temple girl who had such a good voice."

"Did he really say that, Miss Minnie?" Jessie found herself excited that, even as a boy, Elvis would compliment her singing.

"He certainly did."

"Yep. I remember that now," Billy added. "He was showing us the medal he won."

Jessie, trying to imagine Billy growing up in the little three-room house, glanced about the yard with its azalea bushes out near the street and the row of hydrangeas, brown now and autumn dry, growing just beyond the roof's overhang. She could almost see him coming home from school down the gravel lane, his thin frame burdened by a stack of books—and Minnie waiting for him on the front porch.

128

"Billy was always a good boy when he was growing up, Jessie," Minnie said, almost as though she had sensed what was on Jessie's mind. "He never gave me a minute's trouble. Always did his chores without being told to."

Billy rocked forward in his chair, resting his elbows on his knees. "Before you put my name in for sainthood, you might want to tell Jessie about that Halloween we locked the preacher's milk cow inside the schoolhouse all weekend."

"Oh, goodness!" Minnie shook her head. "I'd almost forgotten about that! What a mess!"

"I'll bet it was," Jessie added. "Well, nobody's perfect. Not even preachers."

Minnie gazed out across the yard. Her eyes filled with a soft light and her voice became little more than a hoarse whisper when she spoke. "I knew Billy was going to preach the gospel when he was just eight years old."

"But, Mammaw, I wasn't even a Christian back then," Billy protested.

"Didn't matter."

Jessie stared at the puzzled expression on Billy's face and realized that this was the first time his grandmother had told him of this.

"But how did you know?"

"It happened one Sunday night after I had already gone to bed." Minnie turned toward her grandson. "I'd felt this heaviness in my spirit for weeks like I always do when the ol' devil's up to something. During that time I truly believe he was trying to stop me from praying for you. Anyway, after you and me had our prayer time together like we always did, I couldn't sleep."

"Was it the same Sunday that evangelist from

North Carolina preached in the church?"

Minnie nodded.

Jessie could see by Billy's expression that a memory of that particular Sunday had reached out through the years and touched him.

"Anyhow, as I lay there in bed praying—and it was tough going that night—God just up and told me." Minnie wiped the corners of her eyes with a white handkerchief she had taken from the pocket of her apron. "I didn't hear it with my ears—He spoke to my heart—but I heard it just as plain as I hear the two of you now."

Billy reached over and took his grandmother's hand. "Why didn't you tell me this before?"

"I never did feel released in my spirit to do it until now." Minnie's voice held a hushed reverence.

"I wonder why." Billy leaned back in his chair, his eyes narrowed in thought.

Minnie placed the fingertips of her left hand against the side of her chin. "I think sometimes if we know exactly what God wants us to do with our lives—well, we might just mess things up trying to get it done our own way instead of His."

"I managed to mess things up in my life pretty good anyway," Billy grinned.

"For some of us—maybe most of us," Minnie observed in a solemn voice, "that seems to be a necessary part of finding out where He wants us to be."

Billy reached out with both arms toward the ceiling of the little porch. "Hold it!"

"What in the world's wrong with you now?" Minnie's eyes grew wide.

"I just figured out where I'm supposed to be right now." Billy closed his eyes tightly. "Back at the dinner table with a big bowl of blackberry cobbler sitting in front of me."

Minnie shook her head slowly as she got up from the porch swing, then looked back at Jessie. "Every time I think about that boy preaching the gospel, I realize that the good Lord *has* to have a sense of humor."

With a start, Minnie turned toward the ringing of the telephone in the front room. "I declare, I'll never get used to the sound of that contraption!"

"I made her get one so I could keep in touch," Billy said, watching Minnie as she went inside to answer the telephone. In spite of his sudden turn toward humor, his eyes shone with a bright and unmistakable love for his grandmother.

"Billy, it's for you!"

Jessie heard Minnie put the phone down and walk back to the kitchen.

"Okay." Billy tilted his chair forward and went inside.

Through the screen door, Jessie could hear him faintly talking to someone about times and dates and places. His voice held a suppressed excitement.

"Oh, boy!" Billy banged through the door and bounded out onto the porch.

"I gather you got some good news."

"Yes, indeed!" Billy began pacing back and forth. "That was the pastor of a church down in Jackson. He wants me to preach a revival for him."

"That's wonderful!"

Billy walked over and sat down next to Jessie. "I went to a service down there one time when I was in junior high. We were visiting some kinfolk." He gave her a thoughtful stare. "I still remember how beautiful it was."

"The building or the service?"

Laughing, Billy said, "The building. I was more interested in seeing the sights than anything else."

"At least you're honest about it."

Nodding, Billy stood up again, walking to the edge of the porch. "I'll tell you another thing honestly. This is going to be a humdinger of a revival. I truly believe that."

★ ★ ★

"Well, that's where ol' Elvis bought his first guitar." Billy stood on the sidewalk in front of the two-story brick building proclaiming in large white letters that it was home to the Tupelo Hardware Co., owned by George H. Booth.

Jessie stared through the plate-glass window at the display of electrical tape, an assortment of tools, red Radio Flyer wagons, and one blue tricycle. "He really got his first guitar at a hardware store?"

"Sure did," Billy answered, gazing into the murky depths of the store. "Back in January of '46. I remember it well 'cause we never could get him to quit banging on that thing."

"He seems to do all right now."

Billy nodded. "I even remember what he paid for it—$7.75 plus two percent tax. Elvis wanted a .22 rifle, but he didn't have enough money so Gladys told him she'd make up the difference if he'd buy the guitar instead."

"Amazing, the little things that end up having such an effect on our lives."

"Well, we've seen the radio station, the courthouse, the school, and the old neighborhood on the wrong side of the tracks where Elvis and the rest of us poor white trash grew up." Billy stepped over to the door of the hardware store. "You want to go inside and look around?"

Jessie shook her head.

"What's next, then?"

"I think I'd like to see the swimming hole."

"A fine choice. It ought to be pretty down there this time of day."

As they drove along the quiet streets, Jessie gazed at the simple frame houses shaded by old trees. "I like this town. It must have been kind of like growing up in Sweetwater."

"I suppose it was," Billy agreed. "I never made it to your hometown, though."

"Maybe next time you take a day off we could go down there and visit *my* grandparents."

"I'd like that."

As they headed back across the bridge, Jessie stared at the road curving up the long hill from the creek and bending away out of sight among the trees.

Billy turned left onto a dirt road pitted with holes and ruts from the heavy summer rains. Underbrush and briars raked against the side of the car as they bumped along through the woods. At the end of the narrow track a clearing opened up beneath a stand of sweet gum and red oaks. Car tracks crisscrossing the bare ground spoke of the popularity of the place.

Parking on a grassy spot, Billy got out and led Jessie down a narrow path through the trees to the river. "Well, here it is. The ol' swimming hole. I think down here in the South every wide spot in the road's got one."

"We had two or three back in Sweetwater." Jessie walked out into the little glade and sat down beneath the willow.

Sitting down beside her, Billy plucked a grass stem and began chewing on it.

Jessie leaned back against the trunk of a tree, content to enjoy the peace and solitude of the place. Below them the creek, sunlight dancing on its clear green water, gurgled over a fallen log. Wind sighed high in the tops of several tall pines growing on the bank.

After a few minutes, Billy spoke in a voice that was little more than a whisper. "I've got some more news for you . . . that is, if you're interested."

Jessie turned toward him, a puzzled look on her face. "Of course I'm interested."

"The pastor told me on the phone today that several more pastors want me to come preach in their churches." Billy lay back, staring up at the sky.

"Billy—"

"Yep."

"Are you asking me to come along and sing for you? Is that why you're telling me this?"

"Aw shucks, ma'am. You found me out."

Jessie laughed out loud. "Sometimes I just don't know what to think of you, Billy Pilgrim."

Billy gave Jessie an innocent smile. "Not much to think about. I'm just a simple country boy."

"I never know if I'll be talking to somebody who's seven or seventy when you open your mouth."

"I don't think I'm quite sure myself," Billy admitted. He sat up quickly, crossing his legs and staring into Jessie's eyes. "Well, what do you think?"

"I don't know. It's all happening so quickly."

"You think it's quick for you!" Billy rolled his eyes toward the heavens. "Seems like just yesterday I was lucky if I could get three or four people to listen to me for five or ten minutes on some street corner—and now all these preachers with their big churches and highfalutin congregations can't get me to come preach for them quick enough."

Jessie smiled at the mixture of excitement, joy, and bewilderment that poured out of Billy.

"Well, what do you say?"

"I say . . . yes."

"Oh, boy! We're gonna sing and preach a whole bunch of souls right through them pearly gates!"

Laughing again, Jessie let herself soak up the joy that spilled out of Billy as he brought her up to date.

"We're going over to Meridian after we leave Jackson, then to Birmingham and on down to Montgomery." He took a deep breath. "And after that, Mobile and maybe Biloxi. I don't have all the details yet, but I'll be getting letters from the pastors in a week or so."

"I can't tell you that I'll make every one of the services, Billy." Jessie wouldn't allow herself to be completely swept away by Billy's exuberance. "We'll just take them one or two at a time and see how things turn out."

"Sure. I understand," Billy agreed. "I know without a doubt that God's called me to this work, but I don't want to force anything on you."

"Good." Jessie felt something stirring inside her that she had been wanting to get to the surface for some time.

Seeing the change in her mood, Billy reined in his excitement and let her speak her mind.

Jessie decided to get directly to the point. "What changed you, Billy? How did you get this calling on your life?"

Billy's expression became thoughtful, but the light never left his eyes. "Okay if I give you the short version?"

"That'll do for now."

Billy stood up and walked over to the creek bank. Picking up several rocks, he began tossing them into the water. *Plop.* "After I graduated from good ol' Tupelo High, I decided to get out of this hick town." *Plop. Plop.*

"Guess I got the idea from reading Jack Kerouac's *On the Road.*" *Plop.* "Thought I just had to see the big, wide world."

"Did you?"

"Yes, indeed." Billy's laugh was layered with irony. *Plop. Plop.* "I saw it while I was pumping gas for thirty-five cents an hour in a little filling station in Vicksburg, or sleeping off a drunk in some flea-bitten hotel in Shreveport . . . or getting beat up and left for dead in a midnight alley in Dallas."

"Is that where you got those scars?" Jessie had been wanting to ask Billy about the scars on his face, but never could seem to find the right time. Now the question burst forth without her thinking about it.

"No. I got these preaching." Billy said it matter-of-factly as though every preacher had gone through the same experience as part of his training. *Plop. Plop. Plop.*

Billy dusted his hands together, walked back to the tree, and sat down next to Jessie. "I reached the point where I didn't know which way to turn. I guess I had a whole lot in common with the Prodigal Son. As a matter of fact, he was on my mind a whole lot back in those days."

Jessie noticed a change come over Billy as he sat next to her. The excitement of a few minutes before seemed to have been replaced by a deep sense of peace. She could almost feel it radiating from him as he spoke.

"Then one Sunday morning I woke up in a ditch somewhere in the country outside Minden, Louisiana. To this day I don't remember how I got there." Billy took a deep breath, letting it out slowly. "Music—singing I can still hear it just as plain as I did that summer morning."

Jessie watched a single tear, glistening in the slanting amber sunlight, roll down Billy's cheek.

Billy's voice became little more than a hoarse whisper. " 'When nothing else could help . . . love lifted me. . . .' " Clearing his throat, Billy sat up straighter, running his hand through his hair.

"Are you all right?"

Billy nodded and cleared his throat again. "It was just a little white clapboard church set back off the blacktop. I followed the sound of the singing. A couple of beat-up ol' pickups, a Model-T, and a few horses and wagons. I thought for a minute I'd stepped back into the thirties.

"Anyhow, the windows were open so I sat down in the shade of a big oak tree and just listened. I'd heard the same kind of sermon a hundred times before, but . . . this time it was different. I remember the preacher—I never did see what he looked like—read John 5:24. Then he said, 'These are the words of Jesus and He's talking to you. Listen. *Come unto Me all ye that labor and are heavy laden, and I will give you rest.*' "

Jessie tried to picture that Sunday morning somewhere out in the piney woods of north Louisiana. She could almost see the little white church; could almost hear the voices of the congregation lifted in song.

"Something came over me that morning, Jessie. I got down on my knees and when I got back up, I was a new man." Billy's voice had grown strong and clear.

"I knew two things with absolute certainty—that Jesus had come into my heart and that I was going to preach His gospel wherever I could."

Billy said nothing else, apparently content, staring up at the high blue sky.

Jessie felt a serenity settle over the little glade. She listened to the sound of the creek and the wind stirring the leaves on the trees. Somewhere off in the woods, the cry of a whippoorwill drifted on the clear October air.

★ ★ ★

Dozing off, Jessie heard the dry scraping of leaves on the front walk. She sat up in the wicker chair, rubbing her eyes. At first she thought she was still caught in a dream.

Wearing tan slacks and a navy blazer with the Harvard emblem, Austin stepped up on the porch. "I just happened to be in the neighborhood and—"

"Austin!" Jessie sprang from her chair, throwing her arms around him.

Austin reached out with one arm, regaining his balance on a porch column; the other, he used to encircle Jessie's waist, pulling her to him and kissing her hard on the mouth.

Jessie felt Austin's lips on hers, soft yet demanding as she returned his kiss. Breathless after a few seconds, she placed her hands on his chest, pushing herself away. "My goodness! How did that happen so fast?"

"Magic."

Jessie held Austin's hands, standing close and staring into his clear gray eyes. "What in the world are *you* doing in Memphis?" Then she tucked her father's threadbare khaki shirt into the waistband of her jeans. "Goodness! I must look like a street urchin in this get-up."

"You look like a million dollars and change," Austin beamed, touching her on the cheek with his fingertips as though reassuring himself that Jessie actually stood in front of him. "None of those girls at Vassar and Wellesley can touch you."

"You gave them all a chance, I suppose."

"Nope," Austin laughed. "After you, they all look like Ma Kettle on the farm."

Jessie put her arms around Austin's waist, hugging him tightly. "It's so good to see you." She went up on tiptoes, kissing him on the cheek.

"I've missed you, Jess."

"You too." Jessie took him by the hand and led him over to the white wicker chairs. Sitting down, she patted the chair next to her. "Sit here and tell me what you're doing so far away from those ivy-covered halls of learning."

"Thanksgiving," he said, sitting next to her.

Jessie rubbed her eyes, then shook her head slightly. "Gracious! I've been on the road so much lately, I must have lost all track of time."

"You and the Right Reverend Pilgrim."

"How did you know?" Jessie hadn't missed the slight tone of sarcasm in Austin's voice.

"I talk to your folks once in a while." Austin's smile faded. "I think they'd like to see you come back home and finish your music degree."

Jessie looked down at her hands clasped together in her lap. "What do *you* think?"

"I think you ought to grow up and forget about this show business stuff once and for all."

"You think singing at revivals is show business?" Jessie's eyes flashed with anger.

"I can't really say. I never have been to one of the 'Right Reverend's' services."

"Stop calling him that!" Jessie stood up, glaring down at Austin. "You make him sound like some kind of side-show freak. His name's Billy Pilgrim."

"Sorry." Austin took Jessie by the hand. "I really am, Jess. Sit down now."

Jessie pulled her hand away, but sat back down next to Austin. She took a deep breath and brushed her hair back from her face. "He's really a fine man."

"If you say so."

Staring into Austin's eyes, Jessie suddenly realized what had brought the whole thing on. "Why, Austin Youngblood! You're jealous, aren't you?"

"Who? Me?" Austin stood up quickly, walking to the edge of the porch. "You've got to be kidding!" He turned around, but his voice lacked conviction. "Me . . . jealous of a half-crippled, uneducated street preacher?"

"How do you know so much about him?"

"Huh?"

"If he's so . . . insignificant, how did you come to find out so much about him?"

Austin hit the heavy white column of the porch with the flat of his hand. "What difference does it make?"

Jessie merely stared at him with a placid expression on her face.

In a few seconds, Austin returned to his chair. "I asked your mother. That's how," he reluctantly admitted. "And . . . I called Mrs. McLin."

"Oh, Austin!" Jessie stood up and slipped into his lap. "You're just being silly."

"Yeah. I guess so."

"There's nothing between Billy and me." Jessie

harbored an uneasiness even while speaking the words. Somehow, even though nothing had happened between her and Billy to make her think any differently, she felt that her words didn't quite ring true. "He's so dedicated to his preaching, he hardly knows I'm around when we're out on the road together."

Austin gave Jessie a skeptical look. "Nobody's *that* dedicated."

Uncomfortable beneath the intensity of Austin's gaze, Jessie glanced away, not wanting to reply to his comment.

"Jess—"

Jessie could tell by the tone of Austin's voice what was coming next. "Yes."

Austin took her hand, pressing it firmly in his. "We've been seeing each other for four or five years now."

"That's about right, I guess."

"We've come through some pretty rough times and we're still together."

"Uh-huh."

"Well, don't you think it's time we came to some kind of . . . understanding about our future?"

"What kind of understanding are you talking about?" Jessie felt certain that she knew exactly what he was talking about, but hoped that he wouldn't press the issue if she made him spell it out in so many words.

"Marriage."

Well, that certainly backfired! "Do you really think we're ready for that?"

"Why not?" Austin touched her cheek with his fingertips, turning her around to face him. "I'll have my law degree in June and you could graduate in music then if you'd start back in the spring semester."

Jessie felt suddenly as though she were being backed into a corner. *Why's he doing this? We can work all this out another time.* "I don't know why we have to talk about all this now. We've got plenty of time."

"Plenty of time! Plenty of time! You'll be saying the same thing when we've got separate rooms in the nursing home." Groaning in disgust, Austin put his hands around Jessie's waist, lifted her off his lap, and stood up. "I don't know why I even bothered to come by here."

"Don't be so upset!" Jessie placed her hands on his shoulders. "There's no one for me but you, Austin. You should know that by now!"

"Yeah. Me and whoever you happen to run into chasing the bright lights, standing up in front of an audience, or seeing your name in print."

"But this isn't like that!" Jessie pleaded. "I'm not in show business now!"

"Aren't you, Jess?" Austin took her hands gently but firmly from his shoulders and placed them at her sides. Then as he gazed intently at her, his eyes softened. "I'm sorry. I shouldn't have said that."

Jessie tried to speak, but couldn't find the words to express the sinking feeling in the pit of her stomach.

Austin started to speak, then abruptly turned away. Reaching the steps, he took them two at a time and walked briskly past the hedges, through the front gate to his car.

"Austin, wait!" Jessie hurried after him, feeling a terrible sense of darkness and loss come over her.

Austin started the engine of the Thunderbird, revved it, and slapped it into first gear.

Jessie had reached the sidewalk next to the car. "Austin! Please don't leave like this!"

Glancing into his rearview mirror, Austin gunned

the engine and pulled out into the street with a cry of tires on pavement.

Cradling herself with both arms, Jessie watched Austin speed away through the corridor of trees, his white convertible finally disappearing from sight in the shadowy distance.

PART THREE
★ ★ ★

A CHRISTMAS STORY

NINE

AARON

★ ★ ★

Aaron Walters, wearing the expression of a man being led off to the gallows, walked with Sharon along the sidewalk of Dalrymple Drive.

"Will you cheer up a little? This isn't an execution, you know." Sharon waved her hand at the huge live oaks lining the street and scattered about the LSU campus. The afternoon sunlight shattered like glass in their crowns and patterned the ground beneath them with shadow and splashes of shimmering light. "It's a gorgeous day for a concert."

Aaron made a face as he hooked a forefinger inside his shirt collar, tugging at it to loosen his necktie. Then he unbuttoned the coat of his dark brown suit. "It's a gorgeous day, all right. But I can think of better things to do with it than listening to somebody play a stupid fiddle."

"It's *violin*, you barbarian," Sharon teased. She straightened the jacket of the pearl-colored suit Catherine had let her borrow for the occasion.

"It's a fiddle to me."

Feeling very grown-up, Sharon slipped her arm inside Aaron's. "Call it what you want, but I think you're going to be surprised before the day's over."

"You mean that I might actually live through the next two hours with this necktie cutting my wind off?"

"No, I don't mean that." Sharon tried not to smile at the remark. "I mean if you give it a chance, you might enjoy the concert."

Aaron hitched up his trousers that had fit snugly before his customary weight loss during football season. "Yeah. And you might run a kick-off back against Terrebonne too."

They left the street, taking a short walkway that led to the Greek Theater. Its concrete benches, curving left and right in a semicircle and downward to form a bowl built into the side of the low hill, were filling with people dressed in the tweeds and light wools of late fall.

"Thank you." Sharon accepted a program from a college student dressed for a black-tie affair.

Aaron shook his head. "I'll just look on with her."

"Where would you kids like to sit?" Lane, in a herringbone jacket and navy tie, stepped between his daughter and her boyfriend.

Suddenly Sharon didn't feel grown-up anymore. Going up on tiptoe, she whispered in her father's ear. "Daddy, we want to sit by ourselves."

"We'll see ya'll after the concert." Giving Sharon a knowing glance, Catherine took Lane by the arm, leading him off in the opposite direction.

Sharon gave her mother a quick smile. She thought Catherine was as attractive as a schoolgirl in her navy skirt and white sweater. Somehow, borrowing her mother's outfit had put her on the same plane as Catherine. But she came back to reality as she started down the sloping aisle somewhat unsteadily in the high-heeled shoes she was unaccustomed to wearing. One of the heels caught in a crack in the concrete. "Oh!"

Slipping his arm quickly around Sharon's waist, Aaron kept her from falling. "I don't know why girls wear those silly things anyway."

Leaning over, Sharon smoothed her stockings. "You might learn someday, Aaron."

Aaron cleared his throat and looked away as Sharon slid past him and found their seats.

Settling into her seat, Sharon gazed up at the stage holding little more than four folding chairs and two microphones on gleaming chrome stands. The muffled sounds of conversations and shuffling about as the last of the audience seated themselves played against the traffic noises out on Dalrymple.

Sharon knew, however, that on a late-fall weekend with LSU playing an out-of-town game, the traffic would soon thin to little more than a trickle. She opened her program and held it in front of Aaron. "See? The first piece is Mendelssohn's 'Violin Concerto in E Minor.' "

"Little Richard sang that, didn't he?" Aaron asked, grinning mischievously. "I think it was one of his biggest hits."

Sharon sighed heavily. "Do you ever get serious about anything but football, Aaron?"

"I might be getting serious about *you*."

Blushing slightly, Sharon dropped her head toward the program.

From behind a curtained backdrop, three young women in long dresses and a man in his twenties wearing black tie and tails walked across the stage

149

and seated themselves in the four chairs. An announcer stepped to the microphone, introduced each of them, and left.

To the sound of the musicians tuning up, Aaron turned to Sharon. "Is this all there is?"

"What do you mean?"

"No drums or horns or stuff like that?"

"It's a violin concerto, Aaron—not a Fourth-of-July marching band."

"Oh."

"Remember, we're getting extra credit to come here," Sharon reminded him.

"Well, I can use it," Aaron nodded. "You certainly don't need any, though."

As the musicians plucked their strings, Aaron shifted about uncomfortably in his seat. "I think Paul Hornung is gonna make All-American this year."

"Wonderful."

"I bet you don't even know who he is."

Sharon tapped the side of her head with the tip of her forefinger. "Isn't he the new kettle drum player with the New York Philharmonic?"

"Funny girl. Now we're even," Aaron drawled. "He's just the best running back in the whole country."

"Really?"

"Yeah. Really."

"What do you think about Johnny Unitas?" Sharon asked, then smiled. "Think he'll amount to anything?"

Aaron's eyebrows went up. "Baltimore signed him as a free agent. How'd you know about him?"

"I've got two brothers, and a father who was a college quarterback. That's how."

"Oh, yeah." Aaron stared up at the stage where the musicians were almost ready to begin the concert. "Speaking of your daddy, it looks like Ol' Miss is going to be playing in the Sugar Bowl this year. That is, if they win this last game."

"Uh-huh."

"Well, I guess you know more about football than I do about music."

"Here's your chance to learn something, then. They're about to start."

Suddenly, Sharon heard the lovely, bittersweet strains of the violins. The music seemed to fall over her like a soft rain, soothing her with its warmth and beauty. She closed her eyes, letting the sound flow through her.

"This ain't bad."

"No, Aaron. It *ain't* bad." Sharon felt herself at a loss to understand the feelings that Aaron stirred in her. The two of them were so very different. He was such a physical person, brimming with energy that had to be expended on a playing field or in the carpenter work he did with his father during school holidays and summers. She knew that she could be content with a room full of books and her old typewriter. *And a record player*, she thought, glancing once more at the musicians.

Maybe that's it! Just maybe there's something to that old saying, "opposites attract." Sharon inched over on her seat and leaned against Aaron, feeling the hard, bunched muscles of his upper arm and shoulder. She drank in the music, savored the golden light filtering down through the trees, and smiled as she called back the words he had spoken only minutes before. "I might be getting serious about *you*."

★ ★ ★

"That wasn't so bad." Lane felt Catherine slip her hand into his as they walked along Dalrymple in the throng of people leaving the concert.

Catherine kept her eyes on Sharon and Aaron, a half block ahead of them. "Going to an outdoor concert is supposed to be fun, Lane. You make it sound like a trip to the dentist."

"I think I tolerated it pretty well for someone who was brought up on Jimmy Rogers. Tchaikovsky has his moments, but it's common knowledge that his stuff isn't in the same league with 'My Carolina Sunshine Girl' or 'Peach Pickin' Time in Georgia.'"

Catherine shook her head slowly. "How could someone with your musical taste be the father of a girl who has as much musical talent as Jessie does?"

"Now, wait a minute!" Lane protested with a grin. "I also like Jimmie Davis. You have to admit a song like 'Suppertime' doesn't come along every day."

"Yes, I will admit to that much."

Lane flinched slightly as he saw Aaron slip his arm around Sharon's waist. "I wonder what our little Memphis songbird is doing right now."

"Probably getting ready to sing for a Saturday-night service somewhere or other, I imagine." Catherine clasped Lane's hand a little tighter. "I wish Jessie could get all this show business out of her system."

Glancing down at his wife, Lane's eyebrows raised slightly. "Show business? Singing in revival meetings is your idea of show business?"

"Maybe I'm just old fashioned," Catherine shrugged. "But Velma told me that this Billy Pilgrim character is a little too flashy to suit her."

"I imagine Herbert Hoover is probably too flashy to suit Velma."

Catherine laughed softly. "You may be right about that. I guess mothers are always suspicious about the men in their daughters' lives."

"You certainly don't feel that way about Austin."

"That's different," Catherine countered. "I've known him since he and Jessie were classmates at Istrouma. He's exactly what she needs in her life."

"Sounds like you've got them married already."

Shadows flickered in Catherine's blue eyes. "I'm afraid if Jessie keeps running off every time she gets some kind of silly notion about a singing career, she's going to lose Austin. It's time for her to grow up some."

"I gather Austin's little visit with her in Memphis didn't go too well."

"He didn't say very much about it, did he?" Catherine smiled as she watched Sharon, waiting in the parking lot with Aaron. "Jess could learn a lot from Sharon."

"People have their own personalities, Cath. We can't make them what we want them to be."

Catherine nodded. She and Lane finally caught up with Sharon and Aaron. Not ready for the evening to end, Catherine asked brightly, "Well, children, anybody in the mood for a trip to Hopper's?"

"Sounds good to me, boy!" Aaron answered quickly, putting his craving for Hopper's thick chocolate malts on public display. "I mean, if *you* want to Sharon."

"Sure."

Sharon climbed into the backseat of her father's '39 Ford coupe ahead of Aaron. She found herself slightly uneasy that her mother and father were along on her "date," but somehow the sense of security and belonging that she felt more than balanced the scales in favor of their being with her.

As Lane started the car, picking his spot to pull into the line of traffic, a sudden sense of joy, perfect and complete, filled Sharon's very being. She silently thanked God that He had given her such good and loving parents, thanked Him that He had allowed Aaron to come into her life, and thanked Him for the simple pleasures of times like these.

As they turned onto Dalrymple Drive, Aaron glanced back at the top of Tiger Stadium, towering above the red-tiled roof of Foster Hall. "Boy, I'd like to play *there* someday!"

"Hard work, Aaron," Lane advised him. "Hard work and a boxcar full of desire."

"Is that how you got to be quarterback for Ol' Miss, Mr. Temple?"

"That, and the fact that God gave me a good throwing arm." A faraway look shone in Lane's eyes. "I started college there the same year Knute Rockne got killed in a plane crash."

"He was a coach, wasn't he?"

"Yep. Won a hundred and five games at Notre Dame in thirteen years. That record'll be around for a while."

Aaron leaned forward, placing his arms on the back of the seat. "I wish I was as good as Dalton."

"And Dalton wishes he were as good as Cannon," Lane added. "He can beat him on the hundred, but it's that first forty yards that counts in football, and Billy's a full step ahead of him there. He's a little stronger too."

"Is LSU going to give him a scholarship?"

Lane took the left curve that would take them past the Sigma Chi house and on to the University and City Park Lakes. "I think so. Especially if he does well in the state championship game."

"What about Cass? You think he'll play football?"

With Aaron leaning forward and not able to see

154

her, Sharon gave her mother a look of exasperation at all the sports talk between him and Lane.

Making sure Lane's eyes were on the road, Catherine nodded her agreement.

"Cass?" Lane tried to word his answer carefully. "It's hard to say, Aaron. I sometimes find it difficult to figure out exactly what Cass is going to do from one day to the next, much less predict his long-term interests."

Catherine gave Lane a look of mild disapproval. She usually found herself defending the erratic and sometimes irrational behavior of her younger son.

"Mama, did you hear about the big sale going on down at Rosenfield's?" Sharon had listened to all the football talk she could stand.

Aaron sat back so he wouldn't be caught between Sharon and her mother.

"I sure did." Catherine jumped into the breach opened up by her daughter. "Just about everything in the ladies' department is twenty-five to fifty percent off."

Lane glanced at Catherine. "I bet you and Sharon could spend a month's pay in about twenty minutes."

"Oh no!" Catherine protested, glancing over her shoulder at Sharon. "It wouldn't take *nearly* that long."

"There's a lesson to be learned here, Aaron, my boy." Lane stared out Catherine's window at the wind-rippled surface of University Lake.

Aaron spoke in a somber tone, his face a picture of concentration. "What's that, sir?"

"If you ever want to have any money—don't get married."

"Oh, I won't." He glanced quickly at Sharon. "I mean I will, but I won't—"

155

"He's just teasing you, Aaron," Sharon interrupted. "He couldn't get himself dressed for work in the morning if it wasn't for Mama."

"*That's* for certain." Lane smiled at Catherine, then back at Sharon. "I can't imagine what life would be like without my family. I don't even want to."

"You wouldn't have to wait in line to use the bathroom, for one thing," Catherine chimed in.

"Yeah," Sharon added, "and you wouldn't have to fuss about stockings hanging on the shower curtain."

"You see what I'm up against, Aaron," Lane shrugged. "A poor man hasn't got a chance against these women God made us share His world with."

★ ★ ★

Sharon sat next to Aaron in the front seat of his family's '54 Chevrolet. All around them in the parking lot of Hopper's Drive Inn, the Istrouma student body—and not a few of their parents—were celebrating the district championship. "You were just wonderful tonight, Aaron!"

"You mean the wonderful way I got creamed behind the line of scrimmage—or that wonderful fumble on the twelve-yard line?" Aaron muttered. Using his straw, he angrily punched the thick chocolate malt in its tall, heavy glass. "I oughta be on the tiddlywinks team."

"I didn't know Istrouma *had* a tiddlywinks team." Sharon pursed her lips, her face serious and sober. "Can you win a letter jacket for that?"

"Aw, you know what I mean!" Aaron wore the memory of his mistakes on the football field like a hair shirt. "I was just making a joke."

Pulling her legs up on the seat, Sharon smoothed

her skirt and smiled at Aaron's forlorn expression. "So was I."

"I'm sorry. Guess I'm not much fun tonight." Slowly what passed for a smile forced its way across Aaron's face. "Maybe you should be with somebody else."

"Now, that's a silly thing to say," Sharon replied, sounding like a teacher correcting a wayward child. "You think everything in life is always going to be fun?"

"No, but—"

"And you think I just want to be with you when everything's going great?"

"No, but—"

"And you think I want to be with somebody else tonight because you fumbled a stupid football?"

"Well, I—"

Sharon turned abruptly away from Aaron, staring out her window at their classmates. Boys and girls were visiting from car to car, yelling across the parking lot and generally celebrating not only their school's victory but what the young always have—that sweet and fleeting, wonderful and almost unbearable gift of merely being young.

"What's the matter?" Aaron leaned over and touched Sharon's shoulder.

"You must not think very much of me."

"Are you crazy?" Aaron found himself mired in the mystery of womanhood. "I think the world of you! How could you say a thing like that?"

"Because you obviously think I only like you when you're some kind of hero."

Aaron shook his head slowly. He wondered sometimes if girls were worth all the confusion they created in his life. "I don't know what you're talking about."

Sharon whirled to face him. "You think it makes any difference to me whether you play the perfect game or not?"

"Well, I—"

"You actually think that's important?"

Catching on now, Aaron decided not to try to answer Sharon's rapid-fire questions until she had finished asking all of them. He merely shrugged.

"You think I wasn't telling the truth when I said that you were wonderful tonight?"

Aaron shook his head in reply. He was trying to remember what he had said that had started Sharon on this odyssey of words so that he would never make the same mistake again. Somehow, he felt that behind the bluster and the volume she had his best interests at heart. What he couldn't understand was why she didn't just get to the point.

"Well, at least you know *something*!"

Nodding, Aaron waited for Sharon to finish her confusing explanation.

Noticing the puzzled and almost contrite expression on Aaron's face, Sharon reached over and took his hand. "You were wonderful tonight because you never gave up—in spite of having a bad night. You just got right up and went back and did your best, and you didn't make any excuses."

Aaron merely shrugged, his mind almost numbed by the assault of words.

"*That's* what really matters, Aaron," Sharon encouraged. "Not giving up when things are going terribly for you—not making excuses."

"I guess you're right."

"Oh, my goodness!" Sharon put her hand to her

throat, the words escaping from her in a rush.

Aaron took her by the shoulders. "What's wrong? Are you all right?"

"I just realized something."

"What is it?" Aaron expected Sharon to tell him some awful revelation.

"I sound just like my *mother*."

"You what?"

"I'm only fifteen years old and I already sound just like my mother."

Aaron started laughing—partly because he thought Sharon's expression and concerns were funny and partly in relief that nothing was truly wrong.

"That sounds *exactly* like something she would tell me when *I* get down."

"Well, it certainly made *me* feel better."

"I guess it was worth it, then," Sharon smiled. "I think I'm getting old too fast, though. Girls shouldn't start acting like their mothers until they're in their thirties."

Aaron leaned over and kissed Sharon on the cheek. "I'm sure glad we met." Her heated lecture was already fading from his mind.

Sharon nodded, smiling into Aaron's eyes. "I'll tell you something that I believe, if you promise not to laugh."

"Promise."

"I was doing some research down at the state archives last summer, and I ran across an old letter." The light in Sharon's eyes grew softer with the memory. "It was from a seventeen-year-old Louisiana girl to her boyfriend in the Confederate Army somewhere in Virginia."

Aaron's expression became intent as he grew absorbed in the story.

When Sharon spoke, she struggled to maintain control of her voice as well as her emotions. "She wrote about the weather and how their families were doing. You know, the usual things. Then at the end of the letter she said this: 'I can't wait until I see you again. We'll be so happy together. Or if the war has made you sad, I'll try to make you happy. And if I can't make you happy, then we'll be sad together.' "

Aaron sat very still, staring at Sharon's profile as a soft sigh escaped her lips.

Music piped from the jukebox blared on the outside loudspeakers. The noise level had risen several decibels as more cars had jammed into the parking lot. Honking horns and yelling teenagers added to the din.

Inside the '54 Chevrolet, Aaron felt that he would be violating an unspoken trust if he made a sound after Sharon had spoken of the love of a young Confederate boy and girl almost a century before. He put his arm around her, feeling the silky touch of her hair against his cheek as she lay her head against his shoulder.

After what seemed like a very long time, the bedlam outside seemed to have passed the crisis stage and settled down for the night. From the loudspeakers, the sounds of the Platters drifted across the parking lot.

Only you can make this world seem right. . . .

The fresh scent of Sharon's hair made Aaron think of spring flowers and summer sunshine. "That's how I feel about you."

"I don't think I understand." Sharon turned her face toward him.

"The song."

"Oh. I'm sorry." She settled back against the seat and listened to the song. "I was still thinking about the girl who wrote that letter."

"I really *do* feel that everything's going to be all right when I'm with you."

"Me too," Sharon agreed, but her mind had returned to the girl of the Confederacy and her love for a faraway soldier.

"You want to go steady?"

"I don't think Daddy would let me." Sharon squeezed Aaron's hand.

"Oh."

"But there's nobody else I care about, Aaron." Sharon turned to look into his eyes.

"Me neither."

She settled back again. "Then that's almost as good as going steady, isn't it?"

"I guess so."

Sharon spoke to no one in particular. "I wonder whatever happened to her."

Aaron felt dazed by the realization that he had once more fallen off Sharon's train of thought. "Whatever happened to *who*?"

"The girl who wrote the letter."

"Oh, her."

"Maybe she married her sweetheart and they had a houseful of children."

"Maybe so." Aaron felt that sometimes Sharon concerned herself more with people in books than she did with the people around her.

"Or maybe he got killed in some terrible battle and she died of a broken heart."

"Or maybe she talked about dead people all the time and he married somebody else."

"What?" Sharon sat up and stared at Aaron, then a smile lighted her face. "Oh, I'm sorry. I *do* tend to let my imagination run wild sometimes."

"That's all right," Aaron said, taking off her gold-rimmed glasses. "You're cute enough to get away with it." He kissed her softly on the lips.

Headlights flashed on and off two cars behind them. Aaron quickly handed Sharon her glasses and slid over against the driver's door.

"I think that's Daddy's subtle way of telling us it's time to go home."

Aaron started the engine, slipped the car into gear, and glanced behind him. "It's a real comfort to me just knowing he's back there," he said with a straight face.

Sharon's laughter drifted from the car window as they pulled out of the parking lot.

TEN

THE SILVER MISTING RAIN

★ ★ ★

"What's the matter, 'Pancake' . . . you chicken?" Cassidy, wearing black Converse tennis shoes, Levi's, and a black jacket, stood just inside the Rexall Drugstore near the double door that led into the adjoining A&P.

On Saturday mornings the grocery shoppers, stocking up for the coming week, jammed the aisles and backed up at the check-out counters, keeping the bag boys and the clerks hopping. Customers flowed back and forth through the common door that made it so convenient to shop at both stores.

Staring down at the frayed bottoms of his overalls, Caffey flinched at the sound of his nickname. He knew Cassidy only called him that when he was angry with him. "No. I'm just *careful*, that's all."

Not careful enough, Cassidy thought, noticing the cut at the corner of Caffey's mouth. "Careful," Cassidy repeated sarcastically. "How do you spell that? C-H-I-C-K-E-N."

"I ain't scared!"

"Maybe I ought to get somebody else." Cassidy glanced about the store.

The thought of Cassidy teaming up with somebody other than him ended the debate. "Okay. If you're *really* that crazy, let's get it over with."

"Now you're talking, ol' buddy."

Caffey, glancing around furtively, walked into the A&P ahead of Cassidy.

Following a casual twenty feet behind his big friend, Cassidy eyed the manager, who kept a watchful eye on his store from his glassed-in office.

Caffey stopped at the end of the line of check-out counters, a pained expression on his face. He turned to look back at Cassidy, then quickly jerked his head away.

Cassidy walked up behind his oversized accomplice and carefully took a *Saturday Evening Post* from a rack near the last cash register. Flipping through the pages, he muttered under his breath, "What's the matter?"

Caffey started to turn around.

"Don't look at me, you big dummy!" Cassidy whispered harshly, his eyes still on the magazine.

"I forgot what I was supposed to do." Caffey's face grew slack with defeat.

"Just knock over that big stack of ketchup bottles in the center aisle."

Caffey smiled and plodded off around the counter to his appointed task.

Placing the magazine back in the rack, Cassidy sauntered casually past the dark-haired check-out girl who had been a classmate of Jessie's and greeted her with a smile. By the time he reached the end of the aisle where the cartons of cigarettes were stacked, he heard the reassuring sound of the ketchup bottles crashing to the floor.

Cassidy watched the manager, his bald head shining beneath the fluorescent light, leap from his chair and run out of his office toward the main aisle. Several bag boys and a stock clerk followed their boss's lead.

With a quick glance around the store, Cassidy saw that for the moment, all heads were turned toward the aisle where the noise had come from. He grabbed a carton of Camels from the shelf, tucking it beneath his jacket, and walked unhurriedly through the nearest check-out stand. Noticing the bedlam around the ruined ketchup display, he left through the front door, turned left, and walked on past the Morgan and Lindsey and Western Auto stores to the far end of the shopping center.

Feeling his heart hammering in his chest, Cassidy forced himself to walk slowly and deliberately across the parking lot. He jumped the drainage ditch and continued on a full block down to Seneca, turned left and, after crossing the heavy traffic on Plank Road, walked another block to Wenonah Street.

With a sigh of relief, he sat down in the dusty autumn grass beneath a sweet gum tree and waited. All around him, the dry leaves—a deep scarlet back in October before they fell to the ground—were now the color of dried blood.

Ten minutes later Caffey lumbered down the street toward Cassidy.

"How'd it go?" Cassidy felt the hard bulk of the carton beneath his jacket.

"I got bawled out."

"What'd you expect?" Cassidy grinned, feeling bold and confident.

Caffey sat down heavily next to his friend. "Wasn't as bad as I get from my old man."

"See, you got a good deal out of this," Cassidy insisted. "I take the risks and all you get is a little mouth from the manager. Plus—you get half the cigarettes."

"How come I'm not happy, then?"

Cassidy frowned and stood up. "Come on, you'll feel better after you've had a smoke."

"Where we going?"

"To your place, I guess."

Caffey lowered his head, staring at the ground. "That's the *last* place *I'm* going."

"Your ol' man on another toot?"

Caffey nodded. "He finishes up all his mechanic jobs by Friday night so he can stay drunk all weekend. I learned to stay out of his way."

"I know!" Cassidy snapped is fingers. "We'll go to our garage apartment."

"You're gonna take cigarettes to your house?" Caffey's eyes widened as he stared up at his friend. "Your daddy would skin us both."

"Hardly anybody goes back there anymore since Jessie moved to Memphis."

"I don't know—"

"Aw, come on!" Cassidy reached down, took his friend's hand, and helped him to his feet. "It's *my* house—so it's *my* hide if we get caught."

"Aw right."

Cassidy moved the carton of cigarettes around behind his back and slipped them inside the waistband of his jeans so he could have both hands free. "I look like a criminal walking around with one hand jammed against my coat."

Caffey stared intently into his friend's eyes. "You kinda look like a criminal anyway."

What's he talking about? The simple, direct comment from Caffey, who was incapable of subtlety,
bothered Cassidy in a way that he didn't want to admit. "Come on, let's get a move on."

As they headed north on Wenonah, Cassidy
glanced over at his friend. Caffey's mouth hung
slightly open, his eyes staring glassily down at the
street. *His ol' man must really be giving him a hard
time.* When they reached Chippewa, Cassidy turned
right toward Plank Road.

"Hey, where you goin'?" Caffey asked, his eyes
squinting into the morning sunshine. "I thought we
was going over to your house and smoke some of
these things."

Cassidy didn't bother to explain, knowing Caffey
would follow him anywhere.

When they reached Plank Road again, Cassidy
looked both ways, then turned to his friend. "Wait
here. I'll be back in a minute."

Caffey's face glowed with pleasure as he stared
across the street at the little brick building with the
name and date inscribed in concrete directly above
the front door: Tony's Donut Shop, 1946. "But, I ain't
got no money."

Cassidy staggered backward, grabbing his chest
with both hands. "What a shock!"

With a sheepish grin, Caffey laughed and kicked a
rock along the sidewalk.

Darting across the street, Cassidy stopped on the
other side before going into the shop. Fumbling
through his pockets, he came up with some change.
*Twenty-four cents. I guess Tony knows I'm good for a
penny.*

Caffey stared intently as his friend disappeared inside the shop.

Cassidy emerged from the donut shop carrying a brown paper bag and, without breaking stride, ran easily across the street. "Here you go, big boy."

Caffey took the bag, thrusting his grimy hand inside. Pulling out a donut, he crammed it into his mouth. With his cheeks bulging, he held the bag out to Cassidy and mumbled, "Here. You eat some too."

Cassidy shook his head. He knew donuts were a treat that seldom came Caffey's way since his father had started living inside beer cans and bottles of sour mash whiskey. "No thanks. I had a big breakfast."

The two friends, one moving with smooth and agile confidence, the other burdened by a heavy lumbering gait, walked together in the Saturday morning sunlight, their shadows following on the left, stretching across vacant lots, climbing the sides of buildings, mimicking the actions of flesh and blood.

★ ★ ★

Standing in deep shadow beneath the spreading live oak, Cassidy watched Lane back the Ford out onto Evangeline and drive away. He smiled when he saw his mother's pale hair gleaming inside the car.

"You sure nobody's up there?"

Cassidy walked down the gravel driveway toward the garage apartment located at the rear of their lot. "You saw them leave, didn't you? Quit worrying."

Caffey took in the wide front porch and the upstairs gallery with its scrolled iron railing and white wicker furniture. "You got a nice house."

"Yeah. Better than we had up in Sweetwater, Mississippi. What a hick town *that* was."

"Ya'll go back very much?"

"Holidays mostly." Cassidy remembered the summer days he and Dalton had spent with his grandparents—swimming in the pond and afterward the homegrown watermelons, ice-cold from the freezer on their back porch.

At the back of the driveway, they followed the stepping-stones that turned left away from the house, entered the screen porch, and took the stairs up to the apartment.

Cassidy walked into the kitchen and dropped the carton of cigarettes on the table. Stepping to the counter, he grabbed a box of kitchen matches and tossed them over next to the cigarettes. "What are you waiting for, an engraved invitation? Grab a chair and take a load off."

Caffey glanced around the sparkling-clean kitchen as though he were standing on holy ground. "I'm kinda dirty."

Dragging a chair out with his foot, Cassidy plopped into it, ripped open the carton of cigarettes, and dumped a pack onto the table.

Cautiously, as though whatever he touched might shatter, Caffey joined his friend at the table.

Cassidy tore open the cigarettes, tapped one out, and tossed the pack to Caffey. Then he grabbed a kitchen match from the box, flicked it into flame with his thumbnail, and lit his cigarette. Careful not to inhale too deeply, he drew the smoke into his lungs and let it drift out his nostrils.

Caffey got straight to business without any of Cassidy's flair for the dramatic, holding the cigarette between his thumb and forefinger as he drew deeply on it.

"I assume Daddy bought that carton of cigarettes for you, *Cassidy*."

Cassidy's chair made a scraping sound on the linoleum as he whirled around. "What are *you* doing here?"

"I live here." Sharon sat curled in an overstuffed chair in the shadowed living room, a salient of yellow sunlight gleaming on the opened novel resting in her lap.

"Not back *here*, you don't." Cassidy stood up, dropped his cigarette on the floor, and bent to pick it up. "You can just leave right now!"

"I come back here all the time to read and study." Sharon obviously had no intention of leaving. "I can't even *think* with that racket you call music blaring full-blast on your record player." She returned to her reading. "You little pre-delinquents can just go about your unseemly business."

Cassidy cleaned up the ashes from the floor, dumping them in the sink and turning on the faucet to get rid of the evidence. When he looked up, Caffey had just opened the door. "Hey, wait a minute! Where you goin'?"

Caffey glanced toward the living room. "I don't feel right in here no more."

"C'mon, she's just my goofy sister!"

Shaking his head, Caffey closed the door behind him and tramped heavily down the stairs.

"Now look what you've done!" Cassidy complained. "You've run my friend off."

"I didn't run anybody off. He's just feeling guilty." Shivering slightly, Sharon pulled Lane's heavy gray cardigan sweater closer about her chest.

Cassidy frowned at his sister. "What's the matter with you? You cold or something?"

Sharon shook her head. "Maybe a little." Closing the book, she placed it on the scarred end table that her family had used when they had first moved from

Sweetwater down to Baton Rouge. "I'm worried about you, Cass."

Cassidy drew deeply and defiantly on his cigarette. Then squinting through the drifting blue-white smoke, he snarled, "I don't need *nobody's* worry!"

"You stole those cigarettes, didn't you?"

"I got my own money."

Sharon took a deep breath. "You spend it all on *Hot Rod* magazines and . . . I don't know what else."

"Whadda you know about it?"

"I know I found an empty beer bottle, cleaning up your room the other day."

"You stay outta my room!" Cassidy stepped into the living room. "I guess now you're gonna tattle on me to Mama and Daddy, huh?"

"No."

Sharon's reply seemed to take the edge off Cassidy's anger. He walked over to the sofa and sat down. "Thanks for not telling about the beer."

"You should take those cigarettes back. Smoking's bad enough, but stealing them is worse."

Cassidy stared sullenly out the window at Caffey, who was standing at the end of their driveway, obviously trying to remember which way he had to turn to get home.

"Are you listening?"

"What if I don't?"

Sharon kept a level gaze at her brother. "Then it's just something you'll have to live with."

"You mean that's all?" Cassidy turned to her, a look of relief on his face. "You're not going to tell?"

Shaking her head, Sharon's expression grew solemn. *I think he doesn't know what guilt is.* "I wish you at least *felt* bad about taking them, Cass."

"Oh, I do!" Cassidy tuned down the obvious sense

of relief that his voice carried. "I mean, I really do—but, you see, they just wouldn't understand over at the store if I . . . you know, brought them back, especially with one pack opened and all." He stepped back into the kitchen and dropped his cigarette into the sink, then returned to the living room.

"I can't be your conscience, Cass."

Having escaped the punishment his father would surely have inflicted on him if Sharon had told, Cassidy gladly changed the subject. He walked over and sat down on the couch. "What you reading?"

Sharon picked up her book. "*Lord of the Flies*. It's by William Golding."

"That's kind of a crazy title," Cassidy grinned. "What's it about?"

Staring at her little brother's bright smile, Sharon thought how likable he could be whenever the notion struck him, which hadn't been very often in the past year or so. She felt a deep longing to do something, anything, to stop his drifting into a kind of life that could destroy him. "It's about how *savage* people can become whenever they don't play by the rules of ordinary decency—of everyday humanity."

"Sounds boring to me."

Sharon tried another tack. "Why don't you start going back to Sunday school, Cass?"

"What?" Cassidy sounded incensed at the accusation. "Who do you think that is sitting next to you in the car every Sunday morning?"

"You skip the class and go play the pinball machine down at the drugstore."

Cassidy stood up. "Oh, so now playing a pinball machine makes me some kind of criminal, huh?"

"There's nothing wrong with pinball."

"What is it, then?"

"Deception," Sharon said in a level voice. "There's a *lot* wrong with that."

Cassidy got up and walked back into the kitchen. He picked the cigarette up from the sink, turned the water on, and rinsed all the ashes down the drain. Dropping the butt inside the open carton, he picked it up and tucked it back inside his waistband. "You sure you're not going to tell on me?" He glanced into the living room at Sharon.

With a sigh, she got up and walked into the kitchen. "Cass, you're only thirteen."

Cassidy gave her his best smile. "You don't miss a thing, do you, big sister?"

Sharon couldn't help but smile at the shining face of her brother. "Think about what you're doing."

"Think?" Cassidy rubbed his chin between thumb and forefinger. "Now, that's an idea. I'm always looking for something I've never done before."

Sharon laughed softly. "You're impossible."

"Don't I know it." Cassidy opened the door, then stopped, one foot resting outside on the porch. "You're a good sister, Sharon."

Sharon nodded. "Don't I know it."

Now it was Cassidy's turn to laugh. "But you've got a big problem."

"And just what is that?"

"You worry too much." He turned and ran down the stairs, taking them two at a time.

★ ★ ★

A sadness the color of old pewter seemed to settle on the city with the coming of the cold winter rains. Streets glistened in the early twilight. Across the river, wind clattered through the stalks of sugarcane as tractors and cane buggies roared through the fields and along the dirt roads, rushing to complete the harvest before the first hard freeze.

"You sure your mother doesn't mind taking me home?" Leaving the front entrance of the high school, Aaron carried Sharon's books in one arm and held a black umbrella above their heads with the other. They turned right onto the sidewalk running along Winbourne Avenue. "Mama would have picked me up after basketball practice if she wasn't sick."

"Don't be silly. It's no trouble at all." Sharon wore Aaron's letter jacket over her sweater, but still she shivered in the silver misting rain. "Aren't you cold?" She glanced at Aaron, who was wearing penny loafers with white socks, jeans, and a thin flannel shirt.

"Nah."

Traffic hissed by them, headlights casting yellow reflections on the wet pavement.

Sharon felt like talking to dispel the gloominess of the day. "I got all my homework done while I was in the library. Did some writing of my own, too." She put her hand over her mouth and coughed.

"You okay?"

"Sure. It's just a little cough."

Aaron glanced through a chain link fence next to the sidewalk at the practice football field that was circled by a cinder track and the stands of wooden bleachers, empty now and dark with rain. "You ever get anything else published besides them newspaper articles last summer?"

"Maybe. I'm not sure yet." Sharon had wanted to tell him the good news on some special occasion, but decided she couldn't wait any longer.

"What's *that* supposed to mean?"

"I sent a story to the *Saturday Evening Post* and they wrote me that it would be published in two or three weeks, but that's the last I heard from them."

"They send you any money?"

"Not yet."

"I'd believe 'em when I got the money."

"Let's cross over here." Sharon took Aaron's arm as they crossed the street.

Standing in front of McClure's Drugstore, Aaron glanced at his watch. "We've got twenty minutes. Let's go in and get some hot chocolate."

Sharon smiled her acceptance to the invitation.

As they pushed through the glass doors, cosmetic-scented air washed over them. The shelves held bars of soap and cobalt blue bottles of Evening in Paris perfume stacked in pyramids; pink plastic hair curlers lay in their boxes. Wooden racks held greeting cards and magazines, and postcards of Louisiana's swamps and rivers and public buildings rested in their own racks made of wire.

Walking past rows of toothbrushes and Johnson's Baby Powder, they came to the soda fountain at the rear of the store. Sharon and Aaron sat down on the dark blue leatherette stools that swiveled back and forth.

"What'll it be, kids?" James McClure stared at them through his heavy black-rimmed glasses. His shirt was frosty white under the fluorescent lights.

"Hot chocolate, Mr. McClure." Aaron placed two dimes on the counter.

"Good choice on a day like this." He reached behind him for two heavy white mugs and filled them from a large urn on the shelf next to the mirror.

"You got some marshmallows?" Aaron asked as McClure set the steaming mugs on the Formica counter.

"Sure thing."

Sharon watched McClure place several marsh-mallows in their chocolate, then return to the pharmacy area of the drugstore where he began filling prescriptions.

"You really gonna have a story in the *Saturday Evening Post*?" Aaron sipped his chocolate, leaving a thin brown mustache above his upper lip.

"That's what they tell me. Of course, like you said, I haven't gotten any money yet."

"They'll do it."

"How come you're so sure about it now?"

"'Cause you got real talent. That's how come." Aaron glanced at the posters of malts and sundaes and banana splits taped to the long mirror behind the counter.

Sharon noticed the sudden look of disappointment on Aaron's face.

Almost as though he could read her mind, Aaron said, "I'm just jealous, I guess."

"Of what?"

"'Cause you can do something so good."

"You mean my writing?" Sharon wondered what brought on Aaron's sudden mood change. "*It's* not so good. You don't have to be John Steinbeck to get published in the *Post*."

"Who you trying to kid? That magazine goes all over the country."

"You act like you can't do *anything*."

"I can't." Aaron held his cup close to his mouth, blowing into it, then sipped the chocolate. "Nothing nearly as good as you can write, anyway."

Sharon pushed her cup aside. "This just didn't happen overnight, you know."

Aaron gave her an oblique glance.

"I've sent dozens of stories to magazines over the

last two or three years." Leaning toward Aaron, Sharon placed her hand on his arm. "Do you know how many times I've walked to that mailbox, hoping against all hope that I'd have good news—only to find nothing but another rejection slip? 'Sorry, your story doesn't suit our present publishing needs.' "

Aaron gave her a sheepish smile. "I guess nothing comes easy, does it?"

Sharon ignored the obvious reply. "You say you can't do anything well. What about football? You're on the varsity team and you're just a sophomore."

"High-school ball is as far as I'll go, too."

"You don't know that."

Aaron glanced back at McClure, still bent to his work. "Coach Brown does, and that's what he told me." Aaron ate one of the soggy marshmallows floating in his cup.

"He can't say that for sure."

"Yes, he can," Aaron said in defense of his coach. "He knows his business. He told me if I was four or five inches taller and a step faster on the forty-yard dash . . . well, maybe. But I'm not and there's no use dreaming about things that can't come true. Dalton's gonna play for LSU, sure as anything—not me. I ain't got what it takes."

"Maybe you'll grow."

"Not much chance of that," Aaron muttered. "My daddy's not even as tall as I am." He stared at the rain-streaked plate-glass window. "How about you? Now that you've made the big-time, what's next?"

"I told you, it's not the big-time." Sharon had begun to feel uncomfortable with telling only one person about her moderate success. "Anyway, Mrs. Shay is going to help me get started on a novel. You know, just for the experience."

"She's a nice lady. I made a C in her class 'cause she took up extra time with me."

"She edited my story," Sharon added. "That's probably why it got accepted."

Aaron pointed toward the parking spaces near the street. "There's your mama."

Swallowing the rest of their chocolate, they hurried outside to the black Chrysler and climbed into the backseat.

"You children must have frozen, walking down here from school." Catherine glanced into the backseat as she turned right, onto Winbourne.

"Aaron let me use his jacket." Sharon put her hand to her mouth and coughed, then rubbed the side of her neck with her fingertips.

"And you, young lady," Catherine said evenly, "are going to the doctor with that cough. It's been two or three weeks now, and you're not getting any better."

"I don't have time, Mama," Sharon pleaded. "I've got too much work to finish."

"You won't finish *anything* if you end up in the hospital with pneumonia."

Sharon stared out the window as they passed by the high-school building, its black marble columns wet and gleaming through the pale gray mist.

"Don't look so down-and-out, sweetheart," Catherine smiled. "I just might have some good news for you."

Sharon turned toward her mother.

Catherine picked up an envelope from the seat beside her and handed it to Sharon.

"It's about my story!" One glance told Sharon all she needed to know. She settled down, opened the envelope carefully, and took out a check. "It's too good to be true!"

Aaron moved closer for a better look. "They really *did* pay you! Paid you pretty good too."

"Oh, Mama, this means I'm really a writer!"

"You've been a writer since you were eight years old, sugar." Catherine stopped at the traffic light on Acadian Throughway and smiled over the seat at her daughter. "This just lets the rest of the world know."

ELEVEN

HEM OF HIS GARMENT

★ ★ ★

"How long has Sharon complained of a lack of energy, Mrs. Temple?" Dr. Charles McConnell leaned back against the edge of the walnut desk, eyeing Catherine over his silver-rimmed reading glasses. His white hair and white lab coat contrasted sharply with his lean face, tanned deeply from decades of fishing beneath the relentless south Louisiana sun.

"She doesn't complain." Noticing the concern etched on the doctor's face, Catherine felt a sudden chill at the base of her neck. "Wait a minute! She did mention a couple of days ago about that swelling in her neck, but that was after I had already decided to bring her in for the cough."

Reaching behind him, McConnell picked up a file from the desktop and opened it. Adjusting his glasses with his right forefinger, he shuffled through several sheets of papers, then gave Catherine a level stare. "Your daughter's got an upper respiratory infection."

Catherine wanted desperately for the doctor to

181

stop there, to tell her nothing else about Sharon's condition, but she knew there would be more.

"We can treat that with antibiotics." He closed the file. "Why don't you sit down?"

"I'm fine." Catherine felt sick to her stomach. She steeled herself for what was to come.

"There's no easy way to tell you this." McConnell stared at the window. Early winter light streamed through the venetian blinds, forming pale yellow bars on the opposite wall. "Your daughter has leukemia."

Catherine's strength seemed to flow like water out of her body. Her legs felt dead and heavy, no longer listening to the commands of her mind.

McConnell took her by the arm, leading her over to a leather-and-chrome armchair. Gazing intently into her face, he lay his finger on her wrist and glanced at his watch. "Are you all right? Can I get you something?"

Taking a deep breath, Catherine shook her head. She felt hot tears streaming down her cheeks as the grief, suddenly beyond her control, poured out of her.

Laying his hand on her shoulder, McConnell patted Catherine gently, allowing her to cry out the beginning of her sorrow. After a minute or two, as Catherine's sobs began to subside, he walked over to a white metal table and poured a glass of water from an insulated pitcher. "Here, Mrs. Temple."

Catherine took the water, sipping it slowly. "I'm sorry. I didn't mean to let go like that."

McConnell pulled some tissues from a box on his desk and handed them to Catherine. "Perfectly normal. I may have been worried about you if you hadn't reacted pretty strongly to news like that."

Catherine wiped her face, taking a few breaths to help calm herself.

Pulling a chair over close to Catherine, McConnell sat down, leaning toward her. "I'm sorry if I seemed so brutal telling you like that, but I've never been able to find a better way of breaking bad news to someone than to just go ahead and tell them."

"I understand."

"Now, the worst part is over."

Catherine gazed up at McConnell's face, calm and reassuring, his eyes filled with a light that she recognized as compassion. "There's hope?"

"There's *always* hope, Mrs. Temple."

Catherine nodded, forcing herself to smile. "Yes, I believe that too."

"Now!" McConnell stood up and began pacing back and forth in the confined space. "Now that we've identified the culprit," he stopped and gazed down at Catherine, "we're going to begin to fight him." He picked up the file and took a yellow pencil from a holder on his desk.

Catherine began to feel better. She could almost believe that everything was going to turn out all right as McConnell spoke with such professional confidence.

"Has Sharon been bothered by night sweats?"

"No, not that I know of."

McConnell noted Catherine's answers in the file as he questioned her. "Have you noticed any swelling other than on her neck?"

"No." Catherine looked puzzled. "Shouldn't you be asking Sharon about this, Doctor?"

"Rest assured, I shall," McConnell replied, gazing over the tops of his reading glasses. "Just as soon as we can arrange for her to come in for an appointment." He sat on the edge of the desk and crossed his arms over his chest. "I find that I get more accurate information if I ask other family members and don't rely solely on the patient."

Catherine flinched inwardly at the word *patient* associated with Sharon. "Oh, I see."

"Now, back to business." McConnell sat down in the chair, the file resting in his lap. "Has she been prone to infections, other than this recent respiratory one?"

"No. Not that I know of."

"Good." McConnell made a note in the folder, tapped the pencil's eraser lightly against his upper lip several times, and made some more notes.

"What do we do next?"

"We'll get to that in a moment."

As McConnell pored over his few brief notes and the test results in the folder, Catherine tried not to think about the news she had just received. Her mind turned to the past. She pictured Sharon rushing through the back door into the kitchen holding high a first-grade test paper with "100" marked in bright red at its top. She had taped it to the refrigerator, along with so many others that soon the white enameled door and sides were almost hidden from view beneath a blanket of 100s and A-pluses.

In her mind's eye, all she could see was Sharon—Sharon kneeling next to her by the bedside as they said their prayers together; Sharon smiling brightly as she handed her a Mother's Day present wrapped in pale pink paper with tiny wild flowers on it; Sharon lying in her lap as she rocked her to sleep after awaking from a bad dream.

"Now!"

Catherine leaped back to the present at the sound of McConnell's voice.

"Has she ever complained of pain in her bones or joints?"

"No."

"How long has Sharon shown signs of vague ill health?"

"What do you mean?"

"Just general symptoms—pale, lack of energy, not feeling quite as well as normal—things like that."

Bringing her hands together, Catherine rested her chin on the tips of her fingers and stared at the venetian blinds blossoming with slivers of light. Then she leaned back in the chair. "It's hard to say. I remember right after school let out last year she looked kind of pallid, but she insisted she was all right."

McConnell nodded and made a note of it. Closing the folder, he held it with both hands, placing it across his chest. "I know it may sound strange for me to say this, Mrs. Temple, but in a way we're fortunate."

Catherine was unable to respond to McConnell's statement, though she tried.

"I believe we've diagnosed the disease at its earliest stage."

Catherine merely nodded.

"Secondly, Sharon has lymphatic leukemia, which can be treated with radiation and blood transfusions." McConnell held Catherine's eyes. "We haven't had much luck treating myelogenous leukemia, where white blood cells in the bone marrow replace the red blood cells at an accelerated rate."

"You mean Sharon can be cured?"

McConnell glanced down at the floor. "No."

"But you said—"

"I said she can be *treated*." McConnell glanced up. "We haven't found a cure yet, but treatment can greatly slow down the course of the disease."

A terrible weight seemed to press down on Catherine. She barely had the strength to breathe. McConnell sounded as though he was speaking from a great distance.

"The first thing we'll do is give her some whole blood. She should feel better almost immediately."

Catherine listened to McConnell's words, but their meaning seemed lost somewhere between them, in the air that smelled faintly of antiseptic.

"Later we'll start the X-ray treatments." McConnell reached behind him and pressed his intercom.

"Yes, Doctor."

"Set up an appointment for Sharon Temple as soon as possible, please."

"Yes, sir."

"Mrs. Temple, are you going to be all right?"

Catherine felt almost as though she were standing aside watching the doctor talk to someone else. A numbness in her breast seemed to have replaced the sharp pain of only moments before. "I'm fine."

McConnell's eyes narrowed with concern. "I can have someone drive you home if you'd like."

"No. I'll be just fine."

McConnell nodded.

"Doctor—" Catherine rose unsteadily to her feet.

"Yes."

"I don't want anyone else to find out about this until after you've seen Sharon. I mean, like someone letting it out by mistake or . . ." Catherine took a deep breath, letting it out slowly. "I'll have a talk with my husband when he gets in from work and we'll tell her tonight . . . together."

"I understand."

"I just wouldn't want it getting out—to have her find out another way."

"We're a closed-mouth bunch around here, Mrs. Temple," McConnell said somberly.

"Can she stay in school?"

"Certainly." McConnell rested his arms on his desk. "The disease could go into remission. Sharon could be symptom-free in a few weeks."

"That's possible?"

"Likely, I'd say."

"But I thought it was always—"

"We've got a long time before we have to start thinking about that." McConnell opened the folder, glancing at it and making a quick notation. "I'd like to put her in the hospital and give her some blood and do a complete workup on her to begin with."

"How long would that take?"

McConnell rubbed the side of his neck with his left forefinger. "I'd say about a week."

Catherine nodded. "Would it be all right for her to do her homework so she won't get behind in school? One of her friends could bring it to her."

"I think that would be *more* than all right," McConnell said, and smiled. "I think it would be good therapy for her. We couldn't have her making a 'B' on her report card, now could we?"

"You've been very kind, Doctor." Catherine shook his hand and started for the door.

"Mrs. Temple . . ."

"Yes."

"Anything's possible."

Catherine nodded, a half smile touching the corners of her lips as she left the doctor's office.

★ ★ ★

187

"Funny," Sharon said in a soft voice, "I don't feel very sick." Sitting on her bed next to Catherine, Sharon glanced at Lane, kneeling on the rug next to her. His right hand nervously rubbed the chenille bedspread. Then he stared down at Sharon's feet. She wore heavy cotton socks to keep them warm, except during the hottest part of the summer.

Catherine took a tissue from the pocket of her apron, touching the corners of both eyes. Lane plucked at a loose thread on the bedspread.

Sharon turned toward Catherine, the look of despair on her face as deep as the blue of her eyes. "Mama, am I going to die?"

"No, sweetheart." Taking her daughter in her arms, Catherine rocked her gently back and forth, comforting her as she would a small child. "Don't even think about that." She sat back, touching Sharon's cheeks with her fingertips. "Dr. McConnell said he can treat this. You're going to be just fine."

Lane buttoned the right flap pocket of his khaki shirt for some reason known only to him before taking Sharon's hand. "That's right, baby. We're going to whip this thing together."

"But if I go in the hospital, how can I do my homework?" Sharon appeared more distressed over missing school than she did about being sick.

"Dr. McConnell said we can bring it to you every day so you won't get behind."

Sharon gave her mother a weak smile, then stared at Lane's hard brown hand covering hers. "Good."

"Sharon—"

"Yes, Mama."

"Have you been feeling bad for a while and just not telling anyone about it?"

Sharon shook her head.

"Nothing at all?"

"Well," Sharon rubbed her hand back and forth on her right thigh, "my elbows and knees hurt me once in a while—but not very much."

"Why didn't you tell us?"

"I just didn't want to be a bother."

Taking her by the shoulders, Catherine turned her gently around, gazing directly into her eyes. "Don't you know you could never be a bother to us? We love you so much, Sharon!" Fighting back the tears, Catherine put her arms around her daughter and pulled her close.

Lane turned Sharon's hand loose and sat on the bed next to her, encircling her and Catherine with his arms. The three of them sat that way for a long while, the silence of the room broken by their breathing and an occasional sob from Catherine.

Outside, the sun dropped beyond the great brown flow of the river, the simple board-and-batten cabins of the plantation workers, and the long rows of stubble, blackened and burning in the canefields.

Catherine sat up straight on the bed, blew her nose, and brushed at her cheeks with the back of one finger. "Now, let's get something straight." She took Sharon's face in both, smoothed her hair back, then rested her hands in her lap. "We're going on with our lives, just as we always have."

"But what about the hospital and . . ." Sharon's eyes pleaded for understanding about what was happening to her.

"Oh, I don't mean we aren't going to do what the doctor tells us. We're going to proceed with the treatments and anything else we're supposed to do." Catherine silently prayed for strength. "But, since he said

remission is a very real possibility, that's what we're
going to count on."

"Will it hurt much, Mama?"

Catherine shook her head. "I don't think so. Dr.
McConnell didn't even mention it." She took Sharon's
hand in both of hers, gazing directly into her eyes.
"You've got years and years ahead of you, darling. I
just know you do."

Sharon smiled weakly, nodding her head.

Lane stood up. "So, we'll get everything ready for
the little stay at the hospital, and when that's over it's
back to school and studies and all your friends."

"I guess so," Sharon agreed.

"Remember, darling," Catherine reminded her
with a gentle squeeze of her hands, "we're a family
and we're all in this thing together."

Sharon smiled again and this time the weakness
in it had almost disappeared.

"Lane, why don't you pray for us?"

Without replying, Lane knelt down beside the bed.
Catherine followed him with Sharon kneeling between her mother and father.

"Father, we thank You for Your love, for all the
blessings that You've given us." Lane's voice grew
hoarse. "We need You now, Lord. Our little girl's sick.
We're going to do what the doctor says . . . but as in
all things, we end up depending on You. Lord, touch
Sharon and heal her from this sickness. Jesus, she
needs You just like the woman with the issue of blood.
Let her touch the hem of Your garment." After a few
seconds of silence, Lane's voice was little more than a
whisper as he spoke. "In Jesus' name. Amen."

"Amen," Catherine and Sharon said in unison.

Lane took the hands of his wife and daughter as
they stood up next to him. "Anybody want to go down

and watch 'Gunsmoke' with me?"

"I've got dishes to wash," Catherine said quickly.

"I'll help you, Mama."

Lane frowned at them. "I get the feeling you girls don't appreciate a good shoot-'em-up."

"You're real smart, Daddy."

"We'll all watch 'The Millionaire' together," Catherine said, "after your show's over."

"It's a date," Lane agreed. "I can't wait to see who gets their life ruined by too much money tonight."

After the dishes were done, and the television had gone dark, and everyone had gone to their beds for the night, Sharon sat on the floor in front of her bookcase staring at the titles of some of her favorites: *Tender is the Night, The Yearling, For Whom the Bell Tolls, A Tree Grows in Brooklyn.*

Whenever I've been blue I could always turn to my books. Reading usually made me feel better, but now I can't seem to get my mind to concentrate on anything. Sharon felt a kind of numbness that seemed to be centered in her brain. She had talked with her family tonight, laughed with them, watched television, and eaten ice cream at the kitchen table with her mother. And all the while, it was as though she saw everything through a veil of some kind. Nothing really seemed to come into sharp focus. Nothing seemed real.

Getting up from the floor, Sharon walked over to her desk and sat down. Out in the darkness, the inconstant December wind blew past her window, made a sharp crying sound in the eaves of the house, then died away.

Sharon reached for her Bible resting next to her old Royal typewriter. She ran the tips of her fingers along the white leather cover, remembering that her mother had given it to her for her tenth birthday.

Opening the Bible at random, she read, "I will never leave thee, nor forsake thee." Sharon felt peace begin as a small point of warmth deep inside her breast then begin to spread outward. She had intended to read for a while, but felt somehow that she had read all she needed to read.

Unable to stop the smile that spread across her face, Sharon walked over to her bed, knelt down, and prayed. Then she turned out her lamp, slid between the fresh-smelling sheets, and lay her head on the pillow. In a matter of seconds she had fallen into a deep sleep.

★ ★ ★

"You didn't have to come home just to see me, Jess." Sharon lay in the high, narrow bed, her face almost as white as the hospital gown she wore.

Jessie's face showed the sleepless night she had spent after getting the news about Sharon's illness. "Yes, I *did* have to come see you, baby sister." She took off her heavy wool coat and lay it across one of the chrome arms of the chair next to her. "Either that or go without sleep until I did."

Sharon gave her a weak smile. "Well, you certainly don't have to spend the night up here. Dr. McConnell said I'd be just fine by myself."

"What does *he* know?" Jessie walked over and sat down on the bed next to her sister. "Besides, its been a long time since we had any time together—just the two of us."

"I have to admit it's more fun having you here with me tonight," Sharon admitted. "Mama would have stayed anyway, and she needed to go home and get some rest."

Straightening her red sweater, Jessie gave Sharon

a knowing smile. "I hear you've got yourself a boy-friend."

"Oh, we're just friends."

"That's not how the story I heard goes," Jessie grinned. "Word has it you're courting pretty heavy."

Sharon laughed, pulling the blanket up over her head. "It's not true! I'm too young to court heavy."

Jessie wrestled the blanket from Sharon's hands and pulled it down. "Come on—tell me all about him."

Relenting under her sister's persistence, Sharon fluffed up her pillow, smoothed the sheet about her, and leaned back, resting her hands across her lap.

Jessie noticed with concern that Sharon was breathing much too heavily for such brief exertion.

"Well, he's not very tall, about five-eight, and he's got brown hair in a crew-cut—"

"And he's a football player. Right?"

Sharon nodded.

"Just like Daddy. Girls like boys who remind them of their daddies."

"You've got to stop taking those psych courses of yours seriously, Jess. You might actually start believing that stuff." Sharon shook her head in disapproval. "Anyway, he's not nearly as good as Daddy was, Jess, but he works harder than anybody else on the team. At least, that's what Dalton told me."

"Is he good-looking?"

A slight tinge of color rose in Sharon's cheeks. "I think he's cute as can be."

"Hmm. That's not much of an answer." Jessie tugged at her straight skirt. "I wish I'd thought to stop by the house and get something more comfortable for tonight."

"I've got some of Dalton's old football stuff in the closet," Sharon offered. "He's got so much of it around the house and it's real comfortable. So I brought a couple of his jerseys to the hospital."

"Great." Jessie slid off the bed and walked over to the closet. "Anything beats what I'm wearing." Taking off her clothes, she put on a pair of baggy maroon sweatpants and an oversized white football jersey. Then she dug around on the top shelf, fished out a pair of heavy cotton socks, and slipped them on her feet.

"You look like a hobo."

Jessie climbed back onto the bed, easing Sharon's legs over to one side and sitting cross-legged. "Who cares what I look like? I'm comfortable."

Sharon's face assumed a childlike quality. "I feel like I'm four years old again and you've come into my room to tell me a story before I go to sleep."

"Well, we're going to turn it around tonight," Jessie insisted. "You're going to tell *me* one."

"What kind of story?"

"One about your boyfriend." Jessie held her left hand out, using her fingers to enumerate. "We've established that he's not very tall, he's got brown hair, and he's a football player. Oh, yeah, and he's not good-looking—he's cute as can be."

Sharon giggled in spite of herself.

"Has he got money?"

"Nope."

"Is he smart?"

Shaking her head, Sharon glanced down at her hands, slim and pale and delicate. "Not very."

"Good—you can fool him most all the time, then."

"Oh, Jessie—"

Jessie clasped her hands around her knees. "No money, smarts, or looks."

"Well, that's not exactly—"

"He must be a good kisser, then." Jessie shut her

eyes, puckered her lips, and embraced herself with both arms.

"Jessie, you're awful!"

"Well, there's got to be *something* special about this boy." Jessie sat up straight, her hands held out in front of her, palms turned upward. "We Temple girls don't settle for just any ol' beau that happens along."

Sharon's face turned serious. "He *is* special, Jess. To me, anyway."

"He must be," Jessie smiled. "I've never seen you this way before."

Sharon leaned on her right elbow, placing her chin in her hand. "And now it's time for you to tell me all about this Billy Pilgrim character."

Caught off guard, Jessie reached for one of Sharon's pillows, giving herself time to think.

"C'mon," Sharon insisted, noticing a tender light filling Jessie's eyes. "It's *your* turn now."

Jessie thought of Billy as an enigma wrapped in a riddle. Her feelings for him were almost as puzzling as the man himself. "He's a *great* preacher."

"I'm afraid that's not good enough, Jess," Sharon continued. "I saw your face when I mentioned his name. You're hiding something. Do you love him?"

"No." Jessie's eyes stared at the night table with its stainless-steel water pitcher, glass, and box of tissues. "No, I'm really not hiding anything."

Sharon could see that Jessie was truly undecided about this new man in her life.

"He's like nobody I've ever met before. One minute he's a prophet of God thundering away in the pulpit, and the next he's a little boy getting caught with his hand in the cookie jar." Jessie shrugged. "I don't know how to describe him."

"I think you just did."

"Hmm—maybe you're right," Jessie agreed. "That's probably about as close as anyone could get."

"What about Austin?"

"Oh, nothing's changed there."

"That's not what *I* heard when he came home for Thanksgiving."

"He said things were different between us?" Jessie's eyes held a mild look of panic.

"Not in so many words." Sharon felt she had suddenly become the big sister. "Jess, he's not going to wait around forever. I'm sure a lot of girls have their eyes on him."

Jessie's words burst forth. "Austin's not interested in anybody but me."

Sharon knew she had hit a tender spot, but felt it was worth causing Jessie some pain if it helped keep her from losing the man Sharon believed Jessie was meant to marry. "I think that's probably true, Jess . . . for now."

"What do mean, 'for Now'?" Jessie capitalized the word with her voice.

Briefly holding her sister's eyes with her own, Sharon glanced at the darkened window before she spoke. "I mean that no man, including Austin, is going to wait forever regardless of how much he might love a woman." She felt somehow awkward and uneasy referring to Jessie as a woman although she had already turned twenty-two.

"But we're both still young," Jessie said, defending her position with the usual phrase.

Sharon merely nodded, believing that she was fighting a losing battle with her "young" older sister.

Jessie remained silent for a few moments, then spoke in a subdued tone. "You *really* believe Austin might . . . get interested in someone else?"

"It's really none of my business, Jess." Sharon felt she should have known better than to pursue the subject after her past failures in the same arena and was ashamed now that she had caused the beginnings of doubt that she saw forming in Jessie's eyes.

Silence fell between the two sisters like a heavy, invisible barrier.

Sharon determined quickly that it would not remain. "Don't look so glum, Jess. How could Austin even consider anybody else when he's got the prettiest girl in south Louisiana?"

Jessie gave Sharon a weak smile. "You forgot to mention my marvelous voice."

"That, too," Sharon laughed. She had learned over the years how to restore Jessie's spirits. "Actually, I'm not really worried whether you marry Austin or not."

"For true?"

"Certainly," Sharon replied, tossing her head, her shiny brown hair catching the light. "As long as I get to be the maid of honor in *somebody's* wedding."

TWELVE

THE PHOTOGRAPH

★ ★ ★

"I'm sorry we couldn't go downtown to the Paramount or the Hart tonight." Aaron turned off Plank Road into the parking lot of the Rexall Drugstore across from the Regina Theater. He wanted this to be a very special night—he had worn his short navy gabardine jacket with the two breast pockets as well as his pleated dress slacks, the best clothes he had other than his one good suit that he wore to church, weddings, and funerals.

Although she had been wearing Aaron's heavy wool-and-leather letter jacket since the beginning of the school year, Sharon still considered it special, not only because it belonged to him but also because it kept her warm. "Don't be silly. I've been wanting to see *Picnic* since I first saw it advertised in the newspaper. I just love Kim Novak. She's so pretty."

"Not as pretty as you." Swinging the Chevrolet around in the lot, Aaron stopped, put it into reverse, and backed into a parking spot in front of the little pet store adjacent to Sitman's Drugstore. Shutting off the engine, he laid his arm across the back of the seat and turned toward Sharon. "I mean that, too."

Sharon, an expression of mock concern on her face, took off her gold-rimmed glasses and handed them to Aaron. "Here. You need these worse than I do."

Aaron laughed and gave the glasses back. "Well, I *still* say you've got the prettiest blue eyes in south Louisiana. *Anybody* can see that."

"This time I'll just say thank you for the compliment." Sharon stared across the street at the bright lights of the marquee and the line of people stretched along the sidewalk waiting for the box office to open.

Aaron cleared his throat. "Looks like a lot of other people want to see this movie too."

Sharon sensed in his recent awkward mannerisms whenever they were together what was really on his mind. She also felt that this was as good a time as any to talk about it. "It's all right to ask me about my being sick, Aaron."

"How did you know?"

"I just did. That's all."

Aaron's face colored slightly. "I don't want to make you feel . . . worse or anything."

"I know you've been avoiding this ever since you found out." Sharon spoke almost as though Aaron was the one who was sick, the one who needed comforting. "C'mon. You'll feel better if we get it out in the open."

Aaron's lips grew thin. The muscles along his jawline worked beneath the skin. He turned to face Sharon slowly, his eyes squinting as though he expected someone to deliver him a hard blow. "You're not going to die, are you?"

"Someday," Sharon nodded casually. "But not for a long, long time."

"Whew!" Aaron's body sagged. He lay back heavily against the seat rest.

"See? That wasn't so bad, was it?" Sharon laughed. "All you had to do was ask."

Aaron sat up and gazed directly at Sharon. He shook his head slowly, his eyes narrowed in concentration. "But you don't even *look* sick."

"I know."

"In fact, you look better *now* than you did back in September." He touched her face lightly. "Your cheeks are rosy. You used to look so pale all the time."

Sharon placed her fingertips on the back of Aaron's hand, pressing its hard warmth against her face. "That's because I had a blood transfusion."

Aaron winced slightly. "Did it hurt?"

"Not much."

"Boy! You sure are brave." Aaron sat back against the seat, crossing his arms over his chest. "I've been thinking a lot about this. It doesn't make sense."

"Sickness never does."

"But you're too *young* to be sick. That's for old people up in their thirties and forties."

Sharon laughed softly. "A lot of things in this world don't make sense . . . to us."

"I don't want to talk about this anymore." Aaron sat up abruptly and reached toward his left trouser pocket. "I want to show you something."

"Is it a surprise?" Sharon's eyes grew bright with excitement. Presents, especially when they were unexpected, had always been one of her weaknesses.

"Well, I guess first of all," Aaron paused, sat back, and ran his hand across his bristly flattop haircut, "that maybe I oughta ask you something."

Seeing the look of nervous hesitation on his face, Sharon remained silent.

"Would you—" Aaron glanced at the line of people across the street moving slowly toward the ticket booth. "Do you . . . you wanna be my—"

"Why don't we go steady?" Sharon asked in a calm and deliberate tone.

"You really want to?"

Sharon merely nodded. She was beginning to realize how very difficult it was for Aaron to simply speak what was on his mind. *I wonder if all boys are like that?*

Aaron fumbled in his pocket, coming out with a tiny white box made of slick cardboard. He opened it, took out a small triangular-shaped pin oxidized to a silver-gray color, and handed it to Sharon. "I didn't have a ring or anything."

"What *is* this?"

"It's my Wolf pin from when I was in the Cub Scouts." Aaron reached for it. "Aw, it's just a stupid kid's pin. You don't have to take it."

Sharon pulled back from his reaching hand. "Don't you dare! I think it's sweet."

"Sweet?"

"It means a lot to you, doesn't it?" Sharon turned the pin over in her fingers, watching the dull play of the light on its irregular surfaces. She imagined it to be an ancient artifact used by a boy very much like Aaron centuries before in his own particular rite of passage.

"Yeah, I guess, but—"

"You had to learn some scouting things or make a fire or something to get this, didn't you?"

Aaron raised his right hand in front of him, his forefinger and middle finger extended. " 'I promise to do my duty to God and my country, to be square and obey the law of the pack.' "

"What's that?" Sharon asked bewildered, still clutching the tiny pin.

"The Cub Scout Oath. It's one of the things I had to learn to get the Wolf pin."

Perpetually intrigued by the world of boys, Sharon asked, "What else did you have to memorize?"

Aaron shrugged. "A lot of stuff, I think, but that's all I remember."

Sharon smiled. She thought that in many ways young men like Aaron and her brothers and even older men like her daddy still kept their boyhoods just beneath the thin surface of the men they grew up to be. "You want to pin this on me?"

"I didn't mean you had to really wear it. I just didn't have nothing else."

"I'd rather have this little Wolf pin than a diamond ring any ol' day."

Smiling like a five-year-old on Christmas morning, Aaron eased over on the seat and pinned the tiny gray Wolf to the front of the letter jacket.

★ ★ ★

The threat of rain hung over the city like the Cold War's "A-bomb," but it dampened no one's Christmas spirit. The crowds on Third Street, the heart of Baton Rouge's business and shopping district, seemed heavier than usual in their press to find the perfect gift. It seemed as though every boy in America wanted a coonskin hat or any of the other toys spawned by the Davy Crockett craze, and all the girls just couldn't wait to get their hands on the latest Barbie doll.

"I have absolutely no idea what to get him." Pulling the heavy letter jacket closely about her, Sharon walked along the crowded sidewalk between Catherine and Jessie. "You should know what men like, Mama. You've had twenty-five years of buying presents for Daddy."

Catherine adjusted the red scarf tied about her hair. "Well, darling, it depends on the man."

"I know *exactly* what he needs." Wearing a camel-hair coat over her tweed jumper, Jessie reflected the latest coeds' clothing fads.

Sharon's face brightened at the news. "You do? Well, let *me* in on it, then."

"A pair of shoes."

"Shoes?" Sharon gave Jessie a puzzled look. "He's already got shoes."

"You call those clodhoppers he wears *shoes*?" Jessie shook her head slowly back and forth. "They look like something he bought in a Siberian labor camp."

"Don't you talk about Aaron that way!"

"'Scuse me, please." A burly man in a plaid wool jacket, his arms loaded with presents, shoved his way between Jessie and Sharon.

"And a Merry Christmas to you, too," Jessie called out, stumbling against the side of the building. She regained her balance and took her place next to Sharon. "I don't mean to make fun, but sometimes when it comes to the men in our lives, we women have to take charge in the fashion department."

"Oh." Sharon deferred to her older sister's experience in the shopping-for-a-man department.

"Get him a pair of loafers or something," Jessie suggested, returning the smile of a man in his twenties who stared at her as he walked past. "Those new moccasin-style slip-ons look nice. I bet they're comfortable too."

Sharon turned to Catherine. "What do you think,

Mama? Would he like something like that?"

Catherine noticed the rose flush of Sharon's cheeks. She knew it was only partly caused by the cold air. "It's kind of an expensive gift, sweetheart."

"Oh, don't worry about that," Sharon assured her. "I've got money left over from my newspaper job."

"Well, let's buy something, then." Jessie held her hands in front of her, palms up. "All we've done so far is walk around and look in the windows."

Sharon gave her older sister a mischievous glance. "I know what Austin's got for you, Jess."

Jessie's eyes lighted with excitement. "You do? Well, don't keep it to yourself. Tell me!"

With a quick smile at Catherine, Sharon turned toward her sister. "A whole case of postcards."

Jessie's face fell.

"He said it's the only way he could think of to keep up with you," Sharon grinned, leaning toward her mother for protection, "unless he got in touch with J. Edgar Hoover and had him put some G-men on your trail."

"You think that's funny, huh?" With a quick motion, Jessie took Sharon's earlobe between her thumb and forefinger. "Well, this is even funnier."

"Mama, help me!" Sharon squealed, taking Jessie by the wrist with both hands.

"That's enough, children," Catherine scolded, glancing at the passersby. "People are watching."

Laughing, Jessie released her grip and called out to no one in particular, "My sister, the intellectual, actually has a sense of humor! Fifteen years of being a little cloistered nun and now all of a sudden she's Lucille Ball."

"I can see the two of you need some more etiquette training before I take you out in public again." Catherine's face glowed with joy as she watched her daughters having so much fun with each other. She had hoped they would grow closer as soon as Sharon got old enough to hold her own with Jessie.

"Hey, I know what we can do now." Sharon's eyes sparkled with the thought.

"How about buying some presents," Jessie answered the unasked question. "After all, that's why we're out here braving this freezing weather."

"Come on," Sharon insisted. "This won't take very long, and it'll be fun!"

"Well, she doesn't get this excited very often," Jessie shrugged, turning toward Catherine. "I guess we'd better humor her this one time."

That was all the encouragement Sharon needed. Taking Catherine and Jessie by their arms, she hurried along the sidewalk toward the big Rosenfield's sign a block away. "C'mon! You're going to love this."

Entering the revolving glass doors, Catherine found herself carried along by the press of shoppers. The crowd thinned out near the cosmetics counter. "Is this your big surprise?" Catherine breathed in the heady fragrances of perfumes and powder and colognes.

Sharon grinned and shook her head, pointing toward the rear of the store.

Following the direction of her sister's finger, Jessie's eyes grew wide. "Oh no! Not me."

"Oh, c'mon, Jess!" Sharon sounded like a five-year-old. "It'll be fun."

Twenty minutes later, after standing in a line of two- to ten-year-olds and babes in their mothers' arms, Sharon and Jessie stood in front of a huge white chair trimmed in gold and occupied by a jolly, fat, red-cheeked Santa. His heavy velvet suit was a deep ruby red and his white beard, although obviously fake, was soft and silky looking.

Santa had turned away to hand a little apple-faced boy back to his mother. "Ho, ho, h—" He stopped with his mouth open when he saw the two young women waiting for him, their smiles as warm as the children's.

The store detective, coerced into duty as an elf-photographer for the day, stood behind his tripod, leaning on the bulky black camera. His green uniform stretched across his ample belly. The little silver bell on the tip of his felt cap, drooping to one side, jingled as he spoke to Santa. "I told them this is for kids, Melvin. You want that I should get rid—"

"Did we do something wrong?" Sharon interrupted, her eyes wide with feigned innocence.

Jessie chimed in with, "Is there an age limit? We don't want to break any rules."

"Why—why no," Santa hesitated, glancing at the long line of shoppers. "I just didn't expect you to be as—"

"Well, let's get this show on the road, then." Jessie stepped up on the platform covered with fake snow and plopped down on Santa's knee.

Following her sister's lead, Sharon walked across the artificial snowfall, settling on Santa's other knee. "Gee, your breath smells kinda funny, Santa."

Santa coughed. "Well," he grinned sheepishly, "ol' Santa's been a little under the weather."

"That makes your breath smell funny?" Jessie asked from the other side.

"Medicine, child," Santa snorted, popping a Life Saver into his mouth. "Medicine."

Standing next to the elf-photographer, Catherine watched her daughters enjoying themselves. They both put their arms around the disgruntled Santa, leaned their faces close to his, and smiled into the camera.

Catherine would remember that moment and the joy of it each time she took the photograph from her cedar chest. When she grew old and could no longer recognize most of her visitors, the glowing faces of her daughters and the glassy shine in Santa's eyes would never fail to make her smile.

★ ★ ★

Sharon sat on a tapestry rug on the gleaming hardwood floor of the living room, staring up at the shining angel. The big room was dark but for the glow of the tree. Everyone had gone to bed except Jessie, who had been persuaded to sing at a midnight church service across town. "You know where the angel came from?"

"Bethlehem?" Following Sharon's gaze, Aaron leaned back on his elbows.

"Good guess," Sharon replied with a straight face. "Mama's daddy bought it for her mother a long, long time ago. He was a logger."

Aaron sat up and picked a piece of lint off the new red sweater his parents had given him just before he had left for Sharon's to celebrate the rest of Christmas Eve with her family. "What's *that* got to do with anything?"

"Well," Sharon said with a smile, recalling the story that she had listened to every Christmas since she could remember, "or so my grandmother tells it, Pappaw stopped off from work at the Piggley Wiggley to buy a few things for Christmas dinner and saw the angel. They couldn't afford it but he bought it anyway 'cause Mammaw had always wanted one."

"And . . ." Aaron had begun wondering what the point was to this family legacy of a story.

"And"—Sharon laughed, looking down at the floor and shaking her head back and forth in glee—"Mammaw was so happy she hugged her husband—dirt, grease, and all—and just *ruined* her Christmas dress."

Aaron was now leaning forward, waiting for the big ending. When Sharon stopped and smiled at him, his expression of expectancy died away. "That's it?"

"What did you expect?" Sharon shot back, a little miffed that Aaron didn't find the old tale amusing. "A choir of angels singing the *Hallelujah Chorus*?"

"I don't know," Aaron shrugged. "I just thought it would be funnier."

"I guess your family's like watching 'The Jack Benny Show' everyday, huh?"

"No, but—"

"Well, how can you—" Sharon stopped in mid-sentence, the corners of her mouth turning up slightly. "You know, you're absolutely right."

"I am?"

Sharon lay back on the rug and giggled. "It really *isn't* funny. It isn't funny *at all*."

"Oh, now I wouldn't say—"

"Sure you would," Sharon giggled. "You just did. And you're right."

Aaron stared at Sharon, lying on the floor, staring up at the ceiling. "Maybe if you told it again . . ."

Sitting up abruptly, Sharon scooted over next to Aaron, tucking the skirt of her green velvet dress beneath her. "I'm finally free," she said directly into his face.

"Free of what?" Aaron sat up. As always, he found himself unable to follow the logic of the female mind. He could no more follow Sharon's train of thought

than he could pick up balls of quicksilver from a glass
platter.

"This old story." Sharon's eyes fastened on the
white-robed, golden-haloed angel. "All these years
whenever Mama would tell it, everyone in the family—except for Cassidy, of course—would just *laugh*
like crazy. I wonder now if *anybody* ever thought it
was funny."

Aaron merely stared in silence, a perplexed expression on his face.

"I think these old stories are wonderful," Sharon
continued. She stared at the lights on the tree, bub-
bling with colors of red and green and white, comforted with the thought that these *too* had been on the
family tree since she was a child. "They help bind families together from one generation to the next. But you
can enjoy them without everybody laughing like a
bunch of hyenas." She lifted her hands. "Now that I'm
freed from the bondage of forced laughter, I can just
bask in their glow."

"Yeah."

"Oh, I almost forgot." Sharon scooted over to the
tree and picked up a package wrapped in red paper
covered with jolly Santa faces. An envelope taped to
it bore Aaron's name. Handing it to him, she said, "I
wanted just the two of us to be here when I gave this
to you."

Aaron's face beamed as he hefted the box. "Hey, it's
pretty light for a box this size."

"Well, go ahead and open it, silly." Sharon winced
slightly as Aaron tore into the present. In a few seconds, the paper and ribbon of her painstakingly and
precisely wrapped gift lay in shreds on the floor.

"Boy, these are great!" Aaron unlaced his heavy
shoes and slipped the shiny brown loafers on. Stand-

ing up, he paced back and forth in front of the tree. "Man-oh-man, are these things ever comfortable!"

"They look nice on you."

Aaron sat back down next to Sharon and stretched out his legs, admiring his new shoes in the glow of the Christmas lights. "I *never* had any shoes as cool as these!"

Sharon glanced across the living room at Aaron's thin navy jacket hanging on their hall tree. Since she had been wearing his letter jacket, she had noticed that he never wore a coat to school, but wore sweatshirts under his flannel shirts instead. "Aaron, you really ought to take your letter jacket back."

Aaron's face dropped with disappointment. "You, mean you don't want . . . that we—"

"Oh no!" Sharon saw immediately that he had misunderstood her intentions. "Nothing like that. It's just that January and February are still ahead of us and they're the coldest months, so I thought—"

"Uh-uh." Aaron shook his head, his jaw set firmly. "I want *you* to wear it. Everybody knows you're my girl when they see that jacket."

"But I'm your girl whether I have your jacket or not," Sharon protested. "I'll be your girl from now until . . ." She stopped herself in midsentence, letting the words trail off. Suddenly a chill took her, causing her to tremble in the warmth of the living room.

"What's the matter?" Aaron leaned forward, taking her by the hand.

Sharon closed her eyes, her lips pressed tightly together as she shook her head slowly. "N-nothing." How could she tell him of the terror that sometimes haunted her when she would awaken in bed and stare out into the darkness? She could almost feel the disease inside her like some terrible red-eyed rodent, gnawing her life away. Even kneeling in prayer by the side of the bed, there were times when her words seemed to reach no further than the cloud of fear that seemed to fill the room. A single tear slipped down her cheek, dropping onto her wrist.

Taking both her hands in one of his own, Aaron placed his fingertips beneath her chin, lifting her head up. "Sharon, please! What is it?"

Sharon looked up into Aaron's eyes. They told her more than his words how very much he cared for her. "Sometimes . . . sometimes I get so scared." She thought of the times she had wanted to tell her mother or daddy, but had never wanted to worry them and somehow couldn't bring herself to become a worry to them now.

Aaron sensed that words were not what Sharon needed. He very carefully eased over next to her and embraced her as tenderly as he would an infant.

Feeling his arm around her, Sharon lay her head against his shoulder, taking his free hand between hers. She felt suddenly warm and safe. Staring at the babe lying in the manger beneath the tree and the bright angel, she wondered if He knew, even then, of the sorrow and the fear that was part of the world He had been born into.

PART FOUR

★ ★ ★

THE WHIRLWIND

THIRTEEN

THE CAMEO

★ ★ ★

"Mr. Pilgrim, I thought your sermon this morning was simply glorious."

Billy turned from the middle-aged couple he had been speaking with and gazed at the young woman who had just approached him. No more than twenty, she had carrot-colored hair that flamed in the midday sunlight and fell in soft folds on her shoulders. Her eyes, the color of blue ice, held a startled expression as though someone had just slammed an invisible door behind her. "Glorious?"

"I'm Wynette Reynolds." She held out a gloved hand toward him.

Glancing around, Billy saw the couple he had been talking with making their way down the high front steps of the church. "Billy Pilgrim," he muttered, taking her hand and noticing how her chin tilted up as she smiled.

"I know who *you* are." Wynette Reynolds still held

his hand. "I've been here every night and now it's Sunday."

Billy gazed out over the church parking lot, still amazed at how many late-model Cadillacs and Lincolns were rolling sedately out toward the wide boulevard. "So it is, Miss Reynolds. And a *glorious* one, at that."

Wynette smiled not quite demurely at Billy's obvious reference to her comment on his sermon. "I guess I *did* come on a little strong, didn't I?"

"We'll write it off to the . . . exuberance of youth."

"You're so kind." Wynette caressed the cameo at her throat with the tip of her finger. "Where did you go to seminary, Mr. Pilgrim?"

Billy noticed how the emerald green dress accentuated Wynette's rounded hips. He forced his attention to her question, deciding that the truth would end their brief relationship. "I went to Sidewalk Bible College—majored in curb-and-gutter and minored in drunks."

Wynette's eyebrows raised slightly, but she was not one to be put off lightly. "I believe that response needs some explanation, Mr. Pilgrim."

Laughing, Billy agreed. "You're right. I'm just a street preacher, Miss Reynolds. God did a retread job on me and put me in these big churches."

Wynette nodded, a half smile touching the corners of her crimson mouth.

"The closest I ever got to college was going to a couple of Ol' Miss football games when I was in high school."

"I think that's *fascinating*." Wynette poked Billy's shoulder affectionately to emphasize her opinion.

"You do?"

"Certainly."

Billy merely shrugged, amazed at the things he learned about people every day.

"You actually *preached* on the streets?" She said it as though he could become invisible at will.

Nodding, Billy searched his mind for a way to end the conversation diplomatically.

Wynette stared at Billy's forehead. "Is that where you got this?" With the back of her finger, she lightly touched the L-shaped scar above his left eyebrow. "From one of those—those street people?"

"Yep."

"And this too?" Wynette traced with the tip of her little finger the thin white scar curving upward from the left corner of Billy's mouth.

"That too." Billy decided that it was time to take leave of the much-too-obvious Miss Reynolds.

During the entire week of this revival and several previous ones, the number of unattached young women who had shown more than a passing interest in him had astounded Billy. They had commented on his preaching, his suits—expensive suits bought by members of the congregations who could easily afford them—and one had even complimented him on his limp because she thought it made him look like a war hero. But none of them had the not-quite-tawdry charms of Miss Wynette Reynolds.

Billy noticed that the pastor and his wife had just gotten into their car. Only a few hard-core talkers remained on the church grounds.

"I'd like to treat you to lunch," Wynette offered, "just to show our appreciation."

"Our?" Billy looked around, then back into the foyer. "Is someone waiting for you?"

"I mean the church, silly."

"Oh." Billy watched the pastor's car, its heavy

chrome winking in the sunlight, roll smoothly out into the street. "Well, I'm really pretty exhausted, Miss Reynolds. I even begged off your pastor's invitation today."

"Oh, fiddle-de-dee."

Billy laughed at Wynette's imitation of the consummate Southern Belle. "You might have stolen the part in that movie from Vivian Leigh if you'd had the chance."

"But I don't *want* a part in a movie," Wynette insisted. "I want you to have lunch with me."

Intrigued by the effect he seemed to be having on the women who came to his meetings, and especially the persistent Miss Reynolds, Billy also kept in the forefront of his mind—his calling. "I'm sorry."

"I'll simply *die* if you don't!"

"And I'll simply *die* if I don't get some rest, Miss Reynolds." The week-long meetings, the fourth week in a row, had left Billy frayed and worn.

"But this may be our only chance to get to know each other better."

Billy took a deep breath, letting it out slowly. "Let's don't think about that today."

"What are you talking about?"

"Let's think about that tomorrow," Billy grinned. "After all, tomorrow *is* another day."

"Oh, you!" But Wynette smiled when she said it. "There's just something about you, Billy Pilgrim."

"Must be all my formal education."

"I know a lot of college boys." Wynette touched the cameo again. "They don't do a thing for me."

"Miss Reynolds—"

"Please!" Wynette's voice carried a breath of irritation. "Would you call me Wynette, for goodness sakes!" She regained control, and the breathy overtones returned. "I'm starting to feel like a total stranger."

Billy thought that's exactly what she was, but relented anyway. "Okay, Wynette. I have to go now."

"Maybe we could just go somewhere and have a cup of coffee." Wynette couldn't remember the last time a man had turned down one of her invitations.

Billy shook his head. "I appreciate your kindness, but I really have to go."

Wynette, obviously realizing that she was, in fact, being turned down, merely nodded in defeat.

Taking her hand, Billy held it only briefly. "It's been a pleasure meeting you."

Wynette gazed directly into his eyes. "You too, Billy. Maybe some other time we can have lunch and get to know each other better."

Billy didn't reply as she turned and walked away down the steps. He watched her get into a red Corvette and start rummaging through her purse.

Taking his Bible from the top of a low stone railing, Billy made his way across the parking lot to his Ford coupe parked beneath an ancient cedar. Tossing his Bible on the front seat, he climbed inside the car and turned the key in the ignition. His heart sank as he heard the grinding sound of an engine being turned over by a battery on its last legs. He tried again. The engine ground down to a complete stop.

"What a wonderful way to end a meeting," he muttered. Then something caught his eye. Glancing into the rearview mirror, he saw the red Corvette, gleaming in the sunlight, roll to a smooth stop directly behind him.

★ ★ ★

Elms flanked the white frame house like two ancient sentinels, their limbs spreading stark and bare against the slate-colored afternoon sky. A weather vane creaked on the roof. Flower beds awaited spring planting, the freshly turned earth dark against the dry winter lawn.

Billy opened the gate in the white picket fence, walked between the hedges shuddering slightly in the wind, and climbed the steps onto the front porch. Moments after he rang the bell, a shadowy figure appeared behind the leaded glass of the door. As it opened, he heard a whispery voice.

"Yes. . . ?"

"Mrs. McLin, I'm Billy Pilgrim."

The tiny face merely stared out at him from the shadowy hallway.

"I'm a preacher." Billy pulled his gray topcoat closer about him, shivering in the February dampness. "I picked Jessie Temple up here a couple of times."

"Oh . . . yes." Velma opened the door a little wider. She wore a pink quilted housecoat and soft slippers. "Jessie's gone back to Baton Rouge. Her little sister got sick."

"Yes, ma'am, I know that. I just wanted to find out if you'd heard anything from her."

"Why don't you call her?"

Billy remembered the heavy black telephone resting on a mahogany desk in a pastor's study as well as standing in a Birmingham phone booth talking to Jessie with a light snow falling as he watched a scraggly-bearded Santa ringing a bell on the corner. "I did . . . a couple of times. But I've been on the road for the last three months and most of the time we seemed to miss each other."

The guarded expression faded from Velma's face.

"I remember you now. You're Billy Pilgrim, the preacher."

I thought I just told her that. Maybe not. I'm so tired I can't think straight. "Yes ma'am."

"C'mon in. You must be freezing."

"Thank you." Billy stepped inside, out of the wind.

Velma pointed to a hall tree. "You can hang your coat up if you want to."

"No, ma'am. I can only stay a minute."

"Well, come on back to the kitchen, then, and I'll fix something to warm you up."

Billy listened to Velma's slippers whispering against the gleaming hardwood floors as he followed her down the hallway. Glancing at the framed portraits on the walls, he wondered why so few people in the past century seemed inclined to smile when they had their pictures taken.

"Have a seat." Velma took a quart bottle of milk from the refrigerator and poured some into a pot on the stove.

Billy felt almost at home in the bright kitchen with its black-and-white tiled floor and yellow curtains. After pulling out a chair, he sat down and rested his arms on the table. "You've got a real nice place here, Mrs. McLin."

Velma took a can of Hershey's chocolate down from the cabinet and pried the top off. "Thank you. My husband built it for us back in 1903."

As Billy watched Velma preparing the hot chocolate, he found himself nodding off.

Standing on a lofty pulpit in a dark and ancient cathedral, he gazed down on a sea of uplifted faces. As far as he could see, people waited in their high wooden pews, waited for his words. He opened his mouth to begin the sermon, but found his mind as blank as the high windows looking out into darkness. Reaching for his Bible, he saw that it had somehow vanished. Panic gripped him as he searched frantically—

"Mr. Pilgrim . . ."

"Huh . . ." Billy rubbed is eyes, still bound by the dream and its dark portents. "Oh, I'm sorry. I must have dozed off."

A look of concern on her face, Velma set the steaming chocolate on the table in front of him. "You look like you haven't slept in a week."

Billy picked up the cup and sipped the sweet, rich chocolate. "Umm. That's just what I needed. That wind out there just cuts right through you."

Velma observed him closely, making a clicking sound with her tongue. "You need a long rest, son."

"I'm afraid I won't be able to get one for a few more months," Billy smiled weakly. "I let myself get booked into too many meetings."

A light seemed to click on in Velma's eyes. "I read about you in the newspaper! You've been preaching all over the place, haven't you? And I hear you sometimes on the radio when I can think to turn it on. But how do you get back here to Memphis to preach on the radio when you're going to all those other cities?"

"The programs are syndicated, Mrs. McLin," Billy explained, speaking slowly. "I can tape them wherever I am and they send them out to stations all over the South."

"I declare!" Velma's eyebrows lifted in wonder. "You certainly must stay busy doing all that."

"Yes, ma'am." Billy ran his hand though his hair and rubbed the back of his neck.

"I heard five thousand people came to hear you in that big church over in Atlanta."

Billy nodded. "Something like that. The Lord's really been good to me."

Velma sat down across from Billy. "You used to preach on the streets, didn't you?"

Billy smiled across his cup. "I did do *that*." The look in his eyes reflected a thin memory of the peace he had felt in those simpler and less fretful days that now seemed like such a long time ago. "I *surely* did."

"Jessie told me about that time she met you down at Taylor's Café."

Wrapping his hands around the cup, Billy felt its soothing warmth against his palms. "Have *you* heard from her since she went back home?"

Velma's eyes held Billy's with an intense stare. "I talked to her mama."

"How's Sharon?"

"Looks like the poor little thing's going to be all right. At least, she's feeling a lot better now." Velma's voice carried a tone of indignation against anything that would harm a child. "Such a shame! She's so young."

"And Jessie?"

"She didn't want to leave town until she was sure her sister was going to be all right. I think she's planning on coming back up here pretty soon, though."

Feeling a glimmer of hope that Jessie would soon be accompanying him on the road again, Billy lifted the cup to his lips and took a swallow. The chocolate seemed to taste much better. "I sure hope she *does*."

"Well, we'll know Monday."

Billy listened to the wind moaning outside the house. A sudden gust rattled the panes in the windows that looked out onto the backyard. He felt almost afraid to ask the next question. "She said she was coming back, then?"

Velma shook her head. "Catherine told me that Jessie was going to call and let me know if she was coming back next week." She got up and walked over to the cabinet. Opening a drawer, she took out a wrinkled envelope and read aloud. "She's telephoning on Monday around ten in the morning—and she wants to try and find out where Billy—" Stopping, Velma grinned at Billy. "She wants to try and find out where *you* are so she can get in touch."

Billy felt a deep sense of relief. Somehow Jessie had become in a short time his beacon on the camp-meeting trail. It seemed that she had kept him from foundering on the shoals like a mariner with his eye on a familiar lighthouse. "Good." The simple response was all that seemed necessary.

"Where can I get in touch with you when I find out whether she's coming or not?"

Getting up from the table, Billy took his cup to the sink and rinsed it out before setting it on the counter. "I'll just come over here, if you don't mind. I'm preaching two or three nights here in town anyway."

"Suits me fine."

Billy expressed his appreciation to Velma at the front door, then turned to leave.

"That's a might fancy car you've got there." Holding onto the doorknob, Velma stared past Billy toward the street.

"Uh-huh."

"Never saw one like it before," Velma continued, apparently fascinated by the automobile. "What's it called?"

"A Corvette." Billy stopped at the steps and turned around, a strained expression on his face. "But it's not mine. A friend let me borrow it."

"Must be a pretty good friend to let you borrow a fancy car like that."

Billy didn't answer as he turned away and hurried down the steps. His face burned bright red in the cold February air.

★ ★ ★

Listening to the wiper blades swish back and forth on the windshield, Billy stared out at the high banks covered by thick, gray Kudzu vines, darkening in the rain. He thought back to his childhood and the summertime admonitions of his grandmother to stay away from them and the copperheads and cottonmouths that slithered beneath their jungle of thick green leaves.

Billy smiled as he took his foot off the accelerator and began coasting down He-man Hill. His mind filled with images of Saturday afternoons and swaggering teenage boys longing desperately to be twenty-one. Wearing rolled-up blue jeans, loafers, and white socks, they listened to loud music on car radios, drank from pilfered bottles of beer or cheap wine, and told lies about clandestine encounters with "older women."

As he crossed the bridge at the bottom of the hill, Billy glanced at the swimming hole—then he was once again spinning along the quiet streets of Tupelo. At the corner of North Broadway and Court Street across from the courthouse, he stared at the marquee of the Lyric Theater. Marlon Brando was starring in *On the Waterfront*. Farther on, turning onto Lake Street, he glanced at Lawhon Elementary School. He remembered that Elvis had first sung in public in the school auditorium there.

For some reason he could not explain, it seemed

to Billy as though he had never really left Tupelo. He could almost feel the heavy pull of his schoolbooks as he carried them toward home and the certain, smiling welcome of his grandmother.

An hour later, Billy sat in the little kitchen at the rear of the house. He stared at the funeral-parlor fan, complete with a picture of Jesus holding a tiny lamb in His arms. The fan had been hanging there next to the sink for thirty-five years, a memento of his grandfather's death in a muddy trench in the fierce fighting at Belleau Wood.

"Aren't you hungry, child?" Minnie turned from the sink of dishes she had just finished washing and wiped her hands on her apron.

Billy poked the flaky crust of the huckleberry pie with his fork. "Guess I'm too tired to eat."

Minnie walked over and sat down at the table. Smoothing the red-and-white checkered tablecloth with her damp hands, she spoke in a low voice. "You don't look well, son. What you need is a good rest and some sunshine."

Billy stared at the rain-streaked windows above the sink. "Not much chance of getting any sunshine around here. Looks like it's set in for the rest of the month."

"I still think you oughta stay a few days."

Taking a bite of pie, Billy savored the tart, wild taste of the berries. "Gotta pick Jessie up in Memphis tomorrow, Mammaw. I told you that already."

Minnie sighed. "I know the Lord's called you to preach, but it won't do Him or you any good if you get sick on us."

Noticing the look of concern on his grandmother's face, Billy felt strangely grateful for it. He considered her love for him one of his greatest treasures. "I won't."

The low whining rumble of a truck out on the highway sounded like an anthem for this cold and rainy late-winter day. Above them, the rain pattered on the tin roof with a steady and reassuring cadence.

Billy took another bite. The flavor reminded him of the huckleberries he would pick on the banks along the dusty roads of his boyhood and bringing them home to Minnie in a shiny syrup bucket for her to work her magic with sugar and flour and butter. He felt a sudden great comfort in merely being with her.

"You know I was never one to meddle in other folks' affairs, Billy."

"Yes, ma'am." Billy knew that Minnie's words had understated the fact.

"But I've got something that's been on my mind to tell you for quite a spell now."

Billy glanced up at Minnie's face beginning to cloud over with concern.

"It's time you started thinking about getting married. You need a wife to look out for you."

Placing his fork on the plate, Billy reached across the table and took Minnie's hands. "You don't have to worry about me, Mammaw. *You're* the only woman I need in my life right now." He squeezed her hands and sat back. "You and Jessie, that is. And she'll be back tomorrow."

A rumor of a smile crossed Minnie's lips, lightly seamed by the span of her years. "What *about* you and Jessie? Maybe she's the one."

"Oh, come on, Mammaw!" Billy's voice cracked slightly as he spoke. He cleared his throat.

"Well, why not? I saw how well the two of you got along when you brought her down here."

"We're just friends." Billy shook his head slowly back and forth. "Do you see how pretty she is?"

"And you're not a bad-looking boy yourself, Billy Pilgrim."

Billy thought of the women who had shown more than a passing interest in him over the past few months, believing that it had nothing to do with his looks. He glanced down at the half-eaten pie, wondering where his appetite had gone, then his mind returned to the conversation. "And she comes from a family with a whole lot different background than ours. Her daddy's a lawyer, and I guess that means that their family has money. She wouldn't be interested in me."

"You're too young—I reckon, most men never learn though, no matter how long they live—to know what a woman really wants in a man. A woman that's got good sense anyway, and I believe Jessie Temple does." Minnie gave him a thoughtful stare. "Handsome is a part of it, I guess—in the beginning anyways. But it's certainly not the main part."

Billy listened to the rain, wondering why Minnie had suddenly decided to get him married off. "Well, what *does* a woman want in a man, then?"

Minnie's eyes looked toward the past. "Tenderness . . . kindness." She touched the back of her hair. "Somebody to make her feel special. Somebody to make her laugh when she gets down, somebody she knows will stick by her even when things start going bad."

"Anything else?"

"Yep," Minnie replied quickly. "A man that'll work and support his family . . . whether he makes a lot of money or not. You show me a man that won't work, well, he just ain't a man, and that's the long and the short of it."

Listening to his grandmother, Billy wondered if she indeed spoke for most women—or only for those of her own generation, her own values. He had always considered it a mystery why women seemed so smitten by a particular kind of man. It mystified him even more why lately some of the women at his meetings seemed to be so attracted to him. This was a problem he had never confronted before. "Looks like you've got things all figured out."

"Well, it ain't never *that* simple," Minnie admitted. "Men and women and how they get together sometimes just don't make a lick of sense. Any nitwit oughta know that. But the ones that *stay* together— now, that's a different story."

"This just doesn't seem to be the right time to think about getting married. I'm on the road just about all the time."

"That's *exactly* why you need a wife." Minnie stared directly into his eyes. "And I don't mean just to keep your shoes shined and a clean handkerchief in your pocket either."

Suddenly feeling that his grandmother had shined a searchlight into his soul, Billy glanced away at the windows filled with a smoke-colored haze. The back of his neck felt warm. He shifted uneasily in his chair. When he looked back at her, her face held no hint of condemnation—only the veiled but unmistakable presence of disappointment mingled liberally with sorrow. "I understand."

Minnie went on as though nothing had happened. "I know you've never had much interest in money, son, but there are other things the ol' devil will use to try to trip up a man in your position. One preacher called it the 'glitter.' I reckon what it amounts to is getting the 'big head,' pride—whatever name you call it by, it leads down the road of destruction."

Billy remembered the sermon his grandmother referred to; "The Glitter, the Gold, and the Girls." Somehow she had managed to cover all three of them in just a few minutes. "So you think I need a wife."

"Maybe I'd just like to see another little Billy running around the house, climbing up on my lap, giving me a big hug." Minnie slumped a little in her chair. It appeared as though her conversation with Billy had siphoned off her energy. "A man has to make up his own mind about things like this."

"You forgot to mention one thing, Mammaw."

A thoughtful expression settled over Minnie's face. "Don't know what it could be."

"Love," Billy replied, folding his hands together on the table. "Not much hope for a man and woman without that."

The tinge of disappointment had left Minnie's eyes as she spoke. "I didn't mention making Christ the head of your home either. Some things are so obvious, it just ain't necessary to say them out loud."

FOURTEEN

DESIRE

★ ★ ★

"I thought we never *would* get out of there tonight." A faint, soft April chill hung in the air as Billy walked next to Jessie along the nearly deserted streets.

"The people just wanted to get close to you, Billy." Jessie slipped her hand inside the crook of his arm. "Have you say a word or two to them."

Billy's face glowed with excitement. "Tonight was the best meeting I can remember! There must have been four or five hundred people down at the altar."

Listening to the hollow sound of their footsteps, Jessie thought of the hundreds of people, their faces full of hope, streaming down the aisles of the auditorium where the nightly services were being held.

"You know, it *might* be a good idea to get a bodyguard." Billy gazed thoughtfully at a stray cat perched atop a garbage can at the edge of an alleyway. "Remember last week when that crazy man came busting out of the crowd, screaming about something that I

231

was supposed to have done two months ago? You never know what people are gonna get into their heads."

"But that's just one time," Jessie cautioned. "You don't need to get carried away about something like that. It's not like you're the President or anything."

Shaking his head, Billy continued in a somber tone. "It's happened before . . . three or four times. I just didn't want to worry you with it."

Jessie felt uneasy in a way she couldn't explain. *Why would anybody want to harm Billy?*

"Besides," Billy went on, "it might be a good idea to have somebody around just to help with crowd control." He squeezed Jessie's hand. "You might get hurt accidentally just because people sometimes get too . . . enthusiastic."

Jessie merely shrugged. She watched their shadows lengthen as they walked away from the streetlight behind them, then disappear into the amber shining of the one ahead. "Do you really think we should put so much emphasis on numbers? That's the main thing our flyers and newspaper ads seem to dwell on these days."

"You got something against *everybody* hearing the gospel?" Billy gave her an oblique glance.

"No, I guess not, but—"

"Well, quit worrying just because things are turning out so well for us," Billy countered. "I think I've had my share of rejoicing in persecution and tribulation . . . and I was doing it a *long* time before I met you, Jess. Maybe now it's time to bring the harvest in. Isn't that a reason to rejoice too?"

"Well, certainly, but—"

"C'mon, Jess. Give it a rest, will you?" Billy stopped and took her by the shoulders. "I'm just happy 'cause everything's going great for us now—okay?"

Jessie glanced across the street. Four young men in shabby clothes stood beneath a streetlamp, passing a bottle around. Suddenly one of them broke forth with a stream of obscenities, cursing no one in particular and the whole world in general. She glanced at Billy. *You boys are about to hear a sermon, whether you want one or not*, Jessie thought, actually excited at the idea of once again hearing Billy preach on the street.

Billy gave the lamplit foursome a quick frown, then his face closed over and he continued along the street.

Jessie found herself in a mild state of confusion and dismay. She had never known Billy Pilgrim to pass up so obvious an opportunity to share the gospel.

"Well, there it is, right where the desk clerk said it would be. Remind me to give him a little something extra when we get back to the hotel." Billy pointed to a purple-and-green neon sign in the middle of the next block that bragged 'Fatty's Café—Best Bar-B-Que in the South.' "

"Fatty's not very modest, is he?"

"Who knows?" Billy grinned, quickening his step. "Maybe it *is* the best barbecue in the South."

★ ★ ★

A glare of white neon and the heavy, acrid smell of hot grease welcomed Jessie and Billy into the cramped little diner. Through an open door leading into the kitchen, a slab of a man wielding a lethal-looking cleaver hacked away at a huge chunk of meat. His frayed apron looked as though he had cleaned out the grease trap with it before putting it on.

Wearing a not-quite-as-stained apron, a sallow man in his mid-twenties with dark, greasy hair parted down the middle slouched on a stool at the far end of the long counter. A cigarette dangled from his thin lips.

Billy ushered Jessie into a scarred wooden booth next to the window and slid in beside her. "You think that might be Fatty back in the kitchen?"

Jessie glanced through the open door. "I believe that's a distinct possibility."

The man at the end of the counter stubbed his cigarette butt out on the top of a mayonnaise jar on the counter, picked up a ticket pad lying next to it, and ambled toward his customers. Reaching the booth, he took a stub of a yellow pencil from behind his ear and held it close to the pad. "He'p ya'll?"

Billy glanced at the table, empty except for a stack of napkins and a tan plastic salt shaker. "You think we could have a look at your menu?"

The man shrugged his thin shoulders. "We wouldn't have much of anything left on it this time of night. We mostly use a chalk board in the daytime anyhow." He scratched the back of his neck with the pencil. "Lunch specials, you know."

"Well," Billy urged, "what *do* you have?"

The man's eyes rolled toward the ceiling, fastening on a spider web above the front door. "We got: sliced pork, diced pork, chopped pork, pork loin, pork chops, baked pork with garlic and onion sauce, pork—"

"Hold it!" Billy glanced at Jessie. "Barbecue beef sandwich okay with you?"

Jessie nodded.

"Two barbecue beef sandwiches."

"Hey, Fatty! We got any beef left?"

234

Fatty had traded his cleaver for a hacksaw. Not looking up from his work, he shook his shiny head.

"Sorry, we ain't got no beef."

Crossing his arms over his chest, Billy leaned against the back of the booth. "What do *you* recommend?"

With a furtive glance over his shoulder, the man leaned on the table with his bony hands and whispered, "I recommend you go someplace else to eat. You don't even *want* to know what's left over back there this time of night."

"Two coffees," Billy said quickly.

"That's a good choice." As the man scratched their order onto the pad and turned to leave, Billy stopped him.

"Wouldn't Fatty be mad if he knew you were telling people not to eat here?"

"Don't matter none to me," the man said softly, glancing over his shoulder at his beefy boss. "I done got me a better job anyhow. Startin' first thing Monday morning."

"Doing what?"

"First assistant to the man that picks up trash in the city park." He straightened his shoulders. "He give me my own broomstick with the nail in it yesterday."

"That's real nice," Billy smiled up at him. "Sounds like you're getting ahead in the world."

"Yep." He strolled over behind the counter, took two thick white mugs from a shelf, and began filling them from a huge silver-and-black urn.

Jessie thought Billy had been making light of the man until she noticed his expression. His eyes held a light she hadn't seen since her return to the road with him. "You really *meant* what you told him, didn't you?"

Billy's face was filled with a kind of quiet joy as he replied, "I surely did. He was so happy about his new job—how could I not be happy right along with him?" His eyes turned toward the past. "There was a time I would have been just as excited as he is to get a job like that."

This was the Billy Pilgrim Jessie had first met that day outside Taylor's Café. She had witnessed that special kind of love he had for the people that most of the world overlooked. It was a gift she hoped he would always hold on to.

The waiter who was starting his new job Monday returned with the two mugs of coffee. "Here you go. I *guarantee* you this is better than the food in this place."

"No kidding?"

"Yep. Reason I know is 'cause I make it myself."

Billy looked down at the dark coffee. *Probably tastes like road tar.* After spooning in some sugar, he lifted the heavy mug and took a sip. An expression of pleasant surprise spread across Billy's face. "Never tasted better!"

"Told you," the man beamed. "A woman from New Orleans come through here about six months ago and showed me just how to make it. I'll be right down there on my stool if you need anything else," he called back over his shoulder.

"You're right," Jessie agreed after tasting the coffee. "It *is* good. I guess there's always something worth having even in the worst of places"—she glanced around the shabby little café—"if you're willing to try and find it."

Billy sipped his coffee thoughtfully. "You know who I've been thinking about a lot lately?"

"No." Jessie gazed across the table at the words

carved into the rough wooden surface of the backrest: *Jesus Saves*. There seemed to be something contradictory in causing damage in order to proclaim the message.

"Elvis."

"Have you?" Jessie thought back to that day at Taylor's Café when she had seen him for the third time. "I wish I'd gotten to meet him."

Gazing out the window, Billy watched a bearded man in threadbare overalls shambling along the sidewalk. "Not much chance of that now."

"Why?"

Billy kept his eyes on the bearded man out on the sidewalk, as he leaned against a lamppost, fumbled inside the deep pockets of his overalls, and brought forth a single crumpled cigarette. Sticking it into the corner of his mouth, he continued on his way. "I saw in the newspaper where 'Heartbreak Hotel' hit the number-one spot on the charts last month."

"You think that makes a difference?"

"I think Elvis would just as soon hang around with the same people he always has . . . poor, hardworking carpenters, truck drivers, store clerks, his old school buddies . . . and he'll still stay in touch with some of them, for a while anyway. But I imagine he's caught up in something that he doesn't have much control over now." A shadow crossed Billy's face.

"I wonder if he ever thinks about the time he tried to sing with the Blackwood Brothers. I know he'll never get that love he has for gospel music out of his heart."

Jessie turned toward Billy. His eyes, reminding her as always of the color of the sea, held a weary stare above the prominent cheekbones. A lock of light brown hair hung down across his forehead. "Who knows?" Jessie remarked. "Maybe he'll just have one or two big records and that'll be the end of it."

"Could be," Billy agreed, finishing his coffee. "Anyway, we've got enough on our hands with this preaching and singing we're caught up in."

Billy's words made Jessie think that somehow he felt that *he* was losing control of his *own* life. " 'Caught up.' You make it sound like we're being carried away by a tornado."

" 'Caught up' also sounds a little bit like the Rapture, don't you think?"

"Well . . . yes, I guess."

"So, which is it going to be?" Billy stood up, reached inside his coat pocket and took out a wad of bills. "The Rapture or the whirlwind?"

Jessie knew that Billy had imparted a particular meaning of his own to their conversation, but it was too late at night and she was much too tired to become involved in theological discussions. "Where'd you get all the money?" There appeared to be several hundred dollars in his hand.

"People are always handing me money or stuffing it in my pockets."

"Maybe we ought to set up a better accounting system," Jessie suggested. She noticed the man who was leaving Fatty's for the park system slide off his stool and head toward them.

"What for?" He held his hand toward Jessie to help her out of the booth.

Jessie stood up and fluffed her hair out over the back of her light jacket. "Well, the collections are getting bigger and bigger, and we need to keep track of them better than we're doing. We probably ought to hire an accountant."

Billy shook his head. "We don't need one. No sense

paying somebody for that. What we don't need for expenses, I just give away anyhow."

"We 'preciate the business."

"Best coffee in the South," Billy grinned. He extracted a twenty-dollar bill from the crumpled pile, handing it to the waiter. "Maybe you ought 'ave put *that* on the sign outside."

The waiter stared at the money. "I don't think we got that much change in the register."

"That's for *you*." Billy handed him a one. "*This* is for the coffee."

Dumbstruck, the waiter gaped at the twenty.

"Buy your girlfriend a present, take her out for a nice dinner," Billy suggested. "But don't take her to Fatty's. Especially late at night."

"This is near 'bout as much money as I make in a week." He smoothed the wrinkles from the bill carefully. "I don't know what to say, Mister."

"Don't say anything, then." Billy took Jessie by the arm, then stared directly into the man's eyes. "And remember . . . Jesus loves you."

On the way back to the hotel, Jessie glanced across the street at the group of boys, louder and more obscene than they had been earlier.

Caught up in the whirlwind of the busy schedule that they faced over the next few months, Billy took no notice of the boys. "You know, this meeting in Atlanta is going to be bigger than anything we've ever done. But we've still got the ones in Birmingham, and Knoxville, and . . ."

★ ★ ★

"You're welcome." Wearing a pale green dress that Billy had insisted she buy for tonight's meeting, Jessie handed the sheet music she had just autographed back to the tall, thin brunette standing at the foot of the stage. Dazed by the press of people who had been trying to get her autograph, she took a battered hymnal thrust up at her, hurriedly signing it. "God bless you too." *Finally!* she thought, *only three more left!*

The meeting had been over for an hour and still people milled about the auditorium as though seeking to prolong the spell of the sermon Billy had just preached. The house lights shone down brightly on the crowd, thinning now as a uniformed security officer speaking at the microphone at center stage urged everyone to go on home and to drive carefully.

Jessie glanced at Billy, sitting on the edge of the stage, his legs dangling over the edge as he signed Bibles handed to him, kidded with some of the people, and prayed with others. A quick frown crossed her face as she noticed the burly bodyguard Billy had hired only that morning standing behind a curtain twenty feet away. He wore a dark gray suit and thick-soled black shoes and lacked, she thought, only a black hood and a heavy axe to complete his macabre outfit. Having missed his last name at their brief introduction, she knew him only as "Harold."

Suddenly a chunky, pie-faced man in his early twenties shouldered his way through the crowd toward Billy. As he reached the foot of the stage, his right hand darted inside the breast pocket of his jacket. Jessie had seen only a dark blur as Harold closed the distance. Before the young man could take his hand from his pocket, Harold bent over and grabbed him by one arm and the shoulder of his jacket, jerking him bodily onto the stage.

"Oww!" An expression of shock and pain filled the man's eyes as Harold pinned both of the man's arms behind him and dragged him toward the wings. "I just wanted an autograph! Oww!" He shrieked again. "Let me go! My bus is leaving."

At the noise of the brief scuffle, Billy turned from an elderly woman he had been praying with. Looking back at her, he smiled and patted the woman's hands reassuringly, then made a remark to those gathered around. A smattering of laughter trickled through the crowd, but a few people, muttering among themselves, turned and headed for the exits.

A middle-aged couple, the distinguished-looking man and his fashionably dressed wife passed by close to Jessie on their way out of the building. They were near enough to Jessie that she could hear drifts of their conversation as they moved along.

"Well, he *certainly* is a dynamic speaker," the woman said, taking her husband's arm. Noticing Jessie, she smiled, "You certainly have a lovely voice."

Jessie nodded her thanks.

The husband's eyes fastened on Harold, who had returned to his position on the stage. Then he spoke in a voice loud enough so that Jessie had no trouble hearing him. "I can't argue with that, or with what he preaches. But the whole thing's a little too close to show business for my taste."

Jessie signed the last pages of sheet music held up to her, walked off the stage, and took a seat down on the main floor to wait for Billy. The words she had just heard the man speak forced their way into her thoughts. *Show business!* She remembered her conversation with Austin the previous November on Velma's front porch. *Maybe he was right even back then. Maybe this is too much like show business.*

An hour later, Billy shook hands with his last admirer, then joined Jessie where she still sat on the front row of the auditorium. "Boy, am I ever dog tired." He slouched on the seat next to her, loosening his green tie decorated with tiny white crosses, and unbuttoning his collar.

Jessie's eyes followed the security guard as he ambled down the main aisle toward the lobby.

Billy slipped his shoes off and leaned back in the cushioned chair. "*You're* mighty quiet."

"Just tired, I guess."

"How do you think everything went tonight?"

Jessie thought back on the meeting; of the hush that had fallen over the crowd as they had waited for Billy's appearance. The man in charge of organizing the meeting had decided that Billy would come on stage only after she had finished her three songs. She felt almost like a warm-up act.

"Well—"

"I didn't like it very much."

Billy sat up quickly, turning toward her. "You didn't *like* it! Why not?"

Jessie shrugged. "I don't know really. Something about it just didn't feel right."

Billy leaned back again, placing both hands behind his head and speaking up at the lofty ceiling. "Well, I certainly don't understand that. We had a packed house and as far as I could tell—and I stared out at those faces for over an hour—nobody *else* felt that way."

"I guess it's me, then."

"You're just worn out." Billy's voice held a husky quality from the strain of almost constant preaching. "Maybe you should go home for a while. Get some rest."

Jessie saw the past few months as little more than a blur of hotel lobbies; practice sessions in stuffy basements or dimly lighted stages; row after row of people, their faces turned toward her as she sang; and the endless telephone poles along the endless white-lined highways.

"What do you think?" Billy continued, although his words sounded flat and strained.

"I don't know," Jessie almost sighed from weariness. "I haven't given it any thought."

"Just a suggestion. You don't have to go."

"Who would you get to fill in for me?"

Billy shrugged. "Somebody . . . maybe nobody." Groaning slightly, he sat up in his seat and stared at the platform. "I guess I mean that nobody else I can think of could touch the people the way you do. When you finish singing, *anybody* could get up there and do a good job of preaching."

Jessie knew it was Billy's way of asking her to stay with him. "I'm afraid of where we're heading."

"Afraid?" Billy turned toward her, his brow furrowed, his eyes clouding over. "What's there to be afraid of? How could things be any better?"

Turning her head away from him, Jessie spoke in a voice that was little more than a whisper. "Things just—I don't know, aren't like I expected they'd be."

Billy stared down at his shoes, gleaming dully in the dim lighting of the auditorium. "Sometimes I think the more I'm around you, the less I understand you."

Jessie turned to face him. "It's almost like . . . Hollywood." She had been thinking about the words for days, but only now was she able to speak them out loud. She wished that she hadn't even before they died out in the perfume and powder and after-shave scented air of this place where Billy had just mesmerized his audience with a sermon that she knew full well came directly from his heart. But the words

243

had been spoken now and there was no way she could take them back.

Billy turned slowly toward her, the expression on his face as hurt and vulnerable as a child's. "Is that *really* what you think of me? That I'm doing nothing but *acting*?"

"Oh no, Billy!" Jessie took his hand in both of hers, holding it tightly. "It's not you! It's just these people with all their money and their big cars, chauffeuring us around and taking us out to swanky restaurants all the time." She wanted desperately to convince him that *he* was not the reason she felt as she did. "They're not like the people you and I have always known—the kind of people we grew up with."

"They're just *people*, Jessie—just people." Billy's words sounded hollow and empty. "They've got more money, that's the only difference."

"And we've got these other people working for us now . . . an accountant—"

"That you said we should hire, remember?"

"I just meant somebody we could send the records to," Jessie explained. "Not somebody to travel around with us everywhere we go."

"Jessie, I don't think you realize how complicated things have gotten." Billy ran his hands though his hair in a gesture of weariness. "It takes somebody full time now to count all the offerings, make deposits, take care of all the spending, and keep the records. I just don't have time for it anymore."

"But you've got two front men, or whatever you call them, already working for you."

Billy stood up, stretching his arms above his head. He rubbed his eyes with both hands and explained, his voice growing slightly hoarse. "They've got a full-time job making the arrangements for the halls and ushers and musicians and the choirs and all the other things that go into one of these meetings."

Crossing her arms over her chest, Jessie would not be denied the complaint that had confused and angered her that night. "We don't need Harold."

"What?"

"All these other things you've talked about, I can go along with, but we don't need that brute of a man." Jessie gazed across the auditorium at Harold, waiting patiently next to the side exit like a faithful watchdog.

Billy glanced over his shoulder at the big man. "What's wrong with him?"

"We don't need him."

"Jessie, you see how big the crowds are getting. You never know what's going to happen."

Jessie remained adamant in her cause. "I *certainly* saw what happened tonight."

"Well, he made a mistake," Billy admitted, looking away from Jessie's sparking eyes.

"A mistake." Jessie rolled her eyes toward the ceiling. "His first day on the job and he grabs that poor boy and hauls him off like he was a dangerous criminal."

Billy shrugged, putting both hands in his trouser pockets and staring at his shoes.

Stepping closer to him, Jessie felt the anger go out of her. "Billy, you preached on the streets for years. If you can survive that, you can certainly handle a few people who might get a little too carried away in these meetings."

"You're right," Billy conceded. "I'll talk to him tonight." A half smile crossed his face as his eyes met Jessie's. "Well, maybe I'll wait until tomorrow morning. I'd like to at least give him a full day on the job."

"I think tonight would be better," Jessie insisted.

"You can't preach love and peace and then have some-body like him pull a stunt like he did tonight."

"Jessie . . ."

"Yes."

"I'll tell him tonight that I made a mistake. That I really don't need any security," Billy relented. "You win."

Jessie gave him a tired smile. "I did, didn't I?"

★   ★   ★

Rumbling across the night sky, thunder sounded like distant artillery. Lightning trembled inside the clouds as large raindrops began splattering on the streets and sidewalks, still warm from the hot August sun.

Taking Jessie's hand, Billy led her beneath a can-opied storefront. "I'm sure glad for this. Maybe it'll cool things off a little." He held his hands out into the downpour, then splashed the rainwater on his face. "Maybe we can stay awake long enough to walk three more blocks to the hotel."

"I kind of felt sorry for Harold when you told him you didn't need him anymore after tonight." Jessie thought of the hangdog expression that crawled across the big man's face when Billy broke the news to him.

"Well, I think two weeks' pay for one night's work helped soothe his feelings," Billy added, confused about Jessie's abrupt change of heart toward Harold. *But then*, he thought, *I pretty well stay confused when it comes to figuring out what goes on inside a woman's head.*

Jessie smelled the dank, cool odor of old brick as she leaned against the wall of the neighborhood gro-cery store. Raindrops danced on the street in front of her as the thunderstorm moved across Atlanta.

"I got some news . . . right before I preached to-night." Billy stared out at a small park across from them. "Never thought something like this would happen to *me*."

Jessie shivered as a cold spray blew underneath the store's awning. "Are you going to tell me what this wonderful revelation is?"

Billy took a deep breath, expelling it slowly. "We're going to Madison Square Garden."

"New York?"

"That's where it was the last time I looked," Billy grinned, watching the rain begin to slacken already as the quick summer storm passed them by.

Jessie felt a sudden chill at the back of her neck. She knew it wasn't caused by the damp breeze, but the reason for it seemed just as fleeting and insubstantial.

Billy noticed the light in Jessie's eyes darken. "You don't look very happy."

"I guess I'm a little stunned—that's all."

Disappointed by Jessie's reaction, Billy tried to instill some of his own excitement into her. "We can bring the gospel to twenty-five thousand people a night, Jessie, maybe more."

The glow on Billy's face suddenly lifted Jessie's spirits. She pushed aside the feeling that had come in with Billy's news. "I think it's wonderful! Those folks in New York City will never be the same after they've heard Billy Pilgrim preach."

Billy's face brightened even more. "I was afraid you'd find something wrong with our going there for a minute. Looks like I *finally* did something right."

Jessie felt ashamed that she had complained so much that evening. "You do a lot of things right, Billy." She stepped close to him and placed her arms around his waist. "Most everything, as a matter of fact."

"Well, I don't know if I'd go quite that far." Billy felt Jessie's softness and warmth against him like a dream of all the women he had ever longed for now become flesh in his arms. His fingertips brushed softly against her hair, pale and soft and shining in the glow of the streetlamps.

Desire, as sudden and unexpected as the summer storm, swept over Billy. Tilting Jessie's face upward, he kissed her gently on the lips. Then he stepped back abruptly as though pushed by an invisible hand. "I'm sorry. I shouldn't have done that."

"It's all right, Billy." She moved forward, reached out, and placed the palm of her hand against the side of his face. "Nothing wrong with a kiss between friends."

A thudding sound on the sidewalk behind Billy startled Jessie. She peered at a shapeless bulk in the shadows at the opposite end of the building.

Billy appeared not at all alarmed by what had happened. He held his hand, palm outward toward Jessie. "Wait here. I'll be right back."

Jessie eased along carefully behind Billy as he approached the man crumpled on the sidewalk. Lying on his left side, his legs drawn up against his chest, the man began retching horribly. The smell hit Jessie like a living thing, causing her own stomach to turn over. Ten feet away, she leaned against the storefront and watched.

"You having a rough time, partner?" Taking a clean white handkerchief from his back pocket, Billy knelt next to the man and as soon as he had quieted down, lifted his head and began wiping the vomit from his face.

Jessie saw that the man was white-headed with a

stubbly beard that would have been white had it been clean. His rheumy eyes rolled upward in a plea for help. The smell of the man's filthy clothes and unwashed body was almost more than Jessie could bear. Billy seemed not to notice at all.

Lifting the man into a sitting position, Billy finished cleaning his mouth and face. "Now that we've got you all prettied up, we're going to get you a hot meal and a place to spend the night. How's that sound?"

"I ain't got a penny to my name, mister." The man's voice rasped deep in his throat.

"My treat, partner," Billy smiled. "Next time it'll be on you. Okay?" He lifted the man to his feet, supporting him by slipping the almost limp arm over his shoulders and holding him around the waist. Motioning for Jessie to follow along after them, he began the slow walk toward the hotel.

Jessie felt hot tears slip down her cheeks as she listened to Billy, speaking in a voice as gentle as the soft summer breeze that followed the storm.

"When you get to feeling a little better, I want to tell you an old, old story. It's about a man named Jesus."

FIFTEEN

POPLAR GROVE

★ ★ ★

In 1903 Horace Wilkerson bought a sugarcane plantation located across the river from Baton Rouge, Louisiana. It encompassed thousands of acres of land; a huge, towering sugar mill that operated twenty-four hours a day during grinding season; the big house where the Wilkerson family lived; cabins for the field workers; a commissary; two brick dormitories for seasonal workers; and a sprawling mule barn with two hundred stalls.

September ushers in the first cool front to south Louisiana, dropping the temperature into the fifties. It is an altogether pleasant time, this first taste of dry autumn air, with the thin white light of summer gradually changing to a pale gold as the sun moves southward toward the winter solstice.

On such a September day, on Poplar Grove Plantation, Sharon sat next to her father in his '39 Ford coupe as he pulled away from one of the tin-roofed cypress cabins in the Quarters. Heading west along

Scale House Road, she stared at the long row of identical cabins, each with its own front gallery. Men and women of all ages sat in rockers and ladder-backed chairs talking or visiting back and forth with their neighbors. Children played in the yards, their laughter blended with the barking of dogs and the undertones of clucking chickens as they pecked about on the hard-packed ground.

"That's the Anchorage over there." Lane pointed south toward another row of cabins. "The workers and their families live here rent-free. Even after they're too old to work, they have a home for as long as they want it."

Fascinated by the old plantation village, still thriving in the shadow of the state capitol, Sharon felt as though she had suddenly been transported back to the pre–Civil War South. "I could write a book about this place!"

Lane glanced at this youngest daughter, wearing a straight skirt and white sweater with the sleeves pushed up on her forearms. A blue silk scarf that matched her skirt was tied about her throat. "I think that might be a best-seller—you know, a romantic story of the old South, Cajun-style." He gazed out at the endless fields of sugarcane, rippling like a vibrant green ocean in the afternoon breeze. "We'll call it *Gone with the Hurricane.*"

Sharon smiled at her father, recalling how much time he had spent with her since her illness. At every opportunity he would take her along on short business trips, such as this one across the river. "That's pretty corny, Daddy."

"Ah, well," Lane shrugged. "Good thing I'm a lawyer and not a comedian."

"I sure enjoy these little trips with you." Sharon

stared at the towering sugar mill ahead of them. A tin-roofed maze of pipes and timbers, girders and beams and walkways and the big grinding wheels, it looked about a hundred feet tall. "But anytime you'd rather take the boys hunting or go to Dalton's football practice or something like that, it's all right with me."

"Don't worry. I spend enough time with those boys," Lane countered. "Besides, you're a lot better at conversation than they are." He turned off the dirt road, parking the car next to the sugar mill.

"Well, I just don't want you thinking that—"

"Sharon," Lane interrupted, his eyes lighted with gentle humor as he turned toward her. "Do I look like I'm having a good time to you?"

Sharon nodded. For some reason that escaped her, a vivid memory of her father's homecoming from the South Pacific leaped into her mind. Although only five years old at the time, she could still see the tall, lean, darkly tanned marine that her mother couldn't seem to let out of her sight for a moment. At first she had been afraid, next briefly jealous. Then he had lifted her into his arms, kissing her tenderly on the cheek and holding her close. She could still feel that father's love that seemed to flow into her, leaving no room for fear.

Lane shoved the gearshift up into reverse and turned the ignition off. "There it is." He stared into the vast recesses of the huge mill. "Hard to believe all that pretty white sugar comes from a place like this."

"Show me how it operates." Sharon got out and walked around the car.

Lane joined her, pointing toward the sun's red glare behind a distant stand of live oaks. "Down there at the far end is where the cane's brought in out of the fields and unloaded from the trucks and cane buggies."

Sharon gazed down the long length of the mill where derricks stood, skeletal in the fading light. "Doesn't look like much is going on around here now."

Nodding in agreement, Lane explained, "Those people back there at the cabins know that better than anybody. They're enjoying the final few days before the grinding season starts." He gestured toward the mill. "Then this outfit will be roaring twenty-four hours a day and they'll be working those fields seven days a week to keep it fed with cane."

Sharon made a mental note to try to get her father to bring her over at least once during the harvest to see the mill in operation. She had heard about the tremendous burst of activity that lasted into late December in the rush to get the crop in before the first hard freeze.

Lane began climbing a set of stairs that led up into the mill itself, motioning for Sharon to follow him. "Way down there are the conveyors. The unloaders put the cane on them and it's chopped up by those big sets of knives."

Standing next to her father, Sharon looked out across the expanse of the great structure, its murky shadows softened by the red glow of sunset. She tried to imagine the roaring, clanking, hissing noise of the mill running at full throttle and the tide of workers clambering about to keep it in operation.

"Then the cane goes," Lane continued his brief treatise on sugar production, "through those crushers and the rollers—that's the big iron things with the ribs in them." He glanced at Sharon, her expression intense as she took it all in. "By now, all that's left is the cane juice, and the woody fibers of the cane stalk that's called *bagasse*."

"What happens with that?"

"It's made into a lot of things . . . paper, building materials. In fact, the ceilings in the House and Senate chambers are made of bagasse tiles."

Sharon leaned on the railing of the catwalk where they stood. "Well, we've got it down to juice. What's next?"

"You have to remember now that I'm not an expert on the Louisiana sugarcane business."

"The short version's good enough for me," Sharon remarked, her mind absorbing the layout of the mill. "You never know, maybe one day I really *will* write a story about somebody who works on a sugar plantation."

"Well," Lane continued, his lesson on sugar production drawing to a close, "the juice is heated to almost boiling, purified, goes to the evaporators, and comes out a thick syrup. Then when its boiled, you come up with a mixture of sugar crystals and molasses. This stuff is called *massecuite*."

Never one for things mechanical, Sharon was much more interested in the people and their part in the process of making sugarcane into the stuff of pies and cakes and ice cream. "I thought I was getting the *short* version."

"You have but to ask, O fair one." Lane gave his daughter a quick bow. "The massecuite is put into perforated drums. The molasses is spun away from the sugar crystals. The raw sugar is shipped to one of the refineries like Colonial down at Lutcher where the pure sugar is made."

"Whew!" Sharon puffed out her cheeks. "That's the short version, all right."

"Now," Lane said, concluding the lesson, "you ready to go home? Your mother's probably putting our supper on to cook right about now."

Sharon turned around, propping her elbows on the railing. Giving her father a thoughtful stare, she found herself thinking of their visit to the tidy little cabin in the Quarters. "Daddy, that colored man we went to see today . . ."

"What about him?"

"You said that you knew him from Mississippi?"

"We've known the family for years." Lane watched a thin man in overalls climb a ladder up into the maze of pipes on the opposite side of the mill. Taking a wrench and a hammer from a red tool box he had placed on the wooden floor of the platform, he began working on a coupling. "He brought his wife and children down here to work the cane harvest back before the war. They liked it and decided to stay."

"And you're doing all this legal work for him without getting paid?"

"Yep." With a last glance at the man on the platform, Lane headed toward the stairs at the end of the catwalk.

"Daddy . . ."

Lane turned around, his gaze fastened on the intent eyes of his daughter.

Knowing that it had been her father's habit to do free legal work for people ever since she could remember, Sharon now expected to hear some sage advice about how he allotted time for this. "With all the work you've got to do with your own clients and in the legislature, why come over here across the river for somebody you haven't even seen in years?"

"Because he needed help." Lane obviously saw the matter in a much simpler light.

Sharon had thought there would be more. She felt that her father's simple words were surely only a beginning to an explanation of the charitable life. She had expected to hear something akin to Paul's great chapter on love in First Corinthians, thirteen. *Because he needed help. Is that all there is to it? I'll have to think about that one for a while.*

★ ★ ★

Sharon watched Lane push open the screen door of the Commissary, a small grocery and dry goods store that served the residents of Poplar Grove. He carried a paper bag over to the car, handed it to her through the window, and got in behind the steering wheel.

Watching the dust clouds rising behind them as they headed down Scale House Road toward the levee, Sharon held the bag on her lap. "What've you got in here, anyway?"

"Nabs and Orange Crush."

Sharon reached into the bag and pulled out a dark brown bottle, beaded with cold drops of water. "My favorite drink in the whole world."

"Imagine that." Lane stared down the dusty road at the tops of the willow trees rising on the river side of the levee. "Sure made a lucky guess, didn't I?"

Every time he buys me an Orange Crush, we make the same silly remarks, Sharon thought. *It's almost a family legacy now, like the Christmas Angel story.* She took out two round packs of crackers wrapped in cellophane. "I thought you said you bought some Nabs . . . or something like that."

"That's what you're holding in your hand, young lady."

257

Sharon held them toward her father. "They're peanut butter crackers."

"Nabs. Capital N-a-b-s," Lane corrected her. "Short for Nabisco. That's what we always called them in Mississippi. I'm afraid your education is sadly lacking, sweetheart."

"You may be right," Sharon said with a straight face. "I'm sure that 'Define Nab,' is the first question on every college-entrance exam . . . at all the best schools, of course."

Lane stopped at the River Road intersection. The sounds of a choir singing "Throne of God" drifted from the open windows of the Poplar Grove Chapel on his left. "Sounds like they're getting ready for the Sunday morning service." He pulled across the blacktop and parked on the shoulder. "C'mon, let's go take a look at the river. It oughta be pretty this time of day."

Sharon climbed the gentle slope of the levee alongside her father. The grass, still tall and green in the mild September weather, felt soft and cool brushing against her legs. The bottles clinked together inside the paper bag.

Stopping on top of the levee, Sharon gazed across the mile or more of muddy water toward the city. The limestone walls of the Capitol building, rising against the deep blue sky, gleamed with shades of rose and peach in the sun's afterglow. Down below her, even the water's surface, shadowed by the levee and the willows along the bank, took on a silver gleam rather than the yellowish brown of full daylight.

"Looks nice from here, doesn't it?" Lane sat down on a piece of driftwood someone had dragged up from the water's edge. Its smooth surface, polished by weeks in the river and bleached by sunlight, had the appearance of old bone. "You'd never imagine the things that go on inside the Capitol, just looking at how pretty it is from this side of the river."

Taking an Orange Crush from the bag, Sharon sat down next to her father. "Are things going any better with the gambling problems?"

Lane opened the bottle with a blade of his pocket knife and handed it back to Sharon. "I think we've about got it under control now. A couple of years ago some of the legislators were carrying suitcases full of money around the Capitol, thinking they were so well-protected by the big money boys that nobody could touch them. A few of them got surprised." Opening the other bottle, he took a big swallow. "You're right, sugar. This *is* the best drink in the whole world."

Sharon opened a pack of the Nabs and took one out. "I'm not so sure about eating these things with a Crush."

"I can see you're a woman of taste." Lane held the round cracker between thumb and forefinger, his pinkie raised daintily. "And you're absolutely right. Nabs demand an R. C. Cola to be savored properly. Moon Pies go with Crush." He dropped the Nabs back into the bag and took another long swallow.

"Oh, the life of a child burdened with an uncultured father." Looking toward the cobalt blue sky, Sharon placed her hand against her throat.

Lane smiled at Sharon's theatrics. "Speaking of uncultured, does Jessie tell you much about this Pilgrim character?"

"Why do you think he's uncultured?"

"He's from Mississippi, isn't he?" Lane straightened his necktie with an exaggerated gesture. "Being a native myself, I know something about these things."

"Jessie says he's the most dedicated—I think

anointed was actually the word she used—preacher that she's ever seen."

Lane stared at the wind-rippled surface of the river. "He may be the greatest thing since Paul preached on Mars Hill, but he's *still* from Mississippi."

"You're just afraid Jessie might marry him and stay gone all the time."

"So, you've taken to reading minds, have you?" Lane turned the bottle up and finished it. "Well, I'm just glad that she's come home for a couple of weeks before they go to New York. Who'd have ever thought a good ol' boy from Tupelo would be preaching in Madison Square Garden?"

"Who'd have thought another good ol' boy from Tupelo would have four number-one records in the past five months?"

"You're right there," Lane nodded, swinging the brown bottle loosely in his fingertips. "I guess Mississippi turns out a winner now and again."

"Like Faulkner?"

"Him too." Lane's eyes softened as he gazed at his daughter. "By the way, how's ol' Aaron getting along these days? I haven't seen much of him since school started."

Sharon's cheeks colored slightly. "Oh, he's just as happy as can be. Since Billy and Dalton both graduated, he's first-string halfback. That boy eats, lives, and breathes football. Hardly knows I'm around anymore."

Lane shook his head slowly back and forth as he watched the last glow of sunset play against the bottle's smooth surface. "I know better than that. And I'm not too old to remember when *I* was sixteen. That's about the time I met your mother." He patted Sharon on the knee. "He's a good boy, isn't he?"

"Yes, Daddy"—Sharon smiled, knowing what was on her father's mind—"he's a *good* boy." She gave him a thoughtful glance. "Are you really worried about Jessie?"

Lane gazed at the evening star, bright now above the darkening walls of the Capitol. "A little—I guess." He held Sharon's eyes with his. "I think what bothers me most is that she might lose Austin. What they have together might not come again . . . for either of them."

Sharon sensed what was on her father's mind. "Like you and Mama."

★ ★ ★

Just as the ferry blew a final blast on its whistle, the Ford coasted across the parking area at the bottom of the levee, its tires crunching on the white shells. It bumped up the ramp and onto the iron deck. Coming to a stop directly behind a bright blue '55 Studebaker Hawk, Lane shut off the engine and shoved the gearshift up into reverse. "You want to get some air?"

Sharon nodded and got out on the passenger's side. Walking over to the rail, she stood next to her father, staring down at the ferry's bow rushing across the roiling, muddy surface of the Mississippi. She imagined the tons and tons of melted snow and the heavy spring rains that would send it rising almost to the top of the levee system. The city of New Orleans, a hundred miles downriver and five feet below sea level, had kept the river at bay for almost two hundred years.

"What's on your mind?" Lane glanced at Sharon lost in thought.

"Just thinking about all this water . . . where it came from and where it's going." She stared at the top of the newspaper building, rising above the levee: *State Times—Morning Advocate* in stark black letters was etched against the tan brick. Beyond it, the spire of St. Joseph's Cathedral glinted in the last rays of sunlight. "And the things it passes along the way."

"You've got a unique way of looking at the world, Sharon." As the captain cut power on the ferry's big diesels, Lane watched a huge freighter plowing southward directly in front of them. A man wearing a denim shirt and a black knit cap leaned on a rail above them, staring down at the ferry. "Not much doubt you'll be a writer someday."

Sharon returned the wave of the man standing at the freighter's railing. "I think that's what I'd *like* to be." The breeze off the river swirled her hair about her face. "But most everybody says it's just a phase I'm going through."

"Don't worry about what *everybody* says, sugar." Taking his necktie off, Lane folded it and slipped it into his left coat pocket. "Oh, it's all right to listen to advice—once in a while, that is—from somebody you know who's got good sense. But in the end it's your life and you have to make your own decisions."

Lane turned toward Sharon, leaning one elbow on the railing. "Your mother watched you walk to that mailbox week after week when all you got was rejections. I think it hurt her almost as much as it did you. But you didn't let it get the best of you. Even if the *Post* or some other magazine hadn't published your story, you won anyway because you didn't give up."

"I sure thought about it a lot, though."

"You got other stories in the mail now?"

"Yes, sir."

Lane merely nodded, a quick smile lighting his eyes as he turned to watch the stern of the freighter pass by them. The ferry's engines revved up and they continued at full power toward the opposite shore. Lights were coming on all over the city. To their left, the spotlight atop the Capitol flashed on, shining down on the statue of Huey Long that marked his grave.

"You think Dalton can make the first team next year, Daddy?" Sharon felt that few things in the world could match football for sheer boredom, but she also knew how much Dalton's scholarship meant to her father.

An expression of mild surprise came to Lane's face as he turned his head toward Sharon. "Wouldn't surprise me a bit. Billy's gonna make it for sure, but he's stronger and a step faster than Dalton."

"Dalton surely does work hard," Sharon added. "Lifting weights and running all summer."

Nodding with satisfaction, Lane looked as though he had just seen his son burst across the goal line for the winning touchdown. "Nobody on the team's got more . . . guts than your brother, Sharon. *Quit* just isn't in that boy's vocabulary."

"I don't know what kind of team they've got, but the coach sure is cute," Sharon grinned, having reached her limit of serious football talk.

"Dietzel *is* pretty, isn't he?" Lane half agreed. "We'll find out in a year or two whether he's a coach or not."

"Cassidy told me he's going out for track in the spring," Sharon said, changing the sports scene. She had agonized for months over the fact that she had not told her mother and father about the trouble Cass had been getting into, hoping that he would grow out of it—afraid that he would not. As usual, she tried to speak about him in a positive light. "He's always been quick as a bunny. Maybe he'll do okay."

"This is news to me," Lane shrugged. "With Cass . . . who knows. That boy's moods change faster than a traffic light." His brow furrowed in thought. "Track would probably be the right sport for him, though. He's never been a team player and running is something you have to do on your own."

Sharon was not surprised that Cassidy hadn't told Lane that he had decided to try to make the track team. He had been reluctant, even as a child, to open himself up to others—even his own family. She often wondered what went on behind those blue eyes of his.

"You know," Lane admitted, his face brightening with the realization, "now that I give it some thought, maybe ol' Cass is on to something, after all. He always did have speed to burn. I could tell that when he was just a kid playing around in the yard with his buddies."

Sharon felt a glow of happiness that her father seemed excited about Cassidy's decision. "Dalton barely beat him when they ran back during the summer. I saw them over at the Istrouma track one day."

"He did?" Lane raised his eyebrows slightly, although the reaction belied the excitement registered in his eyes. "Dalton's one of the fastest backs in the SEC—even as a freshman. In fact, Billy may be the only one who's faster."

"Cassidy's been running since school let out to get in shape, Daddy," Sharon said. "I think Dalton called him a sissy or something one time when they had an argument. Said he didn't have what it takes to be an athlete."

"Well, I'll be!" Lane shook his head back and forth slowly. "You just *never* know what it'll take to motivate somebody. I've been trying to get that boy interested in sports for *years*—never had a bit of luck."

"He's real fast, Daddy. *Real* fast."

Lane smiled at Sharon. "How'd Dalton take it when his little brother almost beat him?"

"He looked about as surprised as you do now," Sharon laughed. "But I could tell he was real proud of Cass. He's already started telling him how to work out so he'll do his best when the tryouts start after New Year's."

"This might be the best thing that ever happened to that boy. It'll give him something worthwhile to do with his time, teach him discipline . . ." Lane let his voice trail off. "Who knows? He might even get a scholarship if he works hard enough."

A shadow flickered across Lane's eyes. "I sure wish he'd told me about this. You and Dalton—and even Jessie when she's around—have always been pretty good to tell me what's on your mind. But Cassidy . . ."

Sharon watched her father's face, still glowing with happiness at the prospect of Cassidy's success in sports. At fifteen, she had already begun to realize that not every child had parents who were as concerned about their children as hers were. "I sure have enjoyed being with you today, Daddy."

Lane put his hand on her shoulder, kissing her quickly on the cheek. "Me too, sugar. We're going to do a lot more of this too; don't you worry about that."

Sharon smiled, then stared up at the stars winking on in the deep-blue sky. She and her father had talked for hours and not once had he mentioned her illness. It still weighed on her mind; made her uneasy that he wouldn't talk to her about it, but she felt better remembering the words of her mother. *Don't blame him, sweetheart. I've lived with your father almost twenty-five years, and this is the only thing I've ever seen that he can't come to grips with. Just give him a little more time.*

SIXTEEN

UNSPEAKABLE KNOWLEDGE

★ ★ ★

Baton Rouge was still part of Spanish West Florida in 1805 when Elias Beauregard envisioned what he hoped would become the premier residential section of town. North, South, and East Boulevards provided the man-made boundaries, along with the Mississippi River to the west. By September 1956 the area had largely been abandoned in favor of suburbia, except for those who still had a love for the quiet grace of the mid- to late-nineteenth-century houses that remained there.

"Well, there it is." Austin pulled the convertible over to the curb in front of the white, hundred-year-old cottage on Napoleon Street. Gray shutters flanking the tall front windows matched the gray slate roof. "What do you think?"

Jessie tossed a quick smile in his direction. Then she gazed at the brick walk that led between overgrown flower beds up to the gallery, extending across the front of the house and part of the way down one

267

side. At the south end, a weathered porch swing hung in front of a trellis spilling over with wisteria, its bright purple blossoms and lush vines now given way to autumn dryness. Between the swing and the front door, two ladder-back rockers sat together like old friends enjoying the morning sunlight. "I think it's . . . absolutely charming."

"I was hoping you'd say that." Getting out of the car, Austin walked around and opened Jessie's door, then loosened his tie and unbuttoned the collar of his white oxford button-down. He watched Jessie's pale hair catch the morning light as she slid across the seat; noticed her skin, smooth and warm and glowing with good health, as she stood up close to him.

Since Austin had picked her up on ten minutes' notice, Jessie still wore the clothes she had thrown on for breakfast: scuffed saddle oxfords, jeans—faded and rolled up above her white socks—and one of her father's old dress shirts, its long tails hanging halfway to her knees. Walking over the old bricks toward the house, Jessie asked, "Who does it belong to?"

"Me," Austin replied matter-of-factly, never breaking his stride.

Jessie stopped dead in her tracks, a dazed expression fixed on her face. "You?"

Austin turned, still speaking in a casual, off-handed manner. "Couldn't resist it. I always thought that when I got my own place, it would be here in Beauregard Town."

"But—I'm on the road so much now with Billy. . . ." Letting her words trail off, Jessie suddenly caught not only the meaning that lay at the center of Austin's words but also his intentions. They were mirrored in his clear gray eyes. "You mean to tell me that you've already bought this place?"

"Yep." Austin turned and continued on toward the house, dappled with light which spattered through the leafy overhang of an ancient sycamore.

Jessie caught up with Austin as he stepped up onto the gallery and sat down in one of the old rockers. "Don't you think you should have let me in on your little secret before you actually bought this house?"

"Why?" Rocking slowly back and forth, Austin appeared amused by Jessie's obvious confusion.

"Well—" Jessie suddenly realized the predicament she had gotten herself into. Austin had bought a house. *So what?* He was single and worked at a law office only two blocks away. Although they weren't even engaged, by her own words she had inserted herself into the equation of his creation; had made herself an equal partner with him in whatever the purchase of a home portended. "You know *very well* why!"

Austin responded with the creaking of the rocker on the gray-painted floor of the porch. After a few moments he glanced up at her, his face as innocent as a babe's. "I *do?*"

Agitated that she had let herself be trapped by yet another of Austin's games, Jessie stepped over to the front door and peered though the glass into the shadowy interior of the house. Hearing no response from Austin but the sound of the rocker grating on her nerves, she blurted out, "Well, are you going to let me see the rest of it?"

"Thought you'd never ask." He got up and pushed the door open.

"You don't even lock the door?"

Stepping inside, Austin shook his head. "This part of town is so safe, there's really no need to." He rubbed his chin thoughtfully. "Could be the proximity to the courthouse, the police station, and the jail. That might give a would-be burglar cause to stop and meditate on his job choice."

Jessie joined Austin in the living room, noticing the gleaming floors constructed of heart pine lumber. It somehow gave her a feeling of security knowing that not only was the wood impervious to termites and other insects but that, even if left out in the weather, it would never rot. She took in the ten-foot ceilings complete with crown moldings, the fireplace with its carved mantel, and the long windows letting in the morning light.

"C'mon, let's see the rest of it." Austin pointed out the adjoining dining room, the two bedrooms, bath, and finally the bright, sunny kitchen with gas range, Frigidaire refrigerator, and pale blue cabinets.

After Jessie had inspected everything, she wandered out onto the screened back porch. At one end, inside a utility room with a built-in table for folding clothes, sat a new washing machine and dryer. The other side of the porch had been designed as a kind of sitting room, decorated with hanging baskets and potted plants. White wicker furniture with flowered cushions formed a cozy conversation grouping.

"Well, someone certainly did a nice job out here," Jessie admitted reluctantly.

"Now if we could only find somebody to handle the *inside* of the house." Austin held the screen door open for Jessie. "Want to see the backyard?"

"Might as well," she shrugged, taking the back steps down to a weathered concrete walk that led around to the side of the house. "I've come *this* far." The first thing her eyes fastened on was a huge fig tree near the brick wall that surrounded the backyard. On the opposite side, sunlight shimmered like a waterfall on the downward sweep of willow leaves, stirring in the breeze off the river. Beneath a mimosa tree, a stone bench stood at the edge of a small brick patio.

Jessie walked over to the bench and sat down. The morning air, still carrying the dampness of the night, felt soft against her skin. She watched the play of light on the willow leaves; listened to the sound of a tugboat whistle out on the river; felt the hard, cool stone against her back. Staring at the overgrown flower beds along the wall and the back of the house, she pictured them blazing with spring colors; could almost smell the fragrance of the sweet olive tree standing near the screen porch.

"You like it?"

"Hmm."

Austin sat down next to her. "I think the right person—whoever that might be—could make this backyard a real showplace." He pointed to the back of the house. "You see where that big gable is up there over the back porch?"

Jessie nodded, squinting up at the slate roof, higher than the modern ones because of the ten-foot ceilings and also because the house itself rested on pillars instead of a concrete slab.

"I was thinking about building a second-story room up there to use as a study. I could run the stairs up right there on the back porch inside the wash room." He glanced at Jessie. "That way, it wouldn't disturb the overall integrity of the house. You think that would work?"

"I don't see why not," Jessie shrugged. "Then if you wanted to have some friends over to watch a football game, they wouldn't disturb . . . whoever happened to be downstairs, with all their whooping and hollering."

"That's kinda what I figured," Austin agreed. "And I thought I'd build a good-sized plate-glass window into the gable with a little sitting area. Anybody who took a notion could sit there and look at the ships or watch the sun going down behind the cane fields across the river."

Jessie stared up at the big gable, imagining herself curled up on a cushioned seat, drinking hot tea while winter rain streaked the window. Beyond the ivy-covered brick wall at the rear of the lot, she could almost see ships, drifting like ghosts in the heavy fog.

"See that sunny spot over there next to the wall? That'd be a fine spot to put in a vegetable garden."

Jessie looked at Austin in surprise. "A vegetable garden? What do *you* know about gardening?"

"Not a thing," Austin admitted, inspecting the palms of his hands. "It's just something I'd like to try." He stared reflectively at the fig tree. "I think I got the idea from eating all that home cooking of your mother's: fried okra, field peas in that good dark pot licker, tomatoes and onions, and the best corn bread in the world. Yes sir, fresh vegetables straight from Austin's garden to the kitchen table."

Austin kept his eyes on the fig tree. "And canned figs—on cold winter mornings with hot biscuits and plenty of butter. Nothing like 'em." He glanced at Jessie. "You know how to put up figs?"

Jessie's mind was occupied with picking out furnishings that would compliment the house. She had just decided on the drapes for the living room. "What? Oh, figs. Well, I helped Mama a dozen times when she did it. I guess I could get by in a pinch."

"Hmm." Austin lapsed into silence. A blue jay landed on the brick wall at the back of the yard and began celebrating the new day with its raucous song. The leaves of the banana plants beneath him clattered softly in the wind. Two minutes later and twenty feet away, a gray cat appeared like a puff of smoke atop the wall, ending the jay's brief performance. In a flash of sunlit blue wings, he took to the trees.

Jessie had almost selected the bedroom suite when the bird's flight distracted her. She remembered that she only had one more week before returning to Memphis and from there, back on the road with Billy. "Austin . . ."

"Yeah, Jess."

"Billy's going to New York next month—to preach at Madison Square Garden."

"I heard that somewhere."

Jessie cleared her throat. "He really believes that I should be there with him." She glanced at Austin, his eyes still on the fig tree. "He says my singing is just as important as his preaching."

"Okay."

"I hate to let him down."

"Yes sir, I think I'm going to enjoy living in this house. I can take walks along the river or down to the Capitol grounds and the lake. Third Street's only five or six blocks away for shopping and movies; the courthouse is even closer." Austin stood abruptly. "You want to drop me off at the office?"

"I guess so," Jessie replied, surprised by the suddenness of Austin's actions. "Sure."

"Then you can pick me up for lunch." Austin turned and headed for the house, calling back over his shoulder. "I'll take you home after we eat."

Jessie got up slowly, following along after Austin. It occurred to her that in recent months far too many of their conversations had ended with her staring at his back.

★ ★ ★

273

"He actually bought a house without even letting you see it first?" Sharon wore a red plaid dress and penny loafers. She placed her stack of books on the kitchen counter, folded her arms across her chest, and faced her sister. "I'm not sure that's the best way to start a marriage."

Catherine, wearing a long-sleeved dress the color of ripe dewberries, sat across the table from Jessie, a cup of steaming tea in front of her. Surprise registering in her eyes, she said, "You didn't tell me Austin asked you to marry him!"

Jessie set her cup down. After lunch she had put the old dress shirt and jeans back on, and felt somehow as washed out as her outfit. "Well, he didn't actually come right out and . . ." The words faded on her lips. "Oh, you know how Austin is, Mama! Sometimes he just talks in riddles. It's impossible to get any sense out him when he does that."

"Well, what exactly *did* he say?" Sharon peered over her glasses at Jessie, waiting to hear the answer to her question.

"We just looked at the house," Jessie said simply. "Then went out into the backyard and sat on a bench for a while."

Sharon took the third cup of tea that Catherine had prepared and sat down next to Jessie. "Sounds pretty serious to me," she grinned. "I mean, sitting together on a bench and everything. That's almost as good as getting a ring."

"Oh, hush!" Jessie pouted, pulling one foot up on the seat of her chair and propping her hands on her knee. "I don't know *how* I let myself get into such messes."

Catherine sipped her tea and smiled at Sharon. *In so many ways*, she thought, *she's more like the older daughter than Jessie is. Maybe it's because things have always come so easy for Jessie because of her looks and her talent. Sharon's always worked so hard for her successes in life.*

"Well, just what did the mysterious Mr. Young-blood tell you, Jess?"

Putting her foot back on the floor, Jessie shrugged. "He just talked about the house and how convenient it was to everything and about adding a study upstairs." She stared out the window at the fountain on the back patio. "It really *is* a nice place. Old and homey and comfortable."

Catherine placed her hand on top of Jessie's. "Well, it's obvious—to me, at least—that Austin bought this house for the express purpose of marrying you and making a home there." A slight frown crossed her brow as she continued. "Even if he *didn't* come right out and tell you that in so many words."

"Well . . . he probably would have," Jessie admitted, with a sheepish smile. "If I hadn't told him how important it was for me to go to New York with Billy."

"Well, that's certainly a *great* time to bring another man into the picture, Jess," Sharon sighed. She glanced over at Catherine. "I'm sure that's exactly what Austin wanted to hear while he's showing off your future home. Mama, are you certain somebody didn't switch her for your *real* baby in the hospital?"

Catherine laughed, then noticed that Sharon's humor was lost on Jessie. "Maybe we'd better lay off the one-liners for a little while, Sharon. I think your big sister's got some serious decisions to make . . . soon."

"I've already decided," Jessie replied quickly, leaning on her elbows and staring at her mother. "I'm not going to let Billy down. After all, Austin and I have plenty of time for things like marriage and houses."

Getting no response from Catherine, she asked, "Don't you think so, Mama?"

Knowing that all Jessie wanted to hear was agreement rather than her true opinion, Catherine saw no point in pursuing the discussion any further. "It's *your life*, sweetheart. You'll have to make the decisions."

"Well . . . *that's* a big help."

"Sharon, you solve all your big sister's problems while I answer the phone, will you?"

"Oh, sure," Sharon chirped merrily, "and while I'm at it, I might as well talk Khrushchev into playing a few rounds of golf with President Eisenhower."

Catherine got up and left the kitchen, walking down to the telephone table in the shadowy hall.

Jessie tried not to smile at Sharon's dry wit, but relented. Then she sipped her tea thoughtfully and watched the afternoon breeze stir the leaves on the live oak out in the backyard. Something in the sound of her mother's voice drew her attention. She had heard that same breathy tone before, that certain inflection freighted with an underlying loss of control, that portent of a dark and unspeakable knowledge.

A sudden, jarring chill hit Jessie in the pit of her stomach. She heard Catherine hang up the telephone and listened to the sound of her heels clicking on the hardwood floor of the hallway. Turning abruptly in her chair, she saw her mother's face, pale and drawn, as though the skin had been pulled tighter across her cheekbones. She fought an almost overwhelming urge to get up and rush out the back door into the sunlight, to flee from the shadows she saw in her mother's eyes.

Catherine walked over to the table, knelt down next to her daughter, and took her hand. "Jess . . ."

Jessie felt herself begin to tremble inside. Taking

a deep breath, she fought to regain control. She gazed into her mother's eyes, afraid of the knowledge they held. "It's all right, Mama. You can tell me."

"Jess . . ." Catherine's voice held a whispery hoarseness. "Billy's been killed."

★ ★ ★

Gradually the world began to take shape again. Jessie stared at the picture of Clark Gable, pinned to the wall next to her bed when she was a high-school sophomore. She thought his bright smile looked horribly out of place in a room so full of pain.

Jessie remembered a cloud of darkness dropping over her like a heavy blanket at the sound of her mother's voice bearing the news about Billy. But she had refused to succumb to it; refused to let herself fall into the warm, comforting night.

Rising slowly, she had felt her mother's arms around her.

"I'll be all right, Mama. I just want to go up to my room and be alone for a little while."

"Are you sure, baby?"

"Yes, ma'am. I'm fine."

She had lain across her bed while the shadows lengthened out on the lawn, while the final slanting shafts of sunlight shattered in the crowns of the old trees, while the gathering darkness began to slowly climb the sides of the houses. The numbness was lifting. Now she could feel the pain begin, like sharp tendrils, winding themselves around her heart.

Sitting up and easing her legs over the side of the bed, Jessie stared at the afterglow, drifting like lavender mist outside her window. *I didn't even ask how he died. Strange, the things we think of . . . the things we forget about in times like these. It all seems like some kind of awful dream, but then I guess it's always that way, at first.*

Jessie thought back to that last night in Atlanta. She could see again the tramp on the street, and Billy cleaning the vomit from the man's face, lifting him to his feet. Once again, she heard Billy's words as clearly as she had on that hot August night. *When you get to feeling a little better, I want to tell you an old, old story. It's about a man named Jesus.*

★ ★ ★

The brass-colored light of October seemed to burst into flame as it struck the scarlet leaves of a tall sweet gum tree standing on the hillside among the tilting old tombstones, streaked and blackened with age. Perched on the highest limb of the tree, a mockingbird sang in celebration of the last good month before winter trudged down from the north with its dreary rains.

"What a silly way to die!" Jessie sat in the white convertible next to Austin. She wore a black suit that matched the color of her mood. "I just *know* that after Madison Square Garden, he was going to preach crusades all over the world. Such a terrible—terrible waste!"

Austin leaned slightly forward, slipping out of his charcoal gray jacket and laying it behind him. Then he propped his arm along the back of the seat, gazing at Jessie's brown eyes, bright with tears that she had refused to shed. "I don't imagine Billy deliberately ran his car off the road, Jess."

"I know he didn't—it's just . . ." Jessie's mind returned to the hill outside of town and the steep dropoff down the kudzu-covered right shoulder of the road. *"He-man Hill." It sounds like something from an*

*old Charles Atlas ad in the back of a comic book. That's
probably the reason they called it that in the first place.
How stupid men can be sometimes!*

Austin noticed the distress that registered on Jessie's face. "What's wrong, Jess?"

"Oh, nothing," she sighed deeply, feeling a sense of
desolation nudge her spirit. Memory took her back
again to that day in another October. *Only a year. It
seems like such a long, long time ago.* She saw once
more the long, downhill curve of the gravel road,
heard Billy's words about his friend Jack Piker's record of forty-eight miles-an-hour. *I believe I could take
it at fifty with this Ford. It handles like a dream.*

Austin touched her on the shoulder. "Jess, you sure
you're all right?"

Jessie nodded, gazing across the graveyard, its
grass gone brown and autumn dry. "He could have at
least thought about Minnie. She looked so pitiful today."

The crowd had begun to disperse now, breaking up
into small groups or solitary figures, making their way
back to their cars. Occasionally one or two would stop
before a headstone, point, nod, or perhaps speak a
few words. Their conversations rose from dull murmurings to normal tones when they crossed an imaginary line marking the accepted distance from the
open grave.

"Sure are a bunch of old cars," Austin muttered,
listening to the engines sputtering into life, tires
crunching across the gravel driveways. "I thought you
said ol' Billy was keeping company with the rich folk."

Jessie stared at the mostly thirties- and forties-vintage Fords and Chevrolets; at their owners' rough
clothes, bought in dry-goods stores and goodwill
barns. "Guess the rich folks couldn't find time for a

funeral in a little hick town like Tupelo."

"I'll say one thing for the man. He had friends all over the place," Austin added, noticing the out-of-state license plates. "Tennessee, Alabama, Georgia. I even saw a few from up north—Indiana and Missouri, I remember for sure."

Jessie knew that Billy would have been brimming with joy to know that the outcasts of the cities and the small towns and the gravel road shacks had found their way to his funeral. Their tribute to him brought her a feeling of comfort like time spent in the company of an old friend.

"Jess, you can't let this thing get the best of you." Austin reached over and clasped her hand.

"But it's so senseless!" Jessie almost moaned. "Billy didn't have but four or five years to preach."

Austin squeezed her hand with a gentle and reassuring pressure. His voice softened as he spoke. "I think Jesus had something less than that, didn't He?"

The words seemed to strike at the heart of Jessie's loss. She turned to face Austin.

"I don't think God measures time the way we do—in weeks and months and years." Austin watched the cars moving slowly toward the cemetery gate. "I think He measures our time here on earth in terms of purpose. When Jesus said, 'It is finished,' He meant the work He was sent here to do." He brushed Jessie's hair gently back from her cheek with his fingertips. "Maybe Billy had finished his work, Jess."

Jessie watched a lean man in bib overalls, his face dark against silver-gray hair, begin shoveling dirt into the grave. She leaned over and kissed Austin on the lips. His words had already begun to settle the doubt and turmoil raging inside her. A smile crinkled the corners of her eyes as she watched a pink Cadillac, its heavy chrome flashing in the afternoon sunlight, turn through the cemetery gate onto the blacktop and speed away toward the road that led to Memphis.

EPILOGUE

★ ★ ★

Filtering in through the partially open venetian blinds, afternoon sunlight cast a muted gleam on the chrome and glass and Formica of the soda fountain in Taylor's Café. The waitress with short hair and boyish face sat on a stool at the end of the counter, idly running an emery board across her stubby fingernails. At the other end of the counter, a balding man in overalls nursed a fountain Coke. The muted clatter of dishwashing accompanied by the sound of someone singing "Just a Closer Walk" drifted in from the kitchen.

"I just couldn't face coming back to Memphis to get my things after Billy's funeral." Jessie, wearing Austin's high-school letter jacket against the late October chill, sat across from him in the last booth along the wall.

"I know." Austin reached across the table and patted her on the hand. "It was nice seeing Mrs. McLin again anyway." He slipped out of his black leather jacket and lay it on the seat beside him. "You'd think she was losing a daughter, the way she carried on when you left, though."

"I'm going to miss her. She *was* almost like a second mother, I guess," Jessie smiled, "and believe me, there were times up here when I needed one. Memphis can keep its rock-and-roll record business. I think I'll be happy just to finish my music degree and teach at a school within walking distance of the house."

Austin forked the last dumpling on his plate, put it into his mouth, and chewed it slowly, savoring the rich, spicy flavor. Glancing at Jessie, he swallowed and said, "Almost looks like we're in high school again, wearing these old jackets." His eyes clouded over in thought. "Sometimes I'd like to still be back there. Especially when some client calls in the middle of the night for me to come get him out of jail."

"That might be fun for a while—seeing all the old gang." Jessie had found herself reliving the past year more, she thought, than was good for her. Since Billy's death, there were times she couldn't seem to put the senseless tragedy from her mind. She would try to convince herself that, as Austin had said, Billy had fulfilled his purpose; he had finished his course. But in those times when she would awaken in the night or find herself alone during the day, grief sometimes caught her unawares. Then the bitter taste of desolation and loss returned, like an old copper coin in her mouth.

"You're doing a great job with the house, Jess."

"Thanks. It's such a lovely old place—and so much fun to fix up." Jessie smiled at Austin, thinking as she did dozens of times each day how very fortunate she was to have him after all the years she had sorely tried his patience. "But I have to admit that most of the ideas were Mama's."

Jessie watched Austin push his plate aside and slide a bowl of blackberry cobbler in front of him. *He enjoys food so much. I hope he's got some patience left. He'll sure need it until I learn how to cook.* She turned her left hand over, gazing at the plain gold band set with a solitary diamond. Its simple, quiet beauty somehow made her feel better, even during those hard times when the memory of Billy's death ached inside her like an old wound.

"I wonder if Elvis still comes in here?" Austin glanced across the parquet linoleum floor, reflecting vacant tables and chairs in its gleaming surface.

Jessie merely shrugged, finding it difficult to keep her mind on the conversation. She ran her hand across the red leatherette seat, recalling that this was the same booth she had shared with Billy on the day they met.

"Probably not," Austin continued without Jessie's response. "He's been on 'Ed Sullivan'—and he's making movies out in Hollywood. Why would he come back here?"

Jessie thought of the two friends from Tupelo: the singer, on his way to stardom—the preacher, lying beneath a simple tombstone just outside their hometown. Gazing down at her ring, she heard the faint and faraway sound of someone singing outside in front of the restaurant.

I love to tell the story,
'Twill be my theme in glory
To tell the old, old story
Of Jesus and His love.

A strange and bittersweet joy began to take hold of

Jessie. Her breathing became shallow and rapid. She felt as though she could walk across the restaurant, open the door, and step back in time; back into that day more than a year before when she had first heard the preacher with the mail-order suit and the priceless sea green eyes. "Excuse me. I'll be right back."

"Sure." Austin took another bite of the cobbler. "I'm about finished anyway."

Jessie crossed the restaurant and stopped at the door, feeling the deer-quick beating of her heart. She leaned against the door, her eyes closed, listening to the rest of the song. Then, taking a deep breath, she peered through the polished glass out at the blue-gold October day.

A slim man in his twenties wearing a cheap, slightly wrinkled suit stood on the sidewalk in bright sunlight. His warm brown eyes shone with an intense light. Opening a black Bible, he began to read to the few who had gathered near him. Jessie recognized the red-haired boy on the bicycle, propping his left leg on the sidewalk for balance. *I wonder if he ever goes to school?* A middle-aged couple carrying shopping bags stood next to a telephone pole.

As the preacher began to speak, two big men in business suits rapidly crossed the street toward him. Jessie remembered them well and expected the sermon to be short-lived.

"I don't care what the song says; I don't care what *anybody* tells you—we are *not* all God's children." The preacher's voice carried the undeniable weight of authority. "But we can *all become* God's children."

The two men stood at the curb, staring at each other with perplexed expressions, as though trying to decide why they had both stopped. One of them shrugged; the other gestured with his hands as if to say, *Why not?* Then they sat down on the tailgate of a pickup parked on the street.

The preacher opened his Bible. "John is talking about Jesus in the first chapter of his book. Now listen good, 'cause it's so simple you just might miss the whole meaning." He smiled at the two men sitting on the tailgate, the red-haired boy, and the couple with their shopping bags. Then he began to read. "He came unto his own, and his own received him not."

Suddenly, Jessie knew! She knew why she had come to Taylor's Café at this time on this particular day—and she knew who the preacher was. His left hand, missing the little finger and ring finger, pressed against the back of his Bible. She remembered his face on that day more than a year before with tears streaking the grime and the dirt and the stubble—and his eyes shining with a new light.

Tears streaming down her face, Jessie watched the miracle playing out before her. A still, small voice spoke to her heart: *Not many wise men after the flesh, not many mighty, not many noble, are called. . . . God hath chosen the foolish things of the world to confound the things which are mighty.* At that moment, Jessie knew she would grieve no more for Billy Pilgrim.